TOMB ON THE HILL

TOMB ON THE HILL

SHERIDAN OAKES

A Novel by Sheridan Oakes
Copyright © 2022 by Sheridan Oakes
Lionel A Blanchard, Publisher

First Printing

Hardcover ISBN: 978-1-7923-7670-2
Softcover ISBN: 979-8-88680-207-8

Cover Art and Design by Vincent Chong

This novel is *deadicated*
to my mother, father, and brother.

Ann Mary Sheridan

George Paul Oakes Jr.

Robert Brian Oakes

"I love this view!"

"You say that every morning."

"And you say that every morning."

"Isn't death grand?"

IN THE BEGINNING

The sun rises every day.

Not an original thought, but who am I to question nature?

When unhindered by the marine layer, the sunrise is beautiful enough to look past its repetitive cycle as it begins our daily race with its solar arch across the sky.

I have a clock. By keeping a close eye on this clock, I can slow time in hopes of winning the race. I watch the hands of time move as my own hands attempt to fill the spaces between the ticking seconds with progress. So far, the sun is winning.

IN THE MIDDLE

We bump around like a pinball shooting from one stimulus to another.

IN THE END

We die.

AFTER THE END

Now the fun begins.

INTRODUCTION

My name is Minus Filbert.

I liked the name Sam, but I loved and respected my parents, so I would never do anything to disappoint them. That's why I've spent my life being Minus and striving to be number one.

To do this, I would immerse myself in ventures of a grand design such as, *the cow paddy pen holder.* I felt this was a brilliant concept that would catapult me to become an industry standard. From a financial perspective, the materials were plentiful and free. Artistically, no two were the same, and environmentally they were one-hundred percent biodegradable. Sadly, I failed to appreciate the *ick* factor, which brought *The Pen Paddy* to a demise befitting its origins.

With that scheme safely composted, I moved on to an article I had seen in my local paper about a woman attempting to sell her family's mausoleum. The headline read: *Evicted After Death.* Apparently, she was the last descendant in her lineage and felt the homeowners association wouldn't complain.

As a salesman myself, I'm all for free commerce, and I understand the value of real property. Still, this banishment of the inhabitants of the tomb seemed rather unfair. When I get comfortable for an evening of relaxation, the "Do Not Disturb" sign goes up. So, the thought of kicking back for an eternity and then being told to get up and move to another room is unreasonable, unthinkable, and maybe undoable.

Though, it did seem like an excellent idea for a novel. A declaration on ethics, responsibility, and underground decorating. The subject was infused with ideological and philosophical questions.

Salesmen sell ideas. We manipulate perception while avoiding deception. With this concept, which straddles the line between existence and non-existence, I could take realities and fantasies, and write a book that nobody would understand, but would make me look brilliant. A rather grand endeavor for a school bus salesman, whose writing style is the literary equivalent to outsider art.

Though we've not often crossed paths, I'm not a stranger to death. I can count the people I knew who are now dead on the one hand and all the people I think should be dead on the other. The Filbert Rolodex of the dearly departed included my parents, my brother, a cousin, a dental hygienist I liked a lot, and my childhood dog Zero. I think it best not to go into those on the other hand. Somewhere in that fistful of ghosts, one would think I could channel some graveyard scuttlebutt.

Not wanting to make everything up, I decided to take an intellectually unbiased and completely level-headed approach on the topic. I knew I could always devolve into a hackneyed tale of skeletons running around a cemetery with no clothes on if the publisher insisted.

But, where to start?

Of course, "The Cemetery."

1

THE CEMETERY

My family is buried in a vertical plot.
Stacked underground with a
thin layer of dirt between them for added privacy.
Very much reminiscent of their early days in New York.

I have been inconsistent with paying my respects upon the hallowed grounds of their final resting place. Just across the bay from my home, up on a hill that overlooks the industry of man, the bones of my family lie encased in wood and satin. I'm endlessly traversing the Oakland Bay Bridge for business. Yet, it rarely crosses my mind to take a detour to visit the folks. Maybe it's a sadness of their passing. More likely, I am so self-absorbed by survival that the thought of taking the time to look in on the dead seemed to be a folly that would accomplish nothing.

Life is more time-consuming than death. The dead remain unchanged, while I toil with my existence. Rent is due every month, but through good estate planning, theirs is taken care of.

* * *

Brisbane, California, is like an old European village rising from the bay through winding streets, until the houses are stopped by the open space that keeps us sane. Halfway up this hillside hamlet, my living room window offers me a view of the East Bay where my loved ones reside high on the Oakland Hills, allowing me to always feel connected to my past.

Thinking like this is called "rationalization," which is a reaction to a guilt-inducing situation. I have a bad habit of self-diagnosis.

So, to transcend my shortcomings and hedge my bets with the dead, I've decided to place the ubiquitous flowers on the ancestors' graves in person, like a good son and brother. Diagnose that!

* * *

Sunday morning, when the sun is low in the sky and traffic is almost non-existent, the Bay Bridge feels like a miracle of human invention and a conduit to a world outside of myself. On this day, the pilgrimage to my past began.

With a cold Rosé and a warm breakfast burrito safely stowed in the trunk, I drove east to commune with the dead. To sit upon my family's subterranean condos and ask for guidance. Even if they were unable to share spirit secrets, someone might have connections to a literary agent.

Driving across the bridge into the sunrise reminded me of my early days watching bands at the club Mabuhay Gardens in San Francisco's North Beach district. The incessant strobe of sunlight through the bridge's girders made for conditions as distracting as the nightclub's light show. Time will tell which was more dangerous, driving blind or sitting for hours in a smoke-filled bar listening to loud music.

Having completed the eastward portion of the journey, I turned north to follow the ridgeline through the Oakland Hills. Looking back across the bay, the city was drenched in an auburn glow reminiscent of my skin color after an evening at the Mabuhay.

I stopped outside the cemetery gates to find that the occupants were still getting ready for the day. Posted on the mighty iron portal were the hours: *Dawn until Dusk.* Either the sun was early this morning, or somebody had slept in. So, I filled the time by taking cell phone shots of an anthill in the middle of the road. The industry of these tiny creatures had me wondering if the residents on the other side of the fence had a similar existence.

At fifty-five minutes after dawn, the butler of the dead unlocked the entrance. As I drove through the earthly pearly gates, a sense of home fell over me. Like the calm before sleep. I'm no stranger to nodding off at the wheel, but this sensation had no sleepiness associated. Instead, it was akin to euphoria. Like an antidepressant mainlined into my system. Typically not the emotion I feel when entering a graveyard. It made me want to turn around and try it again.

After extended periods between familial visits, I tend to get lost on the windy roads that snake through these grounds. It's not that anybody's moving around, but the spider web that makes up the road map of the city-of-the-dead was a little too *feng shui* for my sense of direction. At one time, I had considered erecting a tower with a red beacon over the folks' headstones but felt it might confuse small aircraft.

Once ensconced above my ancestors' bones, I opened the wine and unpacked the crystal wine glass I carried in the trunk just in case the need arose. Then I filled said glass with said wine and gave a toast to those who came before and to those who should not have gone before me.

This morning among the souls of my past, I hoped for a sign, but nothing happened. The sky didn't darken with black stormy clouds. A lightning bolt didn't take out the old oak tree that rose above the Finkelman's graves.

What I got was; no visitations, no signs from beyond, not even a breeze through the trees.

The sun continued to dance on the leaves of the Finkelman's tree, but my wine glass did magically empty. This, I believe, was more a sign to be mindful of my alcohol intake than a visitation from the great beyond.

After ignoring the suggestion for moderation, I finished the bottle of Rosé and took a nap upon the natural green carpet that covered the grounds.

I'm prone to naps. As exciting as a school bus salesman's life sounds, it's not. The buses are all yellow and someday end up planted outside Golden Gate Park occupied with three pit bulls and a guy named Grease.

The sun turned to shade as the Finklemans''s tree cooled my resting place. I pulled the plastic Italian-style tablecloth, which I had laid out for the feast, over my chilled bones. Not a snooze goes by without a dream. Supine atop this resting place, I dreamt of life underground. Everyone was there, except the dental hygienist. Still, I could not garner any information that would secure me a Pulitzer.

I heard voices as I lay in my pre-conscious state. Now I can begin my narrative on life after life. I awoke to see that the Finklemans had brought their two sons to the cemetery with a regulation football, who were now throwing it right over me.

Time to go home.

I paid my final respects and headed back to the car.

That was a rather un-ceremonial ending to my private seance. Why would these kids have passing practice using me as the center-line? Maybe there was a meaning in this rudeness, or perhaps they thought I was dead and wouldn't mind. Either way, it was bizarre.

I sat in the car looking out at all the families that had come and gone. Would it *really* matter to any of them if Caltrans decided to put a six-lane freeway, with a full-service rest stop, through their serene village? Greater minds than mine have deliberated this question, though, I'm sure the *rest stop* was an original thought. Unfortunately, they are no closer to an answer than I was sitting in my little red Mustang. It was starting to look like I might have to make everything up.

Running the scenarios for the tale through my head, I realized, I had a better chance of getting a visitation from my dog Zero than I did coming up with a decent storyline. I closed my eyes to lessen the distractions around me. The first image in my mind's eye was the football. I guess I was more bothered by that incident than I had thought. I couldn't get that pigskin out of my head. When I opened my eyes, I thought I saw the ball fly right past my windshield.

I needed to use some creative thinking if I was going to make any sense of my hallucinations. So, how would a football play into this fantasy? Well, it is shaped like a Ouija board pointer with two ends. Maybe it was directing me towards something and away from something simultaneously. I decided to take this nonsensical line of reasoning and head back to the 49ers *Day of the Dead* training camp to see what other fantasies I could conjure up.

When I arrived back at the scene of the annoyance, the Finkleman clan had gone off to bother some other napping visitors. The football, though, had been left behind on the gravestones of my kin.

Three rectangular slabs of marble, set flat into the ground, made up the seating assignment for my family. My brother Brian was the first to go, so he was on the bottom. Next, my mother, Mary. Followed some years later by my father, Paul. I looked at the space above Pops and pictured my headstone:

HERE LIES MINUS FILBERT

FINALLY ON TOP

The football sat between Mom and Pop's stones with each end pointing to a letter. The Ouija metaphor was starting to look promising, though I would have preferred a more direct sign like a spiritual inhabitation or phone call.

The ball was pointing to a T and an S. I made a mental note of the first clue and waited to see if it would move on to the next two letters, but nothing happened. After five minutes, I was back to hoping for a lightning strike, except this time on me. Figuring this could take a while, I went back to the car to get my fake Italian tablecloth to sit on for the duration of the divination. When I got back, the ball had moved. This time pointing at the R and U. That was the limit of what my memory could handle, so I went back to the car to fetch pen and paper. Once again, on my return, the ball had moved and now pointed at Y and O. I sat myself down for the remainder of the show, but the ball didn't move. It looked like this was going to be an exercise in exercise. The ball only revealed its clues when I wasn't there. So, I had to venture to and from the car seven more times before I came back to find the football sitting squarely on my future headstone space. I hoped that this was the end of the message and not a request for me to join the family.

As it stood, I had accumulated the following letters:

TSRUYORUTSOHGTUHT.

Sadly, I was never good with Will Shortz's Sunday puzzles. Still, since my literary career depended on it, I attempted to decipher the clue.

SHOT YOUR THRUST GUT.

Maybe not.

STOUTY'S ROUGH TRUTH.

Still not very helpful.

HOT THUGS RUSTY TOUR.

I've never heard of the Hot Thugs.

I spent the next two hours arranging and rearranging the letters until I came up with:

THRU YOU STRUT GHOST.

Appropriate for the present venue, but not particularly good grammar.

Just as I threw my pad of paper on the ground, a voice came from behind me. "Jesus Christ, Minus, TRUST YOUR THOUGHTS!"

Startled, I swung around to see my brother, looking like a second-grade school teacher with a difficult student. "Trust your thoughts, trust your thoughts," he scolded me, before disappearing.

I stood still, not sure what I had seen and heard. How can I trust my thoughts when I can't trust my eyes? Thank God I had the plastic tablecloth to sit down on because my legs were shaking fast enough to put froth on a frozen Margarita.

"What the hell was that?" I said out loud, feeling like I had just been struck by lightning.

I sat quietly for some time before blurting out, "What the hell was that?" again. This time the answer came into my head: "Trust your thoughts."

I looked around to see if there was another aberration only to notice that the football had disappeared. I wrote down the phrase, "Trust your thoughts," and tried plugging in the letters from the Ouija football experience. After a little more time than I care to admit to, every last letter was used to complete the quote. "Well, why didn't you just say so?" I said out loud, hoping the Finkleman family had truly gone home.

"I did," came my brother's voice in my head.

This time I didn't turn around. Brian wasn't behind me, or next to me, or hovering above me. Damn it, he was in me.

"You're not planning on doing this on a regular basis, are you?" I asked Brian, hoping he wouldn't answer and I could go home.

"I thought you missed me," my sibling replied.

I know the plan was to go to the cemetery and link up with the relatives, but in the real world, this stuff doesn't happen.

"I miss your spaghetti and meatballs," I shot back in the typical manner of our earthly relationship, "you, not so much."

"Well, I've missed your dull wit," Brian calmly informed me.

"How do I know it's really you and not my dull wit talking?"

"Trust me, I could never be as dull as you."

"Yep, it's you," I conceded. "I would recognize that insult anywhere."

"Minus, one of my favorite pastimes in life was messing with you."

"Can I put you on hold?" I inquired, trying to buy some time for my thoughts to catch up with my nervous system.

"You let me in, now you're stuck with me," Brian proclaimed.

I hesitated, but still asked, "24/7?"

"Only if I can stand it," Brian reassured me.

"Do you have a supervisor I can speak with?"

"Yes, but he's busy at the moment."

"Let me know when he's free," I requested.

This is how Brian and I spent eighteen years of our lives. From childhood into near adulthood, we behaved like a vaudeville act, ending with a pratfall usually performed by yours truly.

Brian was a year younger than me when he died. I was now thirty-one years his senior and still sounding like a nineteen-year-old.

"You came here to talk to me about something?" Brian asked.

"If you're in my head, I would think you could read my mind."

"That goes against the privacy laws in the spirit world."

"Good to know I have an advocate in the afterlife. Any chance I have some control over your dialogue?"

"Sure, just stop listening."

"Thanks, I'll work on that," I said, moving on to the business at hand.

2

THE BUSINESS AT HAND

My story idea
seemed a little childish.

I hadn't thought about what I was going to ask the ghost of Christmas past, if the opportunity presented itself. But now that I was in contact with what I had previously considered to be fantasy, I was stumped.

Explaining a plot concept that dealt with the afterlife to my brother's spirit, who in life would have laughed me into the grave, needed to be done with finesse. For a salesman who usually has all the answers, even when I don't, I was dumbfounded. My mind went blank except for the sound of Brian humming "Helen Wheels."

"What are you doing?" I asked.

"I'm killing time while you work out why you're here," Brian said, as he went into the chorus.

I really had nothing to lose. I should just tell Brian the truth. At worst, he would haunt me for the rest of my days using maniacal laughter punctuated with comments about inane story themes. Can't be much worse than watching Fox News.

"How are the folks?" I began.

"You endured the football spelling bee to ask me that?" Brian unceremoniously responded.

"Granted, that's not my main impetus here, but it would be rather rude not to inquire. And by the way, I didn't know who was going to answer the phone. I could just as easily be asking Mom how you are."

"True, but you could also be asking me how I am."

"I'm sorry, Brian. Did I just get you out of the shower?"

"I'll have you know, Minus, not everyone is allowed to plant themselves in their brother's head."

"Pray tell, how did we get to the front of that line?"

"I can't say," Brian replied.

I reloaded my assault weapon and said, "You gotta do better than that, dear brother. Three-word non-answers don't go very far with me."

"Sorry, brother, but I'm in the position of power here," Brian fired back.

I had to stop and think about my position in this narrative. If he leaves my head I'm sunk, and the book goes the way of the agentless writer.

"Okay, I'll lay down my weapons," I said.

"Now that's my Minus being positive."

I kept my thoughts shut about that comment.

"So," I asked, "how are the folks?"

"They're fine," Brian answered, having given up on trying to direct my queries. "Now, what brings you to my headstone?"

I looked around, having forgotten that I was standing among the builders of human history. People who had contributed to the world that I now inhabited.

"I want to write a book about the afterlife," I said. "I thought it would be a good idea to get a little insider information."

"That much I know. But why?"

"If you can't read my thoughts, how did you know that?"

"I can't say," Brian re-replied. "Just consider it one of those cosmic unknowns."

"There are a definitive number of 'knowns' and an infinite quantity of unknowns. I certainly hope we move into the former category soon," I said.

Brian was silent for a moment, so I took this opportunity to carefully construct my reasoning. "Who the hell will read this cock-and-bull story if I don't have some juicy insider poop?" I said.

"Minus, you have to get published for people to read your book."

"You assume I won't get published?"

"It's not a judgment on you," Brian quickly recovered. "You're a school bus salesman, not a liberal arts scholar. I'm afraid you can't just decide to be a *New York Times* bestseller."

"Was that an apology? It almost sounded like one, except for the opinion about being a school bus salesman."

"How can I help with your, *The Ghost and Mrs. Muir* story?" Brian offered.

"Let's hope I get so lucky," I said, not feeling anywhere near as pretty as Gene Tierney. "You seem to have some information on my intentions," I continued, "what else do you know?"

"I know that you want to tell the story of the Kelly property that's up for sale."

"Insightful, any chance you know the winning numbers for the lotto?"

"Yes, I do, but I'm not telling you." Another unknown contributed by Brian.

"So, you've been sent as the PR person for the Kelly Corp.?" I asked.

"Corporations may be considered individuals in America but here they are just soulless entities that someday cease to exist. The Kellys are souls with the right to continue being where they are," Brian said, hinting at his purpose.

"I'll try to fit that in the book, but I'm still not clear why you're helping me."

"Is it necessary for you to know why?"

"I would like to be sure that I'm not inadvertently selling my soul to one side or the other."

"It doesn't work that way. The whole Faust tale was fantasy. There isn't a department here that brokers for human souls. Besides, there are no sides. The concept of duality is a physical construct. There is no good or bad. There just *is*."

"If that statement was designed to confuse me, you get ten points." I rewarded Brian.

"Do you think confusing you is worth ten points?" Brian kindly gave value to my inability to comprehend anything more complex than an omelet.

"Regardless of what both of us think about my intelligence, I still sense a deal being made."

"Very good, Minus, I give you six points for that insight."

"Thanks. May I ask what the deal you're proposing is?"

"It's simple; you save the Kellys' home and I will supply you with information about *THE NEXT WORLD*."

"You say *the next world* like it's all capital letters."

"I'm just trying to sell the idea. Marketing is a big part of my duties. I sometimes get carried away," Brian explained the reason for this tête-à-tête.

"What is the job?"

"My job is to enlist you. Your job is to stop the sale."

"Why me?"

"It's that delicate smile of yours. Don't worry, Minus, you can do it."

Brian may have been only in my head, but he was still the same guy as when he tortured me in life. I now realized how much I missed the son-of-a-bitch. Nobody in my world is as much fun to talk with. I've been trying to train my new dental hygienist, but it's not the same.

"Did I lose you there?" Brian asked, bringing me back to whatever part of my brain this conversation was being held in.

"Yeah, you did. Do people put up with you in the great beyond?"

"There is no good and bad. I'm just accepted for who I am."

"A tolerant group, I must say," I said, still not fully comprehending the concept. "I'm just a school bus salesman, as you've reminded me. Don't you need a lawyer who specializes in condo law or estate planning?"

"That's your job to find them. It's not about right and wrong or good and bad, it's about selling an idea, and you could sell ice to a Maytag repairman."

"I'll take that as a compliment even though I don't know what it means," I said, starting to lose the thread of the conversation. "Still, I don't understand where sales come into this, aside from the land being sold."

"That's it. You fight fire with a fireman, take on the sea with a seaman, and go up against a sale with a salesman. Would you like me to give further examples using airman, doorman, and draftsman?"

"Yeah," I said, egging him on.

"Okay, let's consider my bluff called," he conceded with as little fanfare as possible.

"Is this a common form of logic in the graveyard?" I asked, hoping to make sense out of Brian's logic.

"First off, we don't refer to this place as a graveyard," Brian corrected me.

"No...? Would you prefer *Club Dead*?"

"We prefer, *The Yard*," Brian explained. "And, we are not dead. We are a community of feeling, thinking, and vibrant souls. The next step in evolution. A continuation of existence without the physical limitations of cells and gravity."

"You still seem to be affected by those with cells," I suggested.

"Well, yes, evolution isn't always pretty. There is no growth without challenges. The 'cells' are a ready supply of quandaries."

"So, does that make us your vehicle for growth?" I confronted my mental roommate.

"That's a sticky subject that I would prefer to save for another time when you're not standing around in The Yard looking like a lunatic," Brian said, pointing out my reality.

This conversation had drawn me into myself. I hadn't noticed that the Finkleman troupe were back, looking for their ball.

"Excuse me, sir, have you seen a football around here?" the unexpectedly polite youngest boy asked.

"I'm sorry, I don't know what happened to it," I replied, "but let me get back to you on that."

The boy looked at me like one does to a crazy person who stands around a cemetery, as I questioned Brian if he knew where the kid's ball was.

"It's in the bushes behind the oak tree. I had a squirrel move it there," Brian confessed.

I turned back to the little Finkleman and pointed to a stand of scrub oak and said, "It's over there."

The kid didn't move.

"Go on," I encouraged. "Consider this one of life's little mysteries."

The boy walked over to the bush and stared, seemingly unwilling to venture into the tangle of branches.

"Behind it," I echoed Brian's words from my head.

The future tight end stepped around the oddly located shrub, picked up the ball, and ran like hell.

"You might be right about continuing this conversation somewhere a bit more private," I agreed.

"You'll get used to the strange looks, Minus. It comes with the territory."

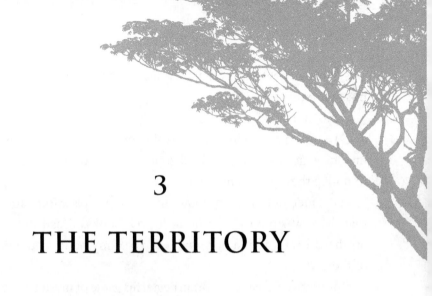

3

THE TERRITORY

As I walked back to the car...
As we walked back to the car...
As the two of us moved from the gravesite to the car,
Brian asked if I would like to have a tour of the Kelly estate.

I had only read the headline of the newspaper article concerning the Kelly tomb. Its location was a mystery to me. Feeling embarrassingly under-prepared for the task I was being conscripted into, I sheepishly asked Brian, "Is it very far away?"

Rarely is there silence in my head, but as I listened for a response from my brother, I could hear only half of a conversation.

"Brian...? You still there...? Brian?"

He used to do this to me when I said something that rubbed him the wrong way, but I would have thought he had gotten past that.

"Are you lying in wait," I tried again, "or have I stepped out of radio range?"

Still, not even static.

"Come on, I was planning on delving into the research once I lined up my writing team."

"I'm sorry, what was that, Minus? I lost you for a moment. Did I miss something?"

"No, nothing," I said.

"I don't have complete control over when we can connect. We may have gone through a dead zone," Brian explained, seeming not to notice the irony in his statement.

I decided not to worry about my lack of preparation, rationalizing that there was plenty of time to hit the books. "Lead the way, dear brother," I said with a bow and a wave of my hand in the direction of the car.

"You can't drive there," Brian began his game of mystery. "You walk."

"I was hoping we could fly," I played back.

"You're too fat to fly. I could try to find you a wheelchair."

"Thanks, but I'd rather drive the Mustang."

"Unless it's four-wheel drive, you walk," Brian repeated.

"Where are we going?" I broke down and showed my cards.

"Face east," Brian directed.

I changed my position ninety degrees and stopped.

"The other east," he said.

"This *is* east," I assured him.

"Where's the sun, Minus?"

"In the west," I answered, assuming it was behind me.

"What's that thing over your right shoulder?" brother Galileo queried.

I turned forty-five degrees to my left to look up the steepest hill in *Poltergeist Park*.

"You were going to send me up *that* in a wheelchair?" I said, pointing at a hill that could have been mistaken for a wall.

"No, the wheelchair was for when you got down." Brian kindly looked into my future.

"Thanks, I might take you up on that."

I began the march up Kilimanjaro hoping to find an ice cream vendor serving popsicles to climbers and their spirit Sherpas.

16

Halfway up the hill, I turned around to rest and take in the scenery. If treetops float your boat, you could sail away on the stand of eucalyptus that shielded the view.

"I can't imagine property values are very high up here," I proposed to Brian, primarily to see if he was still with me or stayed down at ten thousand feet to set up camp.

"Don't be hasty," he chastised me. "You're looking at the bottom of the frame. Save your judgment for the peak."

I turned around to examine my destination. A grassy slope, with the green of spring, stood between me and a place to sit down. Now that my breathing had returned to normal and I had managed to keep a cramp from taking over the lower half of my right leg, I set forth to conquer this hill.

"Stop!" Brian ordered.

"Shit, what's wrong?" I screeched.

"You need to sit down. Now!"

"Why?"

"Just do it!"

I sat on the soft, warm grass facing the wall of eucalyptus. Suddenly the trees began to wave, transforming into an iridescent gray landscape. My imagination went wild. Childhood fantasies played with my thoughts. The sky came alive with cartoon balloons that whirled in the air like autumn leaves before a storm. I again looked at the trees to find they had become bleachers, alive with an audience of humans cheering the balloons that had now taken the form of swashbucklers and buccaneers.

My head buzzed. My toes buzzed. And everything in between vibrated like a tuning fork. I felt like I was a conduit between fantasy and reality, bringing spirit TV to the masses.

Grasping their swords and spears, the characters of this dance darted before my eyes.

Pop! Weeeee! The first strike was made.

The crowd went wild.

I could feel an outside energy surging through my mind, draining my resolve to remain erect.

17

Pop, pop, weeeee, weeeee, two more gone. The bleachers could barely contain the crowd's excitement.

I sat, I watched, I fell asleep.

* * *

"Minus. Yoo-hoo. Wakey, wakey," I heard somewhere between my right and left ears.

I thought about opening my eyes but wasn't sure if I were up for what I would find around me. All I wanted to do was write a book. Hallucinating in a graveyard was not part of the research plan. When I *did* open my eyes, the trees were trees again.

"Good morning," Brian said.

"Very funny. What the hell was that?" I asked, getting right to the point.

"That was entertainment and it is morning."

I sat up and looked for the sun. It wasn't where it used to be. I looked a little further, and it wasn't where it could be, so I looked around to where it shouldn't be, and there it was.

"Damn, they probably towed my car!" was the first reaction to the realization that I had just spent the night in a cemetery.

"Don't worry, I had a word with the guard," Brian comforted me.

"Am I dead?" I asked.

"You should be so lucky. No, you got to experience the semifinals of the balloon popping competition. I'm afraid you missed the end when Captain Henderson's team did a triple skewer against the Berkeley Bubbleheads. It was amazing."

"You're kidding. That was an organized event? It looked like chaos to me."

"Excellent observation, Minus, but everything is chaos. That's what gives interest to both worlds. Are you going to just sit there, or can we get back to our mission?"

"I'm going to sit here until you tell me what happened."

Brian was silent for a moment before saying, "I'll tell you later."
So, I just sat there.

"Let's go," Brian urged me to get off my ass.

I just sat there.

We seemed to be having a face-off. I had control over motor functions and Brian had control over driving me nuts.

"Just stand up and walk, please. If you're hoping to outwait me, I think your growling stomach is going to win." My bodiless brother showed he still had the upper hand.

Stand I did to the fanfare of my joints popping loud enough to wake the dead. After lying on the ground all night, I was amazed that standing was an option.

Cresting the hill, I was relieved to finally be on level ground. Before me stood a modest stone building barely big enough to house a thought, much less a generation of Kellys. The hilltop was huge. Large, *live oaks* were sprinkled upon the expanse of groomed lawn that was punctuated with a dozen, or more, white marble headstones.

"Welcome to the Kelly residence," Brian's voice came into my head, almost knocking me down the hill. The beauty of this place had calmed my mind and filled my thoughts with a peacefulness not often found within this head now sharing space with another.

"Is that the building for sale?" I asked.

"The entire hilltop is on the block. The sepulcher, the gravesites, the trees, and what's behind you. Turn around," Brian instructed.

I peeled my eyes off the landscape and focused on the vista that had been hidden by trees.

The ocean and sky created a razor-sharp horizon that was underlined by the tops of the eucalyptus, which still blocked the presence of the city below. Oakland and Berkeley were gone. San Francisco and Marin were equally shielded from view. This felt like the most peaceful place on earth.

"That is a million-dollar view," I said.

"Two point five million to be exact," Brian corrected me.

"Is there a buyer already?"

"Not yet. Patricia Kelly only recently set the price."

"That's a rather optimistic evaluation. Is she hoping to sell to a developer of a shopping mall for the residents?"

"I have no idea what her plans or needs are," Brian answered, giving no credence to my question.

Still unsure why I was being brought into this family squabble, I asked my spiritual adviser, "Why doesn't one of her relatives just pop into her head to work things out?"

"It's not that easy," Brian informed me. "I can come to you because you are in search of help. Ms. Kelly is quite independent and self-assured. There's no getting inside that head."

What did that say about me, I thought as I wandered around reading the names on the headstones. I've always thought of myself as independent and self-assured.

My first stop was the mausoleum. This venerable structure was occupied only by Declan and Margaret Kelly, who looked to be the Adam and Eve of Kellyville. Moving on, I could see the other residents were situated about the grounds with plenty of room between them to maintain family accord.

There were the Kellys and O'Connors, Fishers and Kellys alongside Ryans and Filberts.

"Brian, that isn't our Filbert, is it?" I asked, immediately upon this discovery.

"Yes, Minus, that one attaches us to the clan."

"Is that my ticket to the party?"

"Bingo, big brother."

"Little brother, I think you need to do some explaining."

4

EXPLAINING

I keep a ready list of
restaurants, cafés, snack bars, and food trucks
in my head so that I never go hungry.

Brian's explanation of a convoluted family history was too much for my already overworked brain to follow. After a night of balloon popping and lawn sleeping, I was in no shape to hear who begat whom. My stomach started to speak up again. I suggested reconvening at the Sunrise Café.

Once we had descended the hill, I requested Brian to bring me my wheelchair.

"Sorry, brother, I was joking about the chair."

"Does your supervisor know about this mean streak?"

"He loves my sense of humor."

"I can see now, I'm going to have to go straight to the top with my complaints."

"If you get to the top, you may find you've bitten off more than you can chew," Brian warned.

"Won't be the first time," I said as I (we) slipped into my ruby-red Mustang.

Driving through the gates of the cemetery, I asked, "Brian, how far afield can you venture from your home? You there, Brian? Come on, man, we really have to communicate better about communicating."

No answer, damn. I was hoping to stick him with the breakfast bill.

The café was only a mile and a half from the cemetery as the pony roams. By the time I hitched Ruby up, right outside the restaurant, I was starving.

To avoid a hypoglycemic seizure, I ran in ordering an omelet with everything in it. The coffee came in time to create an artificial heartbeat that kept me going until the protein arrived.

"You eat like a horse," Brian said out of nowhere, causing me to almost choke on a homestyle potato.

"Can you give me some warning when you're going to pop into my head?"

"Would you prefer I sound the trumpets?"

"I would prefer you to not make me jump out of my seat. Can you also let me know when you're signing out? It's bad enough that I'm talking to myself without talking to myself."

"Any suggestions regarding what you would like to hear?" Brian asked.

"How about, 'dear incredible older brother, I wish to leave now?'"

"I think I'll just say goodbye."

"Good enough," I acquiesced. "By the way, where did you go?"

"Your driving scares the hell out of me. I thought I would just meet you here."

I ate my breakfast while Brian went on about the benefits of being dead. Not wishing to delve into family history, until the sun had a chance to supernova, I practiced developing my ability to tune him out.

Once the waitress had cleared my plate and the sun still shone through the windows, Brian began his history of history.

After two and a half minutes of incomprehensible family lineage, I asked if he could write it down for me.

"Do I look like I can hold a pen?" Brian shot back at me.

"Don't get me started with pen holders," I quipped. "Are you able to take over the use of my hand to do the writing?"

"I can, but it's frowned upon."

"By whom?" I couldn't resist asking.

"My supervisor."

"Well, apparently, he doesn't seem to be around much."

Brian instructed me to get a pen and paper to map out over a century of lives, lived.

"I'm ready when you are," I said to my spiritual genealogist, "go ahead and take over."

"Minus, I'm left-handed, please change hands with the pen."

"You're kidding, you still have physical limitations?"

"Old habits die hard. By the way, your handwriting is terrible no matter which hand you use."

"Fine," I conceded, "this way I can keep drinking my coffee."

I watched as Brian created an outline of the Kellys' world before my time. I was impressed by the quality of his drafting skills. That should have been of no real surprise since he had gone into the military as a draftsman. Although he had ended up a rifleman.

I, on the other hand, couldn't draw a family tree if my family tree depended on it.

After five minutes of filling in little boxes with the names of people I had seen on the hill, Brian turned the paper over and proceeded to document the Filbert clan. Two trees, one future.

"Now you can see where you fit into the picture," Brian said, giving me back the use of my left hand.

"Yes, I see it. But I'm pretty well removed from the Kellys, at least legally."

"I don't expect you to file a lawsuit. I hope that you will have enough influence as *family* to stop the sale."

"According to your chronology, Patricia and I are both the end of our lines. Not a lot of family obligations there."

"On the contrary, obligations to your past are more important than ones in the present. Those who have passed no longer have a voice."

"Really? I hear a voice."

"That's because you're open to help."

I studied the maps that sat before me. Between sips of coffee, I tried to visualize the lives of those who had completed their tenure creating these families. Putting this all into the context was difficult. I'm a school bus salesman, not a tombstone arbitrator. All I wanted to do was write a book about dead people. Now, I was being drawn into a squabble between the ancestors and the real estate industry.

"Brian, I need to think about this on my own. May I have a day to contemplate your generous offer?"

"That's a good idea, Minus. If you need any help, just call me."

"Thank you, but I think I'll go home and take a nap first." Then, just to see his reaction, I said, "I'll let you pick up the check."

"Consider it done," Brian answered without hesitation.

"What does that mean?" I asked, hoping I had hidden the worry in my voice sufficiently.

"Don't worry, Minus, I didn't haunt the waitress. The owner's father is a friend of mine in The Yard. He had a word with his son."

"Is this mind planting common? You seem to pull a lot of weight in the breathing world."

"This is an important mission. I've been instructed not to fail. Certain measures need to be implemented," Brian said, sounding like he was back in the military.

That didn't sound like the Brian I knew before he died. "Did you learn to speak like that during the war?"

"I think it's nap time, Minus," he told me before signing off with, "goodbye."

I asked for the check anyway. "That's already been taken care of, sir," the waitress informed me.

With that came the realization that I should stop being surprised by things that aren't normal.

*   *   *

When I got home, the bed was my first stop. Shoes hitting the floor were the last thing I heard before heading into dreamland.

Usually, I have vivid dreams during the night, but this sleep produced none. When I awoke, there was a calm residing in me that no morning had ever offered.

I looked out my window to see the sun still shining. Glancing at the clock, I saw it was earlier than when I had laid down. I had to think about that for a moment before realizing the obvious. I had just slept twenty hours. The next realization was I *really* had to pee.

Once past the proof of life, I staved off death by cooking two poached eggs, toast, and three strips of bacon.

With a full belly and a rested mind, I wondered if my day to think about this new endeavor began back in the café or started when I woke up. According to my watch, I either had twenty-three hours to contemplate my future or forty-five minutes. That's assuming my memory of the previous day wasn't a hallucination induced by an irrational desire to be a famous writer. I wondered if my brother Brian had really blurred the line between life and death.

"Damn," I said out loud, remembering that I had an appointment with the transportation department of the Oakland School District this morning. This possible fantasy was going to have to wait. It's time to make a buck.

5

MAKING A BUCK

That was brutal, I sighed
as I flopped down on the sofa
to the sound of my grandfather's grandfather clock finishing its
Westminster chime announcing seven p.m.

"That was brutal," I said again to myself after my backup band had stopped playing.

I represent the best school busses made and still I get hammered on the price. These busses are designed to keep children out of cemeteries. How can they quibble over price? If my cousin Phillip had been in one of these, he would still be alive today.

"Phillip is doing quite well," Brian's voice came into my head.

"Damn, it wasn't a dream," I said. "I hoped you were just a literary concept."

"Sorry, brother, I'm afraid you don't have the imagination to come up with such a plotline. So, have you thought about helping us?"

"I don't know if you heard my earlier conversation with myself, but today was brutal. I didn't have a minute to myself."

"Good, too much self-analysis is bad for you."

"Really? How does one grow if one doesn't understand who he, or she, is?"

"Wallowing in self-pity is often mistaken for introspection. It's best to open your mind first."

I was starting to like these conversations with Brian. I've often wanted a life coach. Now, I would have a philosophical dilemma with giving him a hard time.

"You know, I'm not planning on writing a self-help book," I told him. "My idea is to get the lowdown on the down-low."

"Clever," Brian said, apparently feeling I didn't fully appreciate the gravity of the situation.

"I thought so!" I said, attempting to hold my ground. "I'm having so much fun with you that I can't imagine turning down this job. Where do we start?"

I think he knew I would say yes, because he immediately said, "Patricia."

With only knowing where Patricia Kelly stood in the family lineage, I asked, "Do you have her phone number?"

"Sorry, Minus, that's your job."

"Email?"

"Ditto, brother."

"Okay then, what's Pat like?"

"I don't want to give you any preconceived ideas or biases, but if you wish to continue to be a baritone, don't call her Pat."

"Great, strike one and I haven't even met her."

"Not to worry, Minus. You'll do just fine," Brian comforted me, to no avail.

* * *

As I was waiting to hear back from the Oakland School District, that they were going to buy the other guy's busses, I decided to take a couple of days off to work on my new career as a spirit intermediary.

The internet would have made this search a breeze if there wasn't a plethora of P. Kellys. Excluding the ones that are no longer with us left half a plethora.

"Okay, Brian, at least tell me where she lives."

"How do you manage to sell busses when you give up so easily?"

"I haven't given up. I've just gotten tired of spinning my wheels. At least give me a country."

"Albany."

"Albania?"

"No, across the bay in Albany."

"Oh, thanks."

That narrowed the search to one. Now I had to either find a phone book or pay an online entity for her personal information.

"You're not going to make me use social media, are you?" I complained to my spirit follower.

"Come on, Minus, you have a Facebook account, use it."

"I have an account because I don't know how to delete it. Please don't make me sign in!"

"Okay, I can guide you to her house."

"Why can't you just give me her address?"

"That would be stalking."

"Excuse me, what part of sitting outside of her house isn't stalking?"

"If I just tell you how to go there, you can go without me, but if I take you, I am there to supervise."

"You spirit guys sure have a lot of rules."

I (we) hopped into Ruby and headed back across the bay. It seems my life is spent driving across the Bay Bridge. I think someday they should name a girder after me.

"Ms. Kelly hasn't ventured too far from the family," I said, fishing for more information from Brother B.

"If you think I'm going to sacrifice Patricia's privacy, you might as well start discussing the weather."

"Is that what all this secrecy is about?" I finally realized.

"She has to make this decision on her own, Minus, not be coerced by her past."

"I'm a salesman, Brian. You're asking a lot."

"I've seen your sales technique. You are a very fair person."

"Yes, but have you seen inside my pockets?"

"That's not a judge of human worth," Brian insisted.

"No, but it is of net worth."

"The spreadsheet of your empty pockets is not a true valuation of your importance as a person, Minus."

"You can see in my pockets?"

"Minus!"

"Yes."

"Never mind. I'll take you to Patricia."

Brian's guidance to Patricia's house was better than Google Maps. Before you could say "stalker," I was sitting outside her home.

"Okay, now what?" I asked my spirit guide.

"Listen, Minus, you have to take charge at some point."

"Really? I quite liked your direction."

"You're on your own now. Goodbye."

"Brian... Brian... BRIAN!"

That "goodbye" thing is *really* getting annoying.

I sat in my conspicuous car for longer than anyone should sit in a red Mustang outside a single woman's house, trying to work out my next move.

I weighed my options:

1   I could knock on her door and tell her my dead brother sent me.

2   I could wait until she came out and tell her my dead brother sent me.

3   I could borrow a puppy and stand outside her house like I was waiting for a friend. That always works as a chick magnet.

I opted for going home.

*　*　*

"Minus… Wakey, wakey." Brian's voice came into the foreground of my mind. "Time to get to work."

"I'm going to complain to the spirit union about you harassing me."

"Aren't we grumpy?"

"What time is it?" I grumbled.

"It's morning," Brian painted with a broad stroke.

"I don't mean to be difficult, but can you be a bit more specific?"

"It's six o'clock."

"Do you people not sleep?"

"I'm sure that was a rhetorical question, so I'm not going to answer."

"What do you want?"

"I want you to do what you said you would do," Brian said with an officious tone.

"Hold on, you set me up for failure and then disappeared."

"I set you up for success. You turned it into failure," he corrected me. "I'll make it easier for you today. Patricia works in the city and I know where she always eats lunch. Let's try that."

"Okay, sounds good to me, but why then are you waking me up at six o'clock in the morning?"

"I thought you might want some time to exercise and work on that belly of yours."

That was the last thing I heard before falling back to sleep until nine o'clock, when I got up on my own.

*　*　*

The lunch establishment that Patricia frequented was a truck situated at a curb in the financial district, with two wheels on blocks to prevent the food from sliding out the window and onto the street. The outdoor seating area consisted of finding whatever short wall or stoop was free.

"She isn't here yet," Brian said. "Let's hang out at the BART subway entrance."

"Us? There is no 'us' hanging out at the subway entrance. There's just me. And I'm not hanging out at the subway entrance. I'm going to keep moving until she gets here."

"All these people you're wanting to avoid are valid human beings too." Brian tried to access my liberal angst.

"That doesn't make them any less annoying." I stuck to my city self-defense.

The streets in downtown San Francisco get very crowded at lunchtime, especially on a beautiful, warm sunny day, unlike today, which was cold and foggy, so it felt like a ghost town. Which is another reason I wanted to keep moving.

I was feeling ill at ease again with this meeting. It still felt like stalking.

"Brian, this is stupid. Is this what they teach you in spirit detective school? I can't just walk up to Patricia and say, 'Hi, I'm your distant cousin, please don't sell the tomb.' I don't think that will be effective. I should just dig up her phone number and call, instead of all this cloak and dagger."

"You would rather pay a small fee to an online directory than accidentally run into a relative you didn't even know existed before two days ago?" Brian accessed my cheap side.

I had to stop and think about that question because it sounded to me that I had just been taught a lesson.

"Did you drag me all over the Bay Area because I wouldn't pay for Patricia's information?"

"Yes!" Brian answered, without hesitation.

"Can I go home now?"

"Yes," my brother repeated, without the exclamation mark.

With that, I turned to head back to my car, almost bumping into the only other soul on the block.

"Minus!" my sidewalk dancing partner said.

She looked familiar, but I thought that was just wishful thinking. "Yes?!"

"Patricia," she reminded me. "We met at a school fundraiser in February."

"I'm sorry, I didn't recognize you in the fog." I made a lame joke instead of a sincere apology.

She laughed anyway and said, "That's okay. Have you had lunch?"

I remembered the occasion when we had met. She and I had talked for an hour or more, about…everything.

"No, I haven't," I said, not one to pass up a meal.

"Let me buy you a chicken sandwich," she offered.

"Sure, thank you."

I went back inside my head and said to Brian, "You set this up, didn't you?"

"Don't look at me. You're the one who met her eight months ago and didn't know it."

"If you don't eat meat, I can get you a veggie burger." Patricia drew back my focus.

"No, I'm good with meat. I only go vegetarian in months with no vowels."

"What a coincidence, that's when I diet."

Patricia is a woman of forty-something who would die of malnutrition if she dieted.

"It looks like vowels have been good to you," I said, not sure if I just sounded stupid.

"Thank you," she reassured me that even if I was stupid, I was still polite.

As we made our way to the four-wheeled luncheon establishment, I said, "As I recall, you're a tenant's rights lawyer. Working downtown doesn't seem to fit with that MO."

"That's only part of what I do. Two months ago, I got a job at a law firm dealing in condo law. Now I can help from both sides."

The line outside the gourmet food truck was surprisingly short. When it was our turn to order, Patricia asked me, "What would you like?"

"I'll have whatever you're having," I said.

She proceeded to order two of everything: chicken sandwiches (fully loaded), vinegar and salt potato chips, and iced tea.

As she handed the truck waiter her credit card, Patricia pointed to an outrageous-looking cinnamon bun and said, "We'll share one of those."

"A lot of vowels in this month," I couldn't resist saying.

She gave the proprietor her name and we stepped to the side to continue our conversation.

"I don't get how condo law helps renters." I picked up where we had left off.

"When renters have a mole in the ministry, they have an in to become homeowners, if they wish," Patricia explained.

"Does your employer know you do that?"

"That's why they hired me. I help the company sell their units and they help me put renters in them."

"I'm not a great believer in win-win situations. It seems to me that one side usually wins better than the other," I said, with my usual cynicism.

"I agree, but I have more success than I did on the outside."

"Do your friends still talk to you?" I was bold enough to ask.

"Most," she answered, with a wilt of regret.

"Patricia," came a disembodied voice from the truck, which at first sounded like Brian.

When she went up to get our order, I checked in with my silent brother. "You still there?"

"I haven't missed a word. Did you really use that 'vowels in the month' line?"

"I think I like you better, silent," I said as Patricia returned with a feast in hand.

"I'm sorry, did you say something?" she asked, catching a bit of my chiding Brian.

"I just said, 'I drink tea better, quiet.' So, can we sit out of the wind?"

"That wasn't even close, brother," Brian goaded me.

"I'll get you for that," I promised, without moving my lips.

We found a doorway out of the wind and proceeded to devour our lunches.

After the last of the mega-cinnamon roll had been consumed and the conversation exhausted, we both sat silently leaning against the Roman-style pillars that framed the doorway to a bank that had more money than God. Neither one of us wished to speak. We both knew it was time to say goodbye.

"Can I give you a call sometime and maybe go out for another gorge fest?" I asked, definitely sounding like an idiot.

"That would be nice," Patricia said, as she wrote down her phone number on the corner of the box that her sandwich had come in.

I knocked a few crumbs off of the biodegradable packaging before slipping it into my pocket.

As she walked away, she turned back and said, "Text me your number."

I nodded.

Once she had turned the corner, I scolded Brian, "You didn't tell me she was pretty."

"I'm not running a lonely-hearts club here, Minus. You have a job to do."

I took out my phone to text Patricia and there was a message from my office. The Oakland School District wanted to move forward with my bid.

Shit, more obligations.

6

OBLIGATIONS

Life was looking up.
As long as
you didn't look around you.

Before returning to Ruby, I sent Patricia my vitals, including the best places to park around my house. By the time I got back to my car, it held a note from the City of San Francisco Department of Motor Vehicles.

"I told you an hour wasn't enough time for the meter," Brian spoke up.

"Do you have any connections in the SFMTA?" I asked, making a mental note to pad my expense account.

Brian was silent for a moment before declaring, "Nope."

My plan had been to go home after lunch and take a nap, but current events with my employment demanded that I drop into the office first. It appeared, the presentation I had made to the Oakland School District was so well received by the superintendent that she was ready to commit to signing up for my biggest sale to date. Granted, I did make some big promises I hoped I could keep, but there's no need to go into the underbelly of the bus business. Why? Really...why? A sale is a sale.

I wondered if Brian had anything to do with this sudden success in my career. It had been such a longshot that anyone would believe that I could deliver thirty busses in four weeks.

Not that it mattered, except that I might owe him a commission.

My mind was so occupied with "business" that I was halfway to the office before I realized that I had either left Brian back at the curb or he was lying dormant waiting for an opportunity to scare the hell out of me.

"Little brother? Wakey, wakey," I said.

"Have you been planning on saying that all day?" His voice materialized in my head.

"No, it was an inadvertent reaction to an annoying event."

"Good, I would have been disappointed if you had worked on that for more than five seconds. Are you *really* going to go to work now?"

"No, I thought we could catch a flight to the Bahamas. You need to work on your tan," I said, figuring that would shut him up now that I'd got him talking.

"I'm not expecting you to shirk your responsibilities for my project, but I did see on your calendar that you have an appointment to attend a school board meeting. I presume in the East Bay."

"Damn, I forgot about that. When were you looking at my calendar?" I asked in surprise.

"I was looking when you were looking."

"You can see out of my eyes?"

"You bet! I saw what you were looking at when Patricia was walking away."

"We need to make some rules moving forward here," I insisted.

"Don't worry, what happens in Minus, stays in Minus," Brian said, attempting to ease my mind.

"What the hell does that mean?"

"It means I won't gossip back in The Yard."

"That's comforting," I said.

"Do you want me to cross my heart and hope to die?"

With that bit of irony ringing in my head, I entered a new destination on the GPS and headed over the Bay Bridge.

* * *

Once home, the sofa greeted and enticed me.

"I need some time off," I said to myself and Brian if he was there,
"or I need to start selling refrigerators. I'm too old to be sucking up
to anyone."

I guess I was just talking to myself. I couldn't believe Brian would
have passed up a chance to comment on my age. So, I took the opportunity to have a shower in private.

After rinsing off a day of raised voices and special interests, I fell
onto the sofa.

"You really should have that mole on your right thigh looked at,"
Dr. Brian Filbert recommended.

"Any chance I can have a word with your supervisor now?" I
asked.

"Sorry, he's visiting relatives in Maine," Brian responded. "You
can do this, Minus. You just need to compartmentalize your goals.
That was a great job you did today. Not only did you make contact
with Patricia, but you sucked up to your clients like a pro."

"I am brain dead right now," I confessed to Brian. "Do you have
any suggestions on my next step with saving the souls on the hill?"

"You can start by going to bed. You look like shit."

"How about your secretary? I could begin with a grievance to
your assistant."

"Go to bed, Minus."

* * *

I had a dream.

I was on a small island with a majestic mountain rising from the center. I sat on the beach facing the horizon listening to the Sirens. Their song called to me. It was emanating from the mountain rather than the rocks beneath the waves.

The base of the mountain was filled with a low rumble of men's voices, rising to the soft tones of alto and mezzo. Tenors and sopranos floated off the peak.

Looking out to sea, I felt content.

Suddenly, the music stopped. I wasn't sure if I had woken up or if the souls of the mountain had gone away, leaving me with a sadness. I felt the absence of home...of friends...of self.

The sadness invaded me with a sense of loss and the emptiness of the sea.

The sadness went through me and out to the endless ocean to relieve a lifetime of pain that had dwelled inside.

I slept in peace until morning.

* * *

I awoke early, long before I opened my eyes. The memory of the dream was still with me, though the peace was gone.

I laid still, not sure I should open my eyes. Unsure if I could. Not willing to try.

"Are you going to lay there all day?" Brian's voice came into my head.

"Supervisor?"

"Still busy."

I raised my lids to reveal another day. Careful to avoid catching a glimpse of myself in the mirror, I sat up as the sun hit the horizon.

"Am I going to wake up to you every morning?"

"Probably, at least until this job is done. Does that bother you, brother?"

"Don't worry. Most things bother me."

Brian suggested that I check my phone for a message from Patricia.

I prefer to wait at least sixty seconds after waking before delving into the day. This discipline keeps me from appearing to be an utter digital addict.

Sadly, my lifeline to the world, the holder of all knowledge, this icon of technological wonder was dead.

Once its umbilical cord had been securely attached, I asked Brian to wait in the living room while I stepped into the bathroom.

When I came out, Brian didn't hesitate to say, "I think your phone has enough charge to work now."

"Coffee first," I said, mainly to tweak him.

With a freshly brewed cup of coffee and a dead brother ready to strangle me, I turned on my phone. "Sorry, kid, no contact yet. Why are you suddenly in such a hurry?" I finally asked, realizing Brian had become quite agitated.

"Patricia had an offer come in late last night and I'm worried she will accept it."

"Why didn't you tell me that earlier?"

"Well, you seemed to be having so much fun making me wait."

"I was, but this is important."

"I'm glad you appreciate how grave this situation is."

"How about I give her a call to see if she would like to have lunch in a sit-down restaurant?" I suggested.

"Rushing things might scare her away," Brian cautioned.

"Under these conditions, breakfast might be rushing things, but lunch could be too late."

Brian was silent for a moment before settling on brunch.

I sent Patricia a text because seven a.m. was too early, by anyone's standards, to call.

Good morning Patricia, Minus here.

I truly enjoyed our lunch yesterday.

Would you care to have an early lunch today, at Tadich Grill?

I would like to speak to you about a business deal.

"I don't know if being so direct is a good idea," Brian warned.

"It's better than congratulating her on the sale of the tomb."

"You're the salesman."

"Thank you for making that sound like a good thing."

My phone rang as I set it on the table. "Looks like it isn't too early for some people," Brian commented.

The caller ID showed *Suspected Fraud*.

"That's the devil trying to horn in on the deal," I joked.

"Nah, he prefers 'land' at a lower altitude," Brian quipped back.

The phone rang again. This time it was my office.

"Hi Kathy," I answered, "how are you?"

"Good morning, Minus. I'm good. The superintendent of schools in Oakland would like to discuss the sale today over an early lunch."

My phone dinged. It was Patricia accepting my invitation.

Brian was silent, letting me decide how to handle this situation.

"Kathy, tell the superintendent that I'm buried in appointments today. I can meet her tomorrow morning at eleven at an East Bay restaurant of her choice. Let her know I eat meat."

"Will do."

"Thanks, Kathy."

"You're not afraid you may lose this sale by putting the client off?" Brian asked.

"If a lunch can break a deal, it was a deal that was destined to be broken."

I quickly responded to Patricia suggesting that we meet at the restaurant.

* * *

Brian and I arrived at Tadich a few minutes early to secure a private booth. While I wanted to order a glass of wine, the lecture I received from Brian on the evils of drinking in the morning caused me to change my request to a mimosa. *Hold the orange juice.*

Tadich Grill is the oldest restaurant in downtown San Francisco. A bit old-fashioned, but you can't beat the attitude. If the servers at the Fairmont are Shirley Temples, the waiters at Tadich are Bloody Marys.

"What are you planning to say to Patricia?" Brian asked.

"Damned if I know. I figure the conversation will find its way."

"You're kidding, you're going to wing it?"

"I'll have you know that I've built a mediocre sales career with this technique."

"You're starting to scare me, Minus."

"Hello," Patricia said, standing at the end of the table, looking like she had just come off a fashion runway. "I'm sorry, were you on the phone?" she asked, having heard me sounding like a schizophrenic with an inferiority disorder.

I jumped up, saying, "I was just practicing a presentation."

Patricia was my age but looked ten years younger. If she dyed her hair, it would take an electron microscope to tell. Her face showed none of the battles she had fought for others, though her posture hinted at a weariness.

She smiled and sat down across the table. "Was it a presentation for me?"

"No, I thought maybe we could work on that one together," I offered.

"That's an interesting concept, having your target help develop the weapon," she commented.

I liked her handle on constructing an analogy on the spot, though the imagery was a little unsettling.

"Well, you know your needs better than I. I'm just a facilitator. A bridge between parties."

"May I ask who the other party is?" she asked, with a firm grip on the conversation.

"That's a little touchy. I would like to ease into the details. Shall we start with ordering lunch and then move on to creating the dialogue?"

"Sure, the suspense is making me ravenous." Patricia gracefully followed my suggestion.

When our waiter arrived, he looked at Patricia then at me. I felt his eyes noticing every wrinkle in my suit. Turning back to Ms. Kelly, he asked, "Would you like something a little stronger than champagne?"

"Thank you, I'll have a mimosa. *Hold the bubbles.*"

The place was filling up, so we took advantage of the waiter being at our table to order before the kitchen staff went into hyperdrive. Patricia opted for the crab Louie and I, with a suggestion from Brian, chose the sea bass.

Having dispensed with the waiter, Patricia locked eyes with me. A rather delicate smile rose on the corner of her mouth that I wasn't quite sure how to read. Was she amused with my playful banter, or was lack of food creating indigestion?

"You're a man of mystery," she softly spoke as her smile extended to the other side of her mouth. "I'm starting to doubt that our meeting was happenstance."

"Suspicion becomes you," I responded. "Insight plays nicely on your face."

Her eyes broke free. "Thank you, that's the strangest thing anyone has ever said to me."

"You can always count on me for strange things," I said to comfort her.

"There are unknowns at work here," I continued, "but there always are. I had hoped to run into you. I just didn't know it was you I wanted to run into."

She momentarily crossed her eyes.

"You think that's obtuse, wait until I start trying to be clear," I said, before becoming transparent. "I had read an article about you, though I didn't realize we had already met."

"This is about the gravesite?" she questioned, with a slight edge in her voice.

"It's about more than real estate. It's about family."

"Yours or mine?"

"Ours."

"Please explain how that works?"

"That I can do. My great-aunt Joan Filbert married your great-uncle Brendan Kelly, around 1910. They can still be found frolicking in The Yard."

"What's The Yard?"

"That's 'their' name for the cemetery."

"That's whose name for the cemetery?" Patricia asked, putting me into damage control.

Brian couldn't resist commenting, "You stepped right into that one, big brother."

Without missing a beat, I answered, "The groundskeepers."

"Well done, Minus, I thought she had you," Mr. Helpful rewarded me.

"I need to slow down a bit," Patricia said, as she sipped her orange juice that had magically appeared on the table. "Are you laying claim to part of the profits?"

"Not at all. I would like to talk to you about reconsidering selling the property. I know you have an offer, which is why I'm rushing things here."

"How did you know an offer had come in?"

"I have connections in low places."

"You *are* very cryptic."

"It comes with the job."

"And, what's the job?"

"Protecting the crypt."

"Hmmm," she hummed, before falling into a silent stare at her orange juice flute.

"I have no judgments of you, me, or the family members who came before us," I said. "It's not about right and wrong. It's about being clear on what is most important in our lives. I don't know your reasons for the sale. I assume, from what I know about you, that they are just."

Patricia completed her study of the orange liquid and locked her gaze back onto my irises. For a moment, I felt like a glass of juice.

"I've gotten a lot of flak over my decision to sell the land. You're the first person not to accuse me of profiteering. What's your motivation?"

"I have an uncanny sense of responsibility to the past," I skirted the question.

"You have an uncanny ability not to answer questions."

"Only the ones that don't help my cause," I said, as our lunch was hitting the table.

"She does have a wonderful smile, even with suspicious eyes," Brian said to me.

"Can we change the subject?" Patricia said, changing the subject. "Before we go into my motivations, I would like to learn a little more about you, Mr. Sea Bass," she said, looking at my lunch. "What drives your conscience?"

Unclear as to the reference to the fish on my plate, I studied it for a moment before admitting, "It does have an uncanny resemblance to my brother, but I sense you were meaning something else."

"That fish is both the present and the past," she said. "You hold a responsibility to the memory of its life not to waste the flesh."

"Excuse me, do you have a magnifying glass I can borrow, I need to study that statement?" I showed my confusion.

"It's not that oblique, but I do carry a magnifying glass. Look, the world we live in is filled with needs. The past has no needs."

"What if the past does still exist?" I began my tutorial in the ways of the dead. "When the flesh of the fish is gone, does that mean it no longer matters?"

"That's exactly what it means," she concurred.

"She got you on that one," Brian said. "I'm not sure comparing us to fish is a good tactic. Maybe try using a primate."

"Okay, expanding on your fish reference might not be applicable here," I confessed, "but isn't the memory of a person as important as the person herself?"

"No!" she said abruptly.

"One more strike and you're in the dugout," Brian kept score.

"How about this?" I continued. "Your parents are no longer with us, correct?"

She nodded.

"If someone disparaged their memory, would you not take umbrage? Maybe even sue, depending on the seriousness of the offense?"

"An insult against my family isn't an assault on me," Patricia answered.

"Is that right?" I questioned. "Since you're an extension of your parents, I would think it important to preserve their honor."

"If only there had been honor!" Patricia Kelly proclaimed, laying her past to rest.

"I don't want to browbeat you." I stepped back. "All I ask is that you give it a little more time before accepting the offer."

"Why?"

I looked down at my sea bass hoping it would have the answer to this one-word question. If it did, the fish wasn't talking. There was only one thing I could say.

"Because."

She put down her fork and picked up her glass.

"I can hold on a little longer, but I have an obligation to meet," Patricia revealed, not wanting to expand on the details.

We raised our glasses.

"With a divergence of opinion and a little understanding, may we create a mimosa," I made a toast.

Clink.

I honored my sea bass by eating *every last bite*, as Patricia did for her crab.

Looking around the crowded restaurant, I wondered how I was able to get a booth, instead of a table near the kitchen.

"Brian? Don't tell me you know the owner's mother?" I asked, going back into my head.

"No, his ex-wife," Brian said.

Patricia's voice drew me back out. "May I ask you a personal question?"

"The last time I was asked that, I ended up a part-owner of a condo in Tampa, but go ahead."

"Where do you stand in your family tree? I'm the last in my direct line. I didn't expect you, an offshoot."

"I've been called a lot of things in my sales career, but never an offshoot," I said, before continuing with an analogy that was even too artsy for me.

"Some family trees are evergreen, others deciduous. I'm afraid mine is in the autumn of its existence and I am the sole dangling leaf."

"That sounds lonely."

"I rarely get lonely. The family is never truly gone."

I paid the bill and suggested we walk over to the waterfront to get an ice cream. On the way, a homeless woman walked up and asked for help to buy food. Patricia pulled a twenty-dollar bill out of her purse and handed it to the woman.

"That was generous," I said as we walked on.

"Well, what would you do?"

"I would have asked for change."

"No, you would not."

"You're right because I wouldn't have given her any money in the first place," I admitted.

"If they feel they need to ask a total stranger for help, they need the money more than I do," Patricia explained her philosophy.

The San Francisco waterfront once had an icon to human corruption slicing through its heart. A raised double-decker freeway running along the Embarcadero, like a pipeline moving oil into the pockets of the rich. It took an earthquake and a lot of good people to bring it down to reveal one of the most beautiful promenades on the planet.

With my double scoop on a sugar cone and Patricia with a triple in a bowl, we sat on a wooden bench watching cargo freighters sail by. To our right rose the Bay Bridge. A suspension-style structure spanning the water to Buena Vista Island, where the road cut through the central hill to reveal a ghostly white span completing the journey to Oakland.

From our perch, I could see the line of eucalyptus trees that shielded the hill from the city. Behind that flora wall was a place I would reside someday. It always seemed like a safe spot that the mortal world protected and even sanctified. I can be so naive.

We stayed on that bench until the ice cream faded from our senses and we spoke no more of the dead.

7

THE DEAD

Another day,
another trip across the bridge.

San Francisco is one of the major cities of the world and still, I have to drive to the other side of the bay to do business. I know there's enterprise happening in this town. I can see all the tall buildings in my rearview mirror.

Kathy had set up a meeting for me with Helen Wheeler, the Oakland Unified School District's superintendent. The plan was to convene at Oliveto's for an 11:30 lunch to discuss the purchase details. This seemed very strange to me. Usually, I meet with a guy named Harry at a bar under a freeway overpass, not the top dog at a fancy restaurant.

"So, Brian," I began the conversation with my meddler brother, "what can you tell me about this situation you've gotten me into?"

"Excuse me, are you insinuating that I have anything to do with this bus sale?"

"I'm lucky if I sell a bus every lunar eclipse and all of a sudden I'm outfitting one hundred and eighteen schools. Hmmm, seems odd!

If I didn't know any better, I would say you're setting me up to buy the hill."

"I'm just hedging my bets, Minus. It's essential that the hill remains as it is," Brian said, his voice dropping a major third to show the seriousness of the statement.

"I hope you're not putting all your money on Minus," I warned him.

"You're our Golden Boy. A lot is riding on you."

"You know, we could end this gambling analogy with me crapping out," I brought home the reality of this venture.

"Minus, you'll do just fine."

I drove to the Rockridge neighborhood of Oakland with its beautiful old craftsman-style architecture. The restaurant, where I was to meet Ms. Wheeler, was on the corner of a large building that housed an upscale food mart. This cooperative of gourmet edibles was like a wet dream of an Italian chef.

Once inside, the hostess took me to the table where the superintendent had already been seated. Rising to shake my hand, with a grip that could crush a school bus, she said, "Welcome, Mr. Filbert, I'm Helen."

"Please call me Minus. I'm not much for prefixes."

"Would you care for a drink?" the hostess asked.

I noticed that Helen was working on a cup of coffee, so I ordered the same.

Helen gave me the chair looking into the room, taking the seat that faced the wall for herself. To me, this characteristic showed a thoughtfulness for others. A quiet sense of self-sacrifice, not usually found in a person of power.

Helen was of African descent. She looked vaguely familiar, though I knew we had never met. Dressed in a professionally conservative pantsuit, I felt myself looking a bit like a slob.

"I hope traffic wasn't too bad," she consoled me.

"I'm not bothered by the traffic anymore. It's like the sun coming up in the morning, you can't change it, so enjoy it."

"That's a healthy attitude. Do you give seminars on how to do that?"

"No, seminars drive me nuts," I said, to a rousing laugh from my luncheon partner.

"Have you eaten here before?" Helen inquired. "I love the menu."

"No, what do you recommend?"

"If you like pasta, you can't miss. If you don't like pasta, we could go down the street to Burger King."

I made the pronouncement, "Pasta it is."

After ordering our pasta, we got down to business.

Helen began, "I'm not going to hold you to your delivery time. That seems quite optimistic, though it did get my attention. But what caught my eye was your name."

"Yes, 'Minus' has gotten me a lot of attention in my life."

"Filbert is what I'm referring to. I knew your father."

"Oh?" I said with great surprise.

"Yes, he was a counselor at my high school. I owe a lot to him. Mr. Filbert was one of those people who comes into your life and never leaves," Helen said, with a tear in her voice. "I was so sad when he died."

"I don't remember you at his funeral. Did you not get notified?"

"I couldn't go. I was too upset to attend," she said with a tear in her eye. "But as you can tell, I'm much better now."

"I can see that. Would you like a tissue?" I offered.

She smiled and said, "Yes."

"I'm feeling a little funny getting this contract in the light of your relationship with my father," I admitted. "I would prefer it was your faith in me."

"Your father has given me faith in you. When I saw your name on the bid, I felt his presence. I remembered how I was going nowhere when I met him and by the time I left high school, I'd been accepted to Brown University. I can still hear his voice in my head."

"Really? I've got my brother's in mine. Want to trade?" I joked.

"That's not funny," Brian quipped.

"No thank you," Helen gracefully declined. "I like his company."

The pasta arrived at the table and the conversation continued with stories of Paul Filbert. May he rest in peace.

*   *   *

After lunch, I decided to visit my father's grave. All this talk of him had gotten me uncharacteristically emotional. I never knew he had such a profound effect on others outside the family.

To touch another person's life is wonderful. To save it is powerful.

"Brian, I would like to talk to Mom and Pops," I said, as I drove through the steely gates of the cemetery.

"It isn't that easy, Minus. I'm allowed to speak to you because we have a job to do. You can't just ring up and say, 'Hi, is Dad home?'"

"Let's look at it this way," I redefined my position, "if you want this job done, I need to talk to them."

"Even here that's considered extortion," Brian complained.

"That's a strong word. I prefer coercion."

Brian conceded, "I'll make a few calls to see what I can do, but the final decision will be theirs."

I parked in my usual spot in the lower lot. Instead of automatically heading to my regular haunts, I decided to wander around the grounds. As much as I have avoided this place, I've been coming here for more years than I should have had to, never having ventured beyond my family's plot. There was too much sadness here. The absence of life, beyond the trees, had no appeal.

Now, these dormant headstones act as place settings for life on some other plane of consciousness. There are souls here who have touched me in the past few days. The words etched into the stones are introductions to strangers, not just markers to witness what once was.

The Yard is a city. Set on the edge of suburban sprawl, it covers acres of the most beautiful land in the Oakland Hills. Groomed beyond nature but keeping the sense of freedom. "Someday, this will be my home," I said to myself.

"And you will be welcome, Minus," Brian's voice came back to me.

"You don't make the newbies cut the lawn, do you?" I said, ruining the moment.

"No, but in your case, I'm sure we can make an exception."

I asked him how he liked being here, attempting to regain the calm of the land.

"There is no way I can convey what it is to be here. This existence is as far away from your understanding as your ability is to understand the life of a cell. I don't mean that as an insult. Knowledge is linear. It builds on itself, so you have to keep walking that line until you get here."

I tried to think of a joke that would allow me not to have to figure out what it was he had just said, but my mind went blank.

"Minus, you still there?" Brian mocked my grammar.

"Yes, I'm sorry, I dozed off for a moment. You were saying?"

"Dad would love to talk to you."

"Really! I don't owe him money, do I?"

"Minus, you make very little sense when you're nervous. Calm down. He doesn't bite, much."

"I'm fine. I just didn't think past asking to speak to Pops. Will you be staying on the line?"

"No, we've found that more than one extra voice in your head tends to drive people crazy."

"You might want to continue that study concerning just one extra voice." I had to get one last jab in before changing stations.

"MINUS!!" came a voice that was larger than life. "How the hell have you been?"

"I'd know that bull horn anywhere. Hi, Pops."

"First of all, I would like to thank you for that great sendoff you gave me. All those wonderful things people were saying about me, I thought I had gone to the wrong funeral."

"It was all true, Pops. The sugar coating was just to make it palatable."

"You're a good boy, Minus."

"You know, Pops, I'm the same age as you when you died."

"Is that right? Other than that gut of yours, you look pretty good."

"Thanks."

"Brian tells me you asked to talk to me. What's up?"

"What? A son can't just talk to his father for no reason?"

"No!"

"Okay, I would like to ask you about Helen Wheeler. I had lunch with her today."

"I know. I had lunch with her last week. She's a great gal. Listen, kid, we're trying to create a win-win situation here. I'm thrilled that you're on the team. I have friends in The Yard whom I don't want to see displaced."

"I've been trying to conceptualize this situation, but most of the information I've gotten so far consists of a lot of popping balloons," I said.

"You were here for that?" Pops said. "I had my money on the colonel. Listen, Minus, we don't tell you everything because that would influence decisions made in pre-life. Even worse, the greedy and manipulative would use it to their advantage."

"Pre-life? I assume that's my existence?"

"I can't expand on that and shouldn't have used the term in the first place," Pops chastised himself.

"It sounds like a marketing scheme to me," I offered. "*Unhappy with your pre-life? Come to 'Souls Wiped Clean' and start a new life in minutes.*"

"I'll suggest the idea to my manager, but for now, can you take this seriously?"

"Sorry."

"You need to have faith, Minus."

"That's not easy for me," I said. "Look at it from my perspective, Pops. Everything that has happened is all in my head. You, Brian, the balloons. I could just be a nut case with a good job."

"Your job is your power. The nuttiness makes you lovable." My father giveth and taketh.

"Thanks, how so?" I kept the conversation moving, hopefully past discussing my mental state.

"Sales! Every interaction is a promotion of some sort. We sell things and ideas, but mostly ourselves. You're a good man, Minus, you sell honesty."

"Is that why I'm always broke?"

"That and you buy expensive cars." Dear old Pops had to bring Ruby into the mix.

"Well, even if I'm crazy, it's a noble challenge." I then changed the subject. "How's Mom?"

"She's great! Just started a watercolor class."

The conversation continued without revealing any more sensitive information. My stomach once again dictated the length of the visit by suggesting it was dinnertime. I invited Pops to join me for a bite, but he declined, citing a metaphysical *tai chi* class he had to get to. I wasn't sure if he was joking.

Pops signed off for the time being, so I went back to my pricey little car and called Patricia.

When the all-too-familiar voicemail picked up, I suggested meeting for an early dinner at Waterbar, a wonderful San Francisco restaurant overlooking the bay. "Oysters are a dollar each during happy hour," I said, trying to tempt her into joining me at a table with a view of the East Bay lights.

Thursday afternoon traffic into the city is like going to the DMV. You stand in line to take a number to stand in another line before you're told, *"The office is now closed. Please come back tomorrow, we open at nine."*

I made it to the restaurant just after the last cheap oyster had been served. Patricia walked in just behind me.

"Your timing is impeccable. We've both missed happy hour," I said. "Care for dinner?"

After putting my name in with the hostess, I turned back to Patricia. The bright, colorful dress she wore was in distinct contrast to the pale, anxious look on her face.

"Are you okay?" I asked. "You look like you've seen a ghost."

"Did you see him too?" she whispered.

"You have some explaining to do," I whispered back.

"You'll think I'm crazy."

"Believe me, once you're done looking crazy, it will be my turn. Let's get a drink."

I went to the bar to order our drinks while Patricia hovered over any table with an empty glass. Since I had put in a request for a window table, it was going to be some time before we saw a menu.

Through good luck and intimidation, we secured a table for two not far from the bar for easy access. Patricia had ordered a Negroni, and I, a Manhattan. Between those two drinks, we could ignite a bonfire.

"Shall we get right to the spooks, or would you like to start with the weather?" I began the conversation.

"Do you take anything seriously?" she asked, getting a handle on my personality.

"Only if joking doesn't work," I gave my stock reply.

"I'm really scared. My life has been invaded," Patricia said, looking around the room.

"Okay, no more jokes. What's going on?"

"It started with a dream. Normally, I never remember my dreams, but this was different, it felt like real life and he was in it."

"I take it you're talking about the fellow you saw tonight?"

"Yes, even though I haven't seen his face, I know it's the same person. Then the dreams kept coming. Every night. I found them unsettling at first, then they became frightening."

"What was he after?"

"He started with planting the seed of selling the gravesites to help finance low-income home buyers. I thought that was a stupid idea, so he began telling me that if I didn't sell the land, he would reveal some indiscretions about my grandfather. I told him to go ahead. It's no skin off my nose. I don't think he liked that, so his next tact was to ruin my career."

"Does he have something on you?" I asked.

"No, I've been very careful to keep my nose clean, but these days that doesn't seem to matter. It appears the spirits have caught on to fake news. He told me the media would spread accusations that I had created an offshore account to siphon off funds from the corporation's clients."

"That isn't true," I quickly acknowledged.

"Of course not. So, I told him to piss off. He didn't seem to like that either, so the next day I was called into my boss's office to fend off accusations of embezzlement."

"How did he do that?"

"I don't know, but my boss had an electronic trail showing their money going into my account. I told him that the account wasn't mine and someone was trying to frame me. Of course, he wanted me to prove my innocence. So, I asked him to give me a day, which bought me the time to agree to sell the land. The next day, my record was clear. Doesn't that sound crazy to you?"

"If you had told that story to anyone but me, they would have either hauled you away or asked for the publishing rights. Now let me tell you how I fit into all of this."

"Mr. Filbert?" I looked up to see the hostess standing next to me. "Your table is ready."

"That was fast," Patricia commented.

"That's my team at work," I said. "They seem to have a lot of connections in the hospitality industry."

Patricia looked confused. Now I had some explaining to do.

Our hostess showed us to a table with a stunning view of the Bay Bridge and the East Bay's lights. As we sat down, Patricia said, "I think there are some spirit spies here."

"Why do you say that?" I asked.

"Did you see the couple we walked past in the bar? The way they looked at us gave me the shivers."

"They aren't aberrations. Those folks had put their name in before us. They were pissed that we were seated first."

We stopped talking for a moment to take in the view. Even after living in this town for over forty years, I never get tired of its beauty. The Bay Bridge with its computerized light show by artist Leo Villareal was mesmerizing. The San Francisco span had a motion reminiscent of a ballerina dancing a pirouette across a mirrored wall. Patricia seemed to be equally drawn into the movement. We sat in silence until our waiter arrived to refresh our drinks and inform us of the specials that the chef had created for our evening.

"You're a unique specimen, Minus," Patricia reopened the conversation with a compliment. I think.

"Thank you. I think."

"I meant it in a good way. You don't make me feel like a pariah."

"I'm still not sure if that's a compliment."

"Let me rephrase it… I like you."

"That I understand. I like you too," I said. "Now, I think I should explain my part in all of this."

I had to think about how I was going to do that. Should I start with the football Ouija pointer, the Finkleman kids, or just jump right into Brian? I opted for calling the waiter over to see how my Manhattan was doing.

"Minus, I don't think there's anything you can say that would shock me." Patricia attempted to ease my mind.

"I know. I just don't want to sound too crazy to myself. Let me start from the middle." I proceeded to fill Patricia in with details that I would have preferred to keep to myself.

"My *mostly* dead brother, Brian, came to me a few days back asking for help in stopping the sale of the tomb. Our meeting was not accidental. The fact that we had met before was either coincidence or metaphysical meddling. Now, after hearing your story, it feels like I was engaged to help you, help the relatives, and eat at some nice restaurants."

Patricia sat waiting for the next installment of my tale.

"Questions?" I asked.

"No, keep going," she nudged me to keep the story moving.

"Okay. It looks like *Team Minus* is working on making it possible for me to buy the tomb from you, if need be."

"Well, get in line," Patricia said. "I'm up to four offers already."

"Really?" I screeched in surprise, an octave higher than comfortable conversation would allow.

"Yep, and they're all over-bids," she said in a hushed voice to counteract my Robert Plant impersonation.

I adjusted my pitch to something below middle C so we could continue our discussion without earplugs. "That makes finding the bad guy more difficult. Has your dream man directed you to one of the buyers?"

"Can we call him something else? That sounds a little too intimate. How about Maurice?"

"That's not really a name I would have pulled out of the air," I said.

"That's the name he gave me. Maurice is a bit full of himself. Obnoxious, really."

"Great, a ghost holding a hand mirror." I set an image to knock him down a notch.

"To answer your question, he hasn't favored anyone. I don't think he wants to show his hand," Detective Sergeant Patricia Kelly hypothesized.

"So, if you sell to the wrong person, including me, Maurice won't be happy."

"I don't think Maurice is ever happy, but yes, I believe he will smite me."

The drinks arrived at our table, distracting me from commenting on the word "smite." It sounded so biblical.

"Are you ready to order?" the waiter asked.

"I'm sorry," I said, "we haven't even looked at the menu."

"Not a problem," the tall, slender waiter who reminded me of my brother said, "absolutely no rush."

"That's not something you usually hear at a crowded restaurant," Patricia observed, as the waiter walked away.

"Brian works in mysterious ways," I continued the biblical theme.

We toasted Brian with our fresh drinks and sat for a moment watching the lights pirouette across the bridge.

Patricia broke the silence. "I don't understand the opposition to selling the land. It seems to me that the souls who inhabited those bodies are free to go anywhere they want to. I know a nice beach on Saint Lucia," Patricia offered.

"Ah, if post-pre-life was that easy," I said, coining a phrase I knew would tweak Brian. "The reality is; unless there's a graveyard on a beach in the Caribbean, the souls go where their bodies go. I don't understand the physics behind being dead. They are quite tight lipped for being skeletons."

"Oh!" Patricia lamented.

I opened the menu after hearing my belly's contribution to the conversation. "Shall we eat?" I suggested. "The dead can wait."

We quietly allowed the menu to reveal its secrets.

*　　*　　*

With the dinner order firmly embedded in our waiter's memory, we returned to our situation.

"I'm feeling like a pawn," Patricia said.

"I think that would be a step up. I equate us more to the guy who follows behind the knight's horse with a shovel and bucket."

"I'm sorry, you lost me there," my fellow chess player said, looking like a deer annoyed by headlights.

"I sense that there is trouble in paradise and we're here to clean up the mess. If this were just a simple case of 'movin' on up,' everyone would be doing it. There would be a special section in the classifieds for 'Properties to die for.' No, we're shoveling poo."

"Was that statement meant to clarify things?"

"It didn't?"

"You could have blown bubbles into your Manhattan and it would have made more sense. I still don't see why Maurice wants me to sell the land."

"I would say the multiple offers are people wanting to do better for their families. I bet Maurice has other motivations."

"Such as?" Patricia was quick to ask.

"Such as... Well probably... It might be... I don't know the reason. I'm shooting from the hip here. I just have a gut feeling that we are in the middle of something that I'd rather not be in the middle of."

"I'll drink to that," Patricia toasted.

With that, we drained our glasses and ordered another round. It was going to be a long night.

8

A LONG NIGHT

*I can't remember the last time
I drank four Manhattans in an evening.
I do remember the first two.
That's where it gets fuzzy.*

After a wonderful meal, we stepped out onto the Embarcadero. Patricia and I agreed it would be prudent to take a walk before attempting to find the ignitions in our respective cars.

"I love the bay at night," Patricia broke the hush. "I can't imagine a place more peaceful. I grew up here with the freeway running along this street. For me, it was as it had always been. But then, when the freeway came down, I saw the beauty of the past. How anyone could take such a magnificent promenade and turn it into an auto duct is beyond me."

"Greed!" I said. "A desire to thrive and flourish beyond what is necessary. Though as you can see, nature and beauty won out."

Patricia smiled and took my arm. "You, I trust."

We walked along the waterfront for an hour, both lost in our thoughts.

When we got back to our cars, a cold breeze created a shiver that ran circles around my chest. Standing next to my Mustang was a ghostly figure. A man with no face, but a presence that could not be ignored. Since I had only walked off two of the four Manhattans, I asked, "Can I help you?"

He didn't move. He didn't say anything. *He did* make a noise that sounded like a cat in heat.

"Sorry, I didn't get that," I said. "Cat got your tongue?"

In that way I have, I managed to annoy the spook who then rose above my car, hovered for a moment, then slammed down on Ruby's hood.

I saw red. I worked my ass off to buy that car. I didn't care if this guy was dead. I was going to kill him. By the time he rolled off the hood, I was in his faceless face. He looked at me, I think.

"Listen, jerk off," I scolded, "you can't intimidate us. I'm going to pull your foreskin up over your head, you toothless pile of shit."

Just as I was about to circumcise Maurice, Brian's voice came into my head. "What the hell are you doing, Minus?"

I stepped back to regain my composure. "What the hell does it look like? I'm square dancing with the ghost of Christmas future, then I'm going to shove a noble fir up his ass."

"Relax, brother, your car is alright. He's messing with your head. He can't physically change anything."

"Tell that to the guys at the body shop. Look at my car."

"I told you, your car is fine. He planted that image in your mind. He can't touch you and you can't tie his penis in a knot."

"Minus?" Patricia came back into focus. "What are you doing?" she said, with a quiver in her voice.

"Good question. Did you see what just happened?"

"Yeah, Maurice just stomped on your car."

"Brian, is she seeing things too?"

"Yes, he planted the same image in both of your minds."

I walked back to Patricia while keeping an eye on the man in black.

"Brian is here," I told her. "He says we're seeing things."

"Yeah! We're seeing your car get destroyed."

"Trust me on this one. I'll explain later."

"Now you're pushing the envelope," Patricia replied.

That made me smile. I love sarcasm in the face of adversity.

"Brian," I turned back to *my* ghost, "how do we deal with this guy?"

"You have to trust what I tell you to think." Now Brian was pushing the envelope. "Look at your car and imagine it as it was."

I looked over at my poor little pony with the broken nose and told myself it was not damaged. That didn't work, so I closed my eyes and imagined making the insurance claim. When I opened my eyes, the car was back to normal.

"I got it, Brian, you're right. My car is fine."

"Of course, I'm right. This is my world."

"Patricia," I called out, "this guy can't hurt you. My car is safe and so are you. Trust what I tell you. Imagine faceless here in a lead box on the bottom of the bay and he will leave your mind."

Patricia closed her eyes and made a little squizzy face. For a moment, I wasn't sure if she was exorcising the demon or needing to pee. When she came back to the present, she said, "He's gone."

"Yes, I don't think he found us very sociable," I said. "Thanks, Brian, we won the battle."

"Is your brother still here?" Patricia asked.

"It takes more than a weak-chinned crusader to get rid of him. I'd introduce you to him, but I'm not sure what channel he's on."

"That's okay. I just wanted to say thank you."

"You're welcome," Brian had me pass on to her.

"Well," I said to my two companions, "that bit of excitement burned off the remaining two drinks. Do you mind if we recap the evening's events tomorrow? I'm ready for bed."

Patricia looked scared. Brian said nothing.

"It looks like I've been outvoted," I surmised. "Shall we reconvene at my place for a nightcap?"

As Patricia followed in her car, Brian and I had a heart-to-heart talk.

"What have you gotten me into?" I asked. "I don't think you've filled me in with all the pertinent information. What do you think, dear brother?"

"You think I knew that there was some other spirit party interested in the property and didn't tell you?"

"Yes!"

"Why would I do that?"

"To not scare me off?"

"That's a good reason, but not correct. I had no idea who was orchestrating this sale. Whoever this faceless guy is, he's not made himself known to me. But, I'm going to find out his identity."

"What else don't you know?"

"I don't know."

"Sorry, that was a really stupid question. By the way, thanks for helping out back there. You saved the day," I said, remembering the politeness my parents had taught me.

"I'm on your side, brother. Just remember that. I'll see you in the morning," Brian began his sign-off.

"You're leaving?" I squeaked. "I invited you over to my place with Patricia."

"Don't worry, Minus, you'll be okay."

* * *

"Please excuse the mess," I told Patricia as she stepped into my house, "my maid came down with leprosy and hasn't been able to hold a dish towel."

"I have a high mess tolerance," Patricia comforted me. "I'm sure it's not that... Oh, my God!"

"I told you, even the roaches won't live here."

"Minus, it's not that bad. I was referring to the Rothko on the wall."

"It's not signed," I confessed. "I dug it out of his garbage. We worked in the same building for a while."

"You're not an average school bus salesman, are you?"

"I have my quirks. Can I get you a drink?"

"I would love a coffee."

"Regular or decaf?"

"Regular please, decaf will make me sleep too late."

"Yeah, me too."

I went about brewing a pot while Patricia had a look around the place. Out of the corner of my eye, I could see she was an art lover. Patricia wandered from room to room, enjoying the eclectic array of paintings, sculptures, and objects that I had assembled over the years.

I may sell school busses, but I collect beauty.

"Your collection is incredible. How long have you been putting this together?" Patricia called out to me as I ground the coffee beans.

"My first piece was a painting my mother did. She had thrown it away because it was just a brush exercise. An absolute abstract masterpiece I thought. I was sixteen when I dug it out of the trash."

"Is that where you get all your art?"

"Only the good stuff," I answered.

"So, you have a creative background."

"Not really. I inherited my mother's love of art and my father's sense of humor. That and a cup of coffee will buy me a relaxing moment."

"You can be hard to understand," Patricia advised me.

"You think this is bad? You should see me with my tax accountant," I said, proving her previous statement.

We sat down on the sofa with our caffeinated nightcaps and delved into this strange new world we occupied.

"Is Brian here?" Patricia asked.

"Not as far as I know. He had an investigation to carry out."

"Does he know who the spook is?"

"Not a clue. It appears Brian was as sideswiped as us. I feel bad accusing him of not being upfront with me. He might be in over his head."

"I'd like to meet him sometime." Finally, Patricia gave me an opening to get inside her head.

"You have to be open to letting someone else in to do that. Your relatives have wanted to talk to you about the sale but haven't been able to penetrate your defenses."

"You say that like I've built a wall around myself."

"I don't mean to sound judgmental. I'm just disseminating what I've heard. The reason I let Brian in was totally self-serving."

"Is that right?" Patricia said, fishing for more information.

"Yes," I said, not giving it to her. "The thing is, since you have a stalker, it might be best to keep your shields up."

"I'm nervous about going to sleep after all that happened tonight. He might come back with a vengeance."

"I have a spare bedroom if you would like to stay here," I said, hoping the offer wasn't too forward.

"Thank you. I really don't want to go home tonight."

I got the spare room set up for my guest—clean sheets, a towel with face cloth, PJs, and a robe. I showed Patricia how to operate the hot water in the shower, and where to find a toothbrush. I turned off all but the hall light. If she needed help, I didn't want to run into a door jamb, coming to the rescue.

"Good night," I said, standing in the doorway to my room. "Remember, Mourice can't hurt you. You are in control of the physical world. Anyway, I'll be in the other room if you need help. I can shove a noble fir up his ass."

"Good night," she said, leaving her door slightly ajar.

I went to bed thinking about the woman in the other room. How can anyone be so strong and comforting at the same time? I felt like the protector and the protected. I didn't know if I was up for either deed.

The night was long. The dreams were relentless. I was fighting something from beneath the hill. They were numberless, tireless, and driven. Tearing at the headstones, these faceless creatures consumed everything.

I woke up in a panic hearing Patricia in a panic. We met between our rooms and held each other to keep the multitudes away.

"Did you see what I saw?" I asked her.

"Probably," she replied. "I feel like a frightened child."

"I look like one," I said. "Would you like some ice cream?"

"I would love some," she answered with relief.

We spent the rest of the night on the sofa, talking about anything that didn't have the word supernatural in the subject line, until we both fell asleep at either end.

* * *

Morning.

Once again.

As expected,

and the cup of coffee that comes with it.

I awoke to see Patricia curled up at the other end of the sofa. The blanket I had given her when she began to shiver was tightly wound up to her lower lip.

Quietly, I slipped off the sofa onto the floor, then up like Homo Erectus in search of caffeine. I avoided looking at her face, feeling it a breach of privacy. Still, I couldn't help but see an innocent, childlike woman.

I went into the kitchen and made a pot of full blast, no holds barred coffee. If this morning's brew didn't melt our toenails, it was only because our stomachs shut down with excitement.

The coffee grinder managed not to wake her, but the redolence of one hundred proof caffeine permeating the air was like an alarm clock with a fire engine siren.

"Minus?"

"I'm in the kitchen."

When there was no response, I peeked into the living room to see her fast asleep.

I sat on the sofa, sipping my morning life.

I was feeling comfortable.

9

FEELING COMFORTABLE

With only
one cup of coffee
inside of her,

Patricia ran off to a business appointment downtown looking as sharp as the moment she had walked into the restaurant the night before. I, on the other hand, was ready to drop my scruffy ass back into bed.

Two hours later, I was awoken by my phone vibrating on the nightstand. The call rang through to voicemail but continued to ring in my head. The prospect of going back to sleep diminished as the possible negative scenarios of the call exploded in my brain.

"Hi Minus, this is Helen," her voice came through the speaker once I had succumbed to my paranoia. "There's been a turn of events with the bus contract. Please give me a call to discuss the current situation. Talk soon."

I hate situations. They are never good. You won't ever hear a cop say, "We have a situation here. Everyone is being well fed." No, situations are bad and rarely go away on their own. I decided to shower before returning Helen's call, in case the Earth imploded in the meantime.

As chance would have it, when I got out of the shower, the world had not been eaten up by a black hole. The time had come to make the call.

"Hi, Helen, Minus here."

"Hi, Minus, how are you?"

"Fine, thank you, I'm enjoying the warmth of the sun."

"It's foggy here. Is it sunny where you are?"

"No, what's up?"

"There's been a change in the bus order."

"Okay...how so?" I attempted to draw out an answer.

"Well...it's been canceled."

This didn't surprise me. After the events of the previous night, I knew I had pissed off somebody.

"Really?" I said. "Did the bottom fall out of the education system, or are they going to paint the old busses paisley and have the kids travel the country offering free love?"

"You're taking it well. You remind me of your father."

"I didn't know he was into free love."

Helen laughed and asked if we could meet over lunch.

"Sure," I agreed, "any chance we can dine in the city?"

"Perfect, let's meet at Stacks. It's comfortable there," Helen said, suggesting a Hayes Valley icon.

"Eleven thirty okay with you?" I offered.

"See you then."

My life, on the whole, has not been filled with excitement. Aside from the time Zero danced an Irish jig on her back legs at my parents' Christmas party, not much of interest has happened. Now, with all this mystery, I was starting to feel so urbane.

Driving into San Francisco to meet with a woman of power, I realized that it takes the deconstruction of a business deal for me to work in the city.

* * *

Helen and I were seated at a window booth looking out on a giant naked woman, made from car parts, fresh from The Playa at Burning Man.

"Now, if they could make a bus that looks like that, I'd be a rich man," I said, looking out the window.

Helen didn't react to my statement. She just continued to stare at the iron lady.

"Are you okay?" I asked.

"No," she answered without the slightest delay. "Your thirty-foot-tall friend there just gave me a look that could melt a Fiat. You didn't see that?"

"No, I must have been excluded from the memo," I joked. "It appears that somebody is sending you a private message. Have you had a falling out with any supernatural beings lately?"

"Not that I know of," she answered, with a question in her eyes.

"Spook spoiling is trending at the moment," I said, trying not to take anything too seriously. "My suggestion is to ignore her. I'm told, on good authority, that really weird things happening are just visions planted in your mind and can't hurt you."

"You sound like you've been talking to dead people," Helen suggested.

"As chance would have it, I was speaking to an old friend of yours yesterday, Paul Filbert."

Helen didn't look at all surprised. Instead, she smiled broadly.

"Isn't it amazing how he is just as loud dead as when he was alive?" she said.

"I noticed that. I was going to ask Brian if there's a volume control."

Now Helen looked surprised. "You've spoken to Brian?" she said, paying my eyes a lot of attention.

"Yes, he's my man underground. Have you met him?" I asked, holding her gaze.

Helen hesitated to answer but didn't break away from our connection.

"No," she finally said, "but your father has mentioned him."

"I've never known my father to merely *mention* anything. He tends to elaborate."

I waited to see if Helen would volunteer any more information. An Irish wolfhound walked past the window, allowing her to disconnect our eyes and the conversation. "Now that's a beautiful dog," she said, deflecting attention to the world outside.

We avoided talking about the elephant in the room by commenting on the array of dogs parading along the avenue. Helen knew the name of every breed. I only recognized the mutts.

Ending the *Best in Show* portion of the meeting, I indelicately asked, "So what happened with the bus deal?"

She took her eyes off of a very excitable Labradoodle and looked down at her hands, which had just grasped each other for protection. "As the superintendent of schools, my job is governed by the wishes of the board of education. I was called into the board president's office yesterday and told to put a hold on purchasing the busses. He wouldn't tell me why, except to say it was out of his hands."

I looked out the window and said, "See all these people walking their dogs? They are unaware that a leash is also around their necks."

"I think most people know it. They just have been bought off by comfort," Helen said, looking out at the world with her hands still comforting each other.

"Let's look at the bright side," I said, "now I can take a few days off."

The superintendent of schools turned her head back to me and smiled. "I thought you would be upset."

"Not at all. I have another project I've been working on and this will give me a chance to focus. And you did say the order is just on hold."

"You are very much like your father."

"I'll take that as a compliment, based on the person that is coming from," I said, knowing a few people with different opinions of Pops.

Helen's hands released each other, and we went on to have a nice lunch.

* * *

I dropped Helen off at Market and Grove. Across the way from the BART station stood the newly constructed main library. Doing a little research in public might just keep me from taking a nap, so I ventured into the keeper of civilization's accomplishments and failures.

I recently applied for a library card just in case I did write a book. Then, I could check it out along with James Joyce's *Ulysses,* helping to give JJ a slight boost in stature.

Brian was absent today, which was very strange. I was getting used to sharing my headspace with him. This was the longest he had been away since occupying the spare room in my head. I felt uneasy. If he was in trouble, I had no idea how to help.

Sitting down at a bank of computers, I could feel a nap coming on. So, I forced myself to walk around the stacks to work off the Reuben I had for lunch. Mostly, I don't want to succumb to snoring in public.

I wandered to and fro, in and out, up and down, here and there, until I ran out of prepositional phrases, where I ended up in the gardening section. This seemed like an odd place since my experience with plants was limited to killing orchids gifted by friends.

I liked it here. The books were pretty and I didn't have to water them. There was a book on orchids that I felt too guilty to pick up, so I grabbed the one next to it that listed drought-tolerant California native plants.

The reading chairs were calling to me. Tempting my weary eyelids to shield me from the world. Skimming through the introduction, I found the chapter on drying flowers. This was worth checking out. A plant that can die without looking dead certainly would fit into my current life.

I was amazed by the number of flowers and plants I had seen before. Many of them during my visits to the cemetery. These plants had been in The Yard for eons before the first bodies were placed. I felt sad thinking that the foliage would continue to grow long after the descendants of those who were buried were forgotten.

The quiet of the library and the beauty of the flowers did their magic. My eyes closed and I was back in The Yard. The grounds were covered in a vast array of wildflowers, some of which I now knew the botanical name. The air was still, not a whisper of wind. It felt like there *was* no air, though I didn't feel the need for it. A path had been made in the colorful ground cover leading off the hill towards the lower parking lot. I followed the floral-lined lane to find Ruby covered in orchids, parked in the handicapped spot.

For the first time, I was scared for Brian. I ran toward my family's graves. Through a giant stand of pink hedge nettle. Through an exceptionally painful growth of Rosa Gymnocarpa. Finally encountering a valley of poison oak. I carefully made my way around that one, to find their graves disturbed.

I woke up to a library assistant checking to see if I was alright. My book had fallen on the floor and I was about to do the same.

"I'm fine," I told her. "I must have fallen asleep. Thank you for your kindness."

I snatched up the flower book and headed to the checkout lane for my first loan.

Saddling my ruby-hued pony, I ventured back across the bridge to make sure all was well in The Yard. Patricia's company would have been welcome on this visit, but she had a real job. When I arrived at the gravesite, everything looked normal. No piles of dirt or bones scattered about the grounds. Relieved, I sat down next to the headstones and cried for the first time since any of them had died. When I exhausted my tears, I sat quietly thinking of wildflowers.

There was a small flowering clover growing next to the graves. I reached over to pick the white-tipped flower and noticed it had already been cut. This seemed strange since the area showed no signs of being recently groomed. Next to the plant, I saw a line in the grass.

A very straight line that continued to create a large rectangle. I had never noticed this bit of geometry on the ground before.

Getting up onto my knees, I took a closer look at this unusual slice in the earth. Taking hold of a handful of grass, I pulled it up to reveal a section of newly disturbed dirt.

* * *

"Patricia, are you free this afternoon," I began my message on her voicemail. "I think Brian is missing and I could use some company and help."

By the time I got back to my car, Patricia had called and said she would meet me at my place.

10

MY PLACE

I pulled up to my house.
Patricia was parked the wrong way
on the far side of the street.

She was still in her car to protect herself from the wind making its afternoon visit. Today's installment was particularly harsh, inching towards vengeful.

"Are you okay?" Patricia asked as we met in the middle of the road.

"I don't know. I think I did something to my knee at the cemetery."

"That isn't what I meant. Are you emotionally alright?"

"Oh! No!"

From the west, cutting over San Bruno Mountain, came a gust of wind so cold and angry that I could feel the specter before its arrival. Taking to the street, this torrent of air tortured the trees along its path until wrapping itself around us with a grip that was suffocating. The branches above our heads cracked then screamed, sending a limb crashing onto the road, not five feet from where we stood.

"Does that happen often?" Patricia asked, noticeably shaken.

I stared at the shattered log lying on the pavement but could not formulate a sentence that didn't end with "we're all going to die," so I said nothing.

Patricia took my arm and led me inside the house and onto the sofa, then went off to the kitchen to pour a little wine.

"It's only four o'clock," I commented, after hearing the cork release its captive. "I don't start drinking until five."

"It's five o'clock in Arizona, now drink your wine," she commanded with an air of matriarchal dominance as she handed me a glass.

My in-house sommelier then took a seat on her end of the sofa.

I proceeded to disseminate my entire day, with all the suspense and drama of an Edgar Alan Poe poem. Then, I showed her my pretty book.

"Did the giant woman really move?" Patricia asked about one of the more impressive parts of my tale.

"I didn't see it, but Helen was quite upset by her steely stare. From my experience, naked women don't pay much attention to me. How's your wine?" I quickly added to move past my previous statement.

My glass had become desperately close to empty, as it was closing in on six o'clock in Phoenix. Patricia offered to do the next pour.

When she returned from the kitchen, with the remains of the white wine and a fresh bottle of Pinot Noir, Patricia asked, "Do you think someone has stolen Brian's body?"

"Yes, otherwise, he would have been back in touch with me by now. Are you hungry?" I asked because I always am.

"I haven't eaten all day," Patricia revealed, having started the day here with just a cup of coffee.

"There's a Chinese restaurant down the road. Would you like to have dinner?"

"Is it Sichuan or Mandarin?"

"It's Chinese! Grab your bag."

Stepping back out into the windstorm, I felt like a moving target. Maybe the weather was dangerously benign, but I was relieved once we had gotten down the street to the restaurant, where the trees were more sociable. The restaurant was nearly empty, so securing a window seat without any help from Brian was a cinch.

"This is a sweet little town you live in," Patricia opened the conversation. "I didn't even know it existed. Brisbane is like a European city on a hillside overlooking the Mediterranean."

"Hills have been playing a big part in my life lately," I segued from her compliment of the town I had grown to love. "I don't know if it's a clue or just coincidence."

"Well, coincidentally, there's a dish here called a *Mountain of Spice*," Patricia continued the theme. "Shall we order it?"

"Why not? I need something to soak up the wine," I said.

After putting in our order, we set our minds to figuring out the next move.

"I'm stumped," I began the brainstorming.

"That's a good start, Minus. Do you care to expand on that?"

"Okay, let me recap. The land was for sale, then it's on hold. The bus deal was clinched, then it wasn't. I was going to help Brian and now he's AWOL. Did I miss anything?"

"No, that pretty well covers it, but may I come at it from a different angle?"

"Sure," I said, feeling cocky enough to think I could hold my own.

"Thank you," Patricia began her slant. "So far, you have stopped the sale of the tomb without buying it yourself, thus achieving the goal for your brother. Did I miss anything?"

"I can tell you're good at your job, but does any of that make sense to you?"

"Not really, but it sounded good," Patricia conceded.

Patricia was right. I needed to change how I viewed our circumstances.

"Maybe we should start from the present," I refocused. "You and I are sitting in a Chinese restaurant about to eat a mountain of spice. Why?"

"Because we're hungry?"

"Was that a joke?" I asked.

"Yes."

I continued with my logic. "What if everything is going as planned? What if we have been led, and are still being led, somewhere not of our choosing? I'm not sure I would have normally ordered a mountain of spice."

"I see your point," Patricia said, clicking into my theory. "Maybe we're being manipulated every step of the way. How do we know when we're making our own choices?"

"Correct," I said. "Let's order potstickers too. I always order potstickers."

"Was that a joke?"

"Yes!"

The *mountain of spice* arrived, looking much like the mountain island in my dream. A mound of sticky rice topped with garlic spinach and spiced meats. The thought of sautéed animal parts singing to me was a little unsettling, but the meal was delicious.

Using our edible peak as a distraction, the conversation wandered from the subject at hand to epic vacations we'd experienced. Patricia was a rugged traveler, spending weeks, if not months, in countries that I find scary on TV. I preferred to stay away from places that include parasites with every meal. For all of Patricia's style and glamour, she certainly was not afraid of getting dirty. Ms. Kelly was a hard bird to grasp.

After dinner, we went back to my place for a nightcap of coffee and chocolates. While I brewed a pot and unwrapped the sweets, Patricia slipped into something a bit more comfortable. She had bought a new dress before her appointment this morning but had not planned to spend another night at the Filbert Estate. The Walt Disney Goofy PJs, which she had worn the night before, were still on the bed ready to come alive.

"You must give me your tailor's name," I joked as she stepped into the living room. "That dog has never looked so good."

"Thank you, I've trained him well."

Several comments came to mind in response to her statement, none of which would have been proper. Instead, I handed Patricia a drink and took my place on the opposite end of the sofa.

"Do you think it all ends here?" Patricia wondered out loud.

"If all what, ends where?"

"This nightmare. Without Brian's help, I don't see what we can do."

"Me neither, that's why we need to find Brian. And, Helen can help with that."

"Are you going to have her get all the kids in the school district out searching for him?"

"I hadn't thought of that. Keep those ideas coming," I encouraged Patricia's creativity. "No, she is our connection to my father."

Helen's connection with my father, although convenient, was mysterious. All the information I had received, regarding communicating with the dead, was in stark contrast to her link with him. I still had much to learn.

Patricia and I stayed up far too late trying to put the pieces together until neither of us could keep our eyes open any longer. "I think it's time for Goofy to go to bed," I said. "Would you like to sleep on the sofa again or back in the guest room?"

"The bed sounds better to me. But if I have any visitations during the night, don't be surprised if you find me in your bed."

I couldn't think of how to respond to that before she said good night and slipped off into the spare room.

I was ready for another chocolate.

* * *

I woke up suddenly. It was deep into the night and *the quiet* was everywhere. I felt something was wrong. Something missing. I reached inside myself, trying to investigate where my resting mind had been. Nothing was there to grasp. I realized; I hadn't been dreaming.

I rarely have dreamless nights. Dreams have always been a part of me. They let me know what I like, what I fear, who I am. A blank canvas all night is like being locked away in solitary.

I sat up and listened for Patricia. Not a sound came from her room. I stayed in my bed feeling it wouldn't be right to peek in on her.

The night was unusually silent. No wind, no owls, no sounds. I cleared my throat to create a noise. But heard nothing. Comforted by the knowledge that I was dreaming about not dreaming, I slept peacefully until just before dawn.

* * *

"Brian!" I yelled out as my alarm began to ring. Confused by the commotion, I sat up with the buzzer continuing to wreak havoc on my nerves.

Patricia rushed into my room and silenced the phone. "Minus, what happened?"

"I heard Brian. He was trying to talk to me."

"What did he say?"

It took me a moment to calm down before I could answer. When my pulse slowed to a fast rate, I said, "Brian's voice was too faint to hear the words, but his panic was palpable."

"Can you remember anything?"

"I thought I had caught a word, but it's gone now. I can feel it in my memory, but it's hidden like a ghost."

We sat in silence hoping my rattled mind would conjure up the word.

"It will probably come back to you in the shower," Patricia sagely suggested.

I took her advice and slipped into the shower while Goofy and Patricia brewed a pot of coffee. The water felt good. It always feels good. That's why my water bill is so high. I languished in the rain until the utility's stock went up two points, but still, the word didn't come to me.

When I came out of the bathroom, Patricia was there with coffee. "My turn," she said, as she handed me the cup and stepped through the door.

Forty-five minutes later, after doing whatever it is that could take forty-five minutes, she emerged. I greeted her with a cup of coffee from the second pot I had brewed.

"Thank you, nice shower. I could have stayed there all day. I now see why you were so long," she said, pre-empting the smart-ass comment I had been working on for twenty minutes.

We sat, once again, on either end of the sofa, enjoying the view. The sun had long since risen. Fingers of fog stretched through the city, tickling the buildings before breaking off to be absorbed by the bay. Again, and again, they attempted to engulf the town. San Francisco resisted their approach, repelled their invasion, and severed their grasp until the sun itself had seen enough and banned the fog to sea.

"That was fun," I said, "it looks like the good guys won."

"Do you get to watch this every day?"

"Every sky is different. This view is like a 365-quotes calendar. I learn something new every morning."

I followed Patricia's gaze as it danced along the Oakland Hills. She seemed melancholy. Her posture had slumped slightly. At that moment, I realized everything had been about me. What I had wanted. I had not checked in on what she was going through.

"I'm sorry," I said, "this must be hard for you. Are you okay?"

"I'm fine," she replied in that knee-jerk human way.

"Are you fine with being manipulated by the dead or with being manipulated by me?"

"I'm fine with the decisions I've made. Everyone is doing what they need to do, as am I. So far, I have no regrets."

"You must give me your therapist's name," I said, almost able to stop myself from saying it. "Still, this is a difficult time. I would like to help. Is there anything I can do to make it easier for you?"

Her gaze shifted from the far-off hills and straight into my eyes. "Thank you, that is all I needed."

She turned her attention back to the view and quietly enjoyed the morning.

"You are always welcome to gaze out my window," I said.

After a short silence, my sofa-sitting companion said, "Thank you."

Time was getting on and one of us had a job to get to. The other, had a job to avoid.

We arranged to meet at Tadich Grill for lunch, hopefully with Helen in attendance.

Patricia headed off to work, leaving me to pour myself another cup of coffee.

*　*　*

"Good morning, Helen," I began my voicemail request. "Would you, by chance, be free for lunch? I would like you to meet someone. We're meeting at Tadich at one. Let me know if that will work for you. Oh, by the way, the waiters can be a bit gruff. You might want to ask your iron lady to accompany you."

Within ten minutes, Helen called back and agreed to come into the city.

"I'm finding it hard to concentrate on work since our last lunch," she said. "A trip into the city would be a welcome escape, but if you don't mind, I would prefer to come solo."

I stayed home until 12:15, which gave me plenty of time to get to the restaurant. It was early in the month, so my next rent payment was a lifetime away. Making a living was taking a back seat to the dead.

Right at one o'clock, I stepped into Tadich. Patricia was already seated at a table near the kitchen, next to the waiter's station, on the way to the bathrooms.

"It's a different experience without Brian haunting the maître d'," I said, greeting her.

"I only hope they don't try to poison us," Patricia set the seed of doubt.

Once we worked out our food testing strategy, we ordered tap water.

"Were you able to get ahold of Helen?" Patricia asked.

"Yes, Helen will be joining us. Sorry, I forgot to give you a heads-up. As you know, the bridge can be a nightmare this time of day. So, we may end up having dinner instead. How about we order a little something to stave off pancreatic shock?"

"That's okay. We may not survive past our waters anyway," Patricia nurtured the seed of doubt.

On that happy note, Helen walked into the restaurant and was directed to our table.

"You made good time," I greeted her.

"Not really. I left right after our phone call. Traffic was so slow that I was able to listen to Mahler's entire third symphony." Helen painted time with a musical brush.

I made the introductions and the two women immediately bonded.

When Helen apologized for being late, Patricia comforted her by stating, "You aren't late until dessert has been eaten."

"Thank you," Helen said, adding, "I love dessert."

I sat quietly while the two women created the chrysalis of a burgeoning friendship. After several minutes, they noticed I was still in the room and apologized for excluding me.

"I didn't feel left out," I said. "I enjoy being a fly on the wall."

"That's not a welcome image in a restaurant," Patricia pointed out I needed to work on my clichés.

Helen then posed a question in my direction. "Other than Patricia and I having a lot in common, why are we here?"

This was my opportunity to explain and vent simultaneously. I had wound myself up thinking about what I had gotten the three of us into. Nothing made sense. Even the menu had vegetables that were out of season.

I began my declaration with a wave of my hand. "All these people around us are living their lives not dealing with the dead. We though, have been drawn into a world we don't understand. My brother, my father, and an unknown phantom have been in contact, leaving us with more questions than answers. I think we deserve an explanation, even if we are just mere mortals."

"Well said," Patricia congratulated me.

"I'm not sure where I fit into all of this," Helen said.

"You have a connection with my father, and we need to contact him to find Brian."

"I didn't know Brian was missing," Helen said, sounding surprised.

"Oh, didn't I tell you?"

"No. It must have slipped your mind." Helen cut me a little more slack than I deserved.

Patricia noticed that Helen was uncomfortable with her new role as seance team leader. She asked, "Is there anything we can do to make you feel better about getting involved with our dilemma?"

"I feel this is also my cause," Helen said. "I owe a lot to Paul Filbert. Pardon my hesitation, I needed to assess my part in all of this. Whether I can be of any help is unclear. But I'm willing to try. What's the first step?"

"The cemetery," I proposed. "Pops is a regular there."

* * *

Having survived lunch, we piled into Helen's car for the long trip across the bridge.

Patricia and I had parked in garages that charged by the nanosecond. However, relegating our vehicles into indentured servitude was preferable to negotiating the iron traffic jam individually.

During one of our momentous six-foot advances, I asked my bridge captives, "Are you familiar with the Bridge Troll?" Neither one had the slightest idea of what I was talking about, so I continued with my favorite Bay Area trivia. "After the Loma Prieta earthquake, legendary East Bay artist, Bill Roan, anonymously attached an iron troll to the new span of the bridge to protect future travelers."

A deafening silence rose from the front seat.

"You didn't hear the media hubbub?" I added, hoping to jar their memories.

Both women shrugged their shoulders, looking like sixth graders at a pop quiz.

"I feel like I'm the keeper of knowledge that would otherwise fade into oblivion. This local lore enriches our lives, creating texture in this place we call home." I paused for a moment. "Did that sound a little too, *six o'clock news?*"

Patricia was the first to comment. "Yes," she said, not mincing the word.

"Helen?" I prodded. "Your thoughts?"

"Minus, you're a wonderful person," was all she said on the subject.

I could tell she was a rising star in the political arena.

We were silent for the remainder of the trip, lost in our own thoughts. Or maybe they were hoping I wouldn't start up with some other obscure Bay Area lore.

Finally arriving at our destination, we were stopped at the gate.

A guard had been posted just outside the hallowed grounds. He stood six feet tall with an attitude that dwarfed his stature.

"Good afternoon," he greeted with a voice twenty dollars above his pay grade, "who have you come to visit?"

"Hi, this is Patricia Kelly," I quickly responded from the back seat. "We've come to visit her family's plot," I continued, preempting anyone in the car from mentioning the Filberts.

"The cemetery closes in half an hour. We will be locking the gates promptly," the guard proclaimed.

"Thank you," I graciously accepted his decree hoping my companions would stay silent, knowing they were prone to telling the truth. A salesman's ability to direct the conversation without technically lying is invaluable.

"I assume you had a reason for your backseat driving?" Helen said with moderate restraint in her voice.

"I think it best to do a little reconnaissance before we start talking to people with stars on their sleeves," I said. "Let's see what's happening in The Yard first."

We drove up to the lower parking lot, where I guided Helen to take my usual spot. The day had moved on substantially since we had gotten on the bridge. Now, the shadows were long, and our visit would be short.

Quickly making our way to the Filbert camp, I suddenly felt nervous. Anything could happen now. My mind was racing with every negative scenario my paranoid little brain could conjure. By the time we got to the gravesite, my imagination had destroyed the Earth.

There was another guard stationed at the Filbert plot. This fellow looked to have the same tailor, though he was only five-six if he stood on a rock.

"Can I help you?" the guard inquired.

Wanting more information, I asked, "Security sure has been beefed up around here. Are you expecting a jailbreak?"

If there was any humor in my statement, it went unnoticed.

"We have a situation here, sir. Are you associated with the Filbert family?"

Before Patricia and Helen could be good civic members, I answered, "No. What's going on?"

The guard stood a little straighter and told us it was best to move on. With that dismissal, we headed up the hill.

"Why didn't you tell him who you are?" Patricia began, with Helen finishing the thought, "He might have shared some information."

"Those guys are private security. I don't trust them. If the true authorities want to get ahold of me, I'm sure they can figure it out."

Once on top, I looked around for another guard. We appeared to be alone. Gazing out at the view, the color of the sky was unreal. If Ford could match that hue of blue, I would consider trading in Ruby.

The serenity on the Kelly hill was calming. A quiet resistance to the mortal angst surrounding it. This place should have no monetary value. Money is beneath its worth.

My companions had split up. Helen wandered the *domain of the dead*, stopping at each headstone to read the inscriptions. She would bow her head, then move on to the next.

Patricia stood transfixed on the mausoleum. Something strong held her gaze. It was nothing I could see or feel. Her own ghosts had a tight grip on the life she couldn't share with me.

We had little time to complete our covert mission. Reluctantly, I gathered the team.

"Helen," I began, "do you have a special bird call you use, or does my father come to you like a freight train?"

"I don't control his visits, but they are always gentle."

"We are talking about the same Paul Filbert? The man who could verbally strip paint off an ocean liner?"

"Only if the ship needed it," Helen stood up for the old man. "He will come when he's ready."

Helen walked over to a bench that faced the sea and sat alone. She had a sadness about her. Not just at this moment, but within our relationship. However, she seemed more at peace in this serene place among the dead.

I felt a kinship with both women. My bond with Helen was different. I didn't know why, other than her connection to my father.

Patricia came from behind to stand beside me, wonderfully too close.

After leaving my place this morning, she had stopped by her own home to change into something even more fashionable.

"I like Helen," she softly said in my right ear.

I turned my head to reply, finding her face dangerously close to mine. Quickly, I turned back to focus on Helen and said, "I like her too."

Patricia's proximity felt uncomfortable. Shoulder to shoulder, I turned back to face her left ear and whispered, "I like you too."

A smile arose across her face.

We watched Helen sit perfectly still while the hue of the sky beyond her changed with the sun's daily decline, easing Ruby's fate.

A voice came through the air. Floating above and around and through the trees. Carried on a breeze that had begun at the ocean, flowing miles down city streets to deliver us a message: "The cemetery is closing. Please make your way to the main gates."

Helen rose from her stone pew, enjoyed another moment of the sun's journey, then returned to complete our trinity.

"Got it!" she said. "I could use a drink."

Helen started down the hill, with her companions in close pursuit.

* * *

I dropped my lovely heroines off at Wood Tavern, one of my go-to restaurants in Oakland, having offered to park Helen's car. I then began the search for a piece of curb.

Because of San Francisco's limited space, I tend to see the East Bay as a giant parking lot with houses and businesses sprinkled about. Today though, my pursuit for a piece of curb large enough to fit Helen's Toyota was reminiscent of parking on Nob Hill.

By the time I had successfully secured a reasonably legal parking space and got back to the restaurant, Helen and Patricia were receiving their wine. After finishing the iced teas they had nursed during my extended absence, it was time to begin the evening. Not wanting to fall too far behind on the festivities, I ordered a Long Island iced tea with two lemon wedges and a Zinfandel. I was sure a burger was in my future.

They had saved me the best seat, facing an open window and looking onto the street. This was my parking reward.

"Thank you for the seat of honor. I will try to live up to its expectations," I said, taking the chair in hand and lowering myself into its view. "Did I miss anything?"

"The first drink," Patricia pointed out.

"That's a temporary condition," I assured her. "I was referring to any of the testimony from on high?"

"We were saving that for you," Helen answered. "I'd rather not go through it twice."

As if the bartender was tuned in to my thoughts, my drink arrived quickly. I looked to see if the server was Brian, but she was a little too short to be my brother.

Before initiating the debriefing, I enjoyed a moment on Long Island.

"I'm ready when you are. The floor is yours, Helen."

Helen sat back in her chair and glanced out the window. A woman with a dog stood outside the restaurant. She was looking at her phone while Scruffy was looking at her.

"You see that woman?" Helen said.

Patricia and I nodded.

"We are the woman, the phone is the cemetery, and Brian is the dog."

"That's what I've always said," I remarked, inciting Patricia's eyes to roll.

"Your father told me Brian appears to have been taken prisoner. Your brother was making a lot of waves with stopping the sale of the tomb. Somebody didn't like that. And that somebody, Paul believes, was coached by an insider to execute the theft. It was too precise to have been mere grave robbers."

"Why would an insider betray their own?" I asked.

"Bad people die, too," Helen shed a little hope for the human race.

"I had hoped they went to hell."

"No, they come from hell. Anyway, let's not get into that. The thing is; they only took Brian's skull."

"They don't need to take the whole body?" Patricia asked.

"The head is the keeper of our consciousness, before and after death," Helen answered. "Our bodies are only the vehicle. That's why beheading was so popular."

"At least now I know I'm going to order the salad," I said.

"Don't you take anything seriously?" Helen asked.

"We can go into that later," I replied. "Please continue as if I hadn't sidetracked the conversation."

Helen looked back at the woman on the street who had put her phone away but still was not connecting with her pooch.

"It's not about the location of the consciousness. It's about directing your thoughts."

As if on cue, the woman looked down at Scruffy, setting his tail into hyperdrive and creating a doggy smile a mile wide.

"If we direct our minds to Brian, and if he's not too far away, we can reconnect," Helen continued.

"That's great, but we still don't know where to direct our thoughts," I said, pointing out the obvious.

"Obviously," Helen concurred, "but that doesn't stop us from opening our minds to your brother."

"I admire your resilience," I said.

All this talk of mind opening was causing my thoughts to close down. I needed some fresh air.

"Excuse me while I go pet Scruffy," I said, as my wine hit the table.

The dog was a mutt. A mix of everything that doesn't work in a canine but is still cute as a button.

I asked the woman, "What type of dog is this?"

She looked down at this mop of a creature and said, "He's pure dog, no additives."

"That was going to be my first guess. May I pet him?"

"Certainly, he finished his rabies shots yesterday."

"How timely," I responded. "I think I'll just wave."

Sitting back down at the table, I said, "That dog reminds me of Brian."

"Your father has information that may help," Helen took up where I had cut her off. "He's been searching the Undernet for who was directing the heist. All he saw was a man on the water. The who and the where are unknowns."

"The dead are good with unknowns," I managed to stereotype an entire group of former people. "By the way, Helen, why are you able to connect with my father? When for me, it takes an act of Congress."

"We have been talking to each other for so long, the connection is natural."

"Was that an answer?" I asked.

"Yes and no," Helen kind of answered.

"Oh, I love yes/no answers. They're so definitive."

"Helen, what do you think we should do?" Patricia cut in, seemingly to save Helen from having to expand on her nebulous answer.

"First, we should get some food into Minus before he starts petting rabid dogs."

How could a statement like that do anything but end a conversation? So, I ordered the salad, as promised, along with a Pino Grigio. I gave the Zinfandel to Scruffy. Helen ordered the lamb and Patricia the halibut.

* * *

With dinner behind us, we agreed to reconvene the next day in The Yard. After a long day, developing a metaphysical geographic strategy seemed a bit optimistic.

Helen offered to drive Patricia and me back to the city. Since it was far too late for Helen to shuttle us home, we opted to be dropped off at a BART station. I was way too tired to stay awake to make sure Patricia didn't fall asleep while keeping an eye on Helen.

On the train, Patricia and I took turns napping until we exited at the Embarcadero station in San Francisco at an hour I would rather not be at the Embarcadero station.

After paying a small ransom to free Ruby, I gave Patricia a ride to her car. Only to find it was in lockdown due to the late hour.

"I have a wonderful pair of Dumbo PJs if you would rather not BART it back home," I offered.

"He's my favorite," Patricia said. "You don't mind?"

"Not at all. I'm happy to share Dumbo with you."

We drove back to Brisbane and fell into our respective beds.

That night my sleep was deep, and my dreams were like secrets.

11

SECRETS

Sunday, I awoke early.
Though my bed refused to release me.

It had only been a week since Brian had come to me. Less than that with Patricia and Helen. Yet my life was not the same. I couldn't imagine going back to a week ago when my biggest excitement was folding used dryer sheets before throwing them out. I don't know why I do that, so don't ask.

I laid within my cloth clam shell, staring at the ceiling. I thought about my life, my job, and the woman in the other room, attempting to reconcile the three. My thoughts kept coming back to buses. I felt that somehow the contract with the Oakland School District played a part in this story of the dead.

Before Patricia came to life, I texted my assistant, Kathy:

Good morning,
Sorry to bother you at home on a Sunday morning.
Can you tell me who requested the quote for Oakland?
FYI, I'm okay with you charging the company time and a half for this.

One of the benefits of being a salesman is; you are a god in the company. Or, in my case, a demigod.

I knew I wouldn't hear from Kathy for a few hours, so I went about my morning making coffee, as quietly as possible, before searching my email for clues.

Going back to the first contact I had received from the Oakland School District, I looked to see where the message had originated. *Noreply* came up in the sender list, along with Kathy. If there is one thing I'm not, it's tech-savvy. I was feeling well out of my digital comfort zone chasing unknowns around the internet.

The coffee machine beeped, enticing me from cyber hell. I set down the phone to go in search of caffeine.

The first coffee of the day is a reward for having survived the night. Morning brings a resurrection and coffee rolls away the stone.

I checked my messages in hopes that Kathy was on the ball, but not so much as an early morning marketing call had come in. I opened a Google page, but had no idea what to Google. The web is excellent for creating confusion and misinformation but investigating supernatural occurrences, not so good.

I enjoyed my coffee until Patricia rose from the dead. The Dumbo PJs were quite striking, though the placement of the ears was a bit distracting.

"Would you like a cup of coffee?" I asked, trying not to look at Dumbo's animated ears.

"That would be wonderful," she said. "Excuse me while I get a robe."

That will help, I thought. Then I went into the kitchen to fetch Patricia some brew.

Once we had taken our places on either end of the sofa, with coffee in hand, Patricia recalled her dreams.

"I spoke with Brian last night," she said.

"How is that possible? Did he dial the wrong number?"

Patricia just looked at me.

"Sorry, but how do you know it was him?" I asked, attempting to save the moment.

"As I didn't trust it *was* him, I asked for proof he was Brian Filbert. He seemed to think about that for a moment before saying, 'Minus is a pain in the ass.' That sounded authentic."

"I appreciate both of your opinions of me, but why would that lead you to trust him?"

"Only a brother would use an insult to gain trust," she hypothesized.

"I'm sure you could find a number of people who would agree with him," I said.

"That proves my theory. You two are so alike. Both, Minus deprecating."

"Now that we've cleared that up, what did he have to say?"

"Your brother couldn't get through to you, so he was trying different avenues."

Patricia looked into her coffee as if it were a crystal ball.

"He doesn't know where he is. His abductors have put him in a box with dozens of other souls. The density of thoughts makes it extremely difficult for him to concentrate. On top of that, Brian continues to be taken farther away, making it even harder to contact you."

"I don't get why he can talk to you but not me."

"He's tried, but someone keeps getting in the way. Minus, your brother wants to talk to you." Patricia took a thoughtful sip of coffee. With both hands wrapped around the mug, she held it close to her mouth creating a puff of steam with every exhalation. "Brian hopes some of what he said got through to you. Eventually, he just gave up trying and started working on me!"

"Wyoming!" I almost shouted. "The word I heard Brian say was, Wyoming."

"Where did that come from?"

"The Algonquin Indians, I believe."

"How do you know that? Never mind," Patricia quickly retracted her question. "Does it mean anything to you?"

"I've been told it's a state in the US, although there's a lot of those places that seem theoretical to me." I flexed my West Coast prejudicial muscle.

"Do you get in trouble saying things like that?" Patricia asked.

"This is my living room. How much trouble can I get in?"

"You never know who's listening these days," Patricia warned.

"Do you think Wyoming has the technology to bug my house?"

"Wyoming's dead probably do."

"That's a good point." I realized what she was getting at. "I will try to be more open-minded about my fellow Americans and their ancestry."

I couldn't imagine that Brian had kept his communication with Patricia to such a short conversation, so I brought the topic back. "Did Brian have anything else to share?"

"He did," she said, then finished her coffee.

I waited to see if that was a complete sentence or if she was planning to add a verb and subject.

Patricia stared deep into her mug.

"Would you like a warm-up on your coffee?" I offered to give her time to gather her thoughts.

"Yes, thank you."

I went into the kitchen to procure the refills. The coffee steamed when it hit the cold cups more than I remember it doing on the first pouring. Frigid fingers ran up my spine. Something was wrong. The room had become cold. Bitterly cold. The curtains began to sway like ghosts, slapping against the sill with a snap. Quickly, I turned to see the back door wide open. "Damn," I said to myself. "I should fix that latch." This was the third time in a week that had happened. I closed the door and went back to the cozy sofa still occupied by Patricia and Dumbo.

"Thank you," Patricia said, as I handed her the cup.

"Are you warm enough?" I asked. "I was increasing global warming through my back door. I hope you didn't catch a chill."

"No. I'm fine. These pajamas are very comfy," she said, reminding me of Dumbo's ears.

"Where were we?" I restarted the preempted conversation.

"You asked about what else Brian said."

"So, I did…and?"

"He was cut off mid-sentence."

"And the half-sentence was?" I pushed.

"All he said was, *'Tell Minus I,'*" Patricia said.

When I had heard my brother was killed in the war, I was numb. The daily number count of the dead on the news couldn't prepare me for his death. This also, I was not ready for. Life is cruel. Death was looking even crueler.

"Are you okay?" Patricia asked.

"No!" I said before my voice had a chance to crack.

She left her safe place on the sofa and gave me a hug. Patricia was warm and soft, tender and strong, real and temporary. For a moment, I was safe.

"Thank you, that was nice," I cried.

"We'll find him," she promised, then went back to her corner.

Once I pulled myself together, I asked, "Now what?"

"Let's start with what we have until we have what we need," Patricia answered.

"Did you just make that up?"

"My father used to say it." Patricia gave a glimpse into her past.

"That's the first I've heard you mention your family. Is this a sensitive subject?"

"It's not something I want to get into right now."

"Understood, but may I ask for a rain check?"

"Yes," she said, giving me the hope of understanding her past.

"What we have is; Wyoming. And what the hell does that have to do with anything?" I asked.

"Maybe you have relatives who like to ski," Patricia contributed to the pool of possibilities.

"There are no bad ideas," I suggested, "but that is verging on one."

"Okay, your turn," she turned it back on me.

"Maybe I have dead relatives with second homes."

"That is a bad idea," she said.

"Yeah, I know. I was just trying to make you look good."

"It worked."

"Maybe it's your relatives stealing my relatives?" I offered.

"Why would...? That's an interesting idea," Patricia acknowledged. "After all, it is my property that is causing this craziness."

"Indeed! So, let me ask you a question. What does Wyoming mean to you?"

"Skiing," she said.

"We're not going to go through that again, are we?"

"It's a reason to go there, and if we dig up a little information, all the better."

"Are you serious? You want to just pack up and go skiing?"

"Sure, do you have something better to do?"

"I have a job."

"Minus, it's nine o'clock in the morning and you're sitting on your couch in your PJs!"

"It's Sunday, Patricia."

"Oh, right. Let's go to Wyoming anyway."

"How can I say no to that?" I replied, admitting it sounded nice.

We had arranged to meet Helen at the cemetery around eleven. The morning was getting on. Patricia went off to retire Dumbo while I had a shower, wishing I were Dumbo.

* * *

There was no guard at the gate when Patricia and I arrived at the cemetery. Still, I felt unseen eyes on us.

"Rather quiet here today," I said, as we drove through The Yard.

"Rather," she replied, not expanding on the comment.

The Filbert gravesite was also unguarded. Helen looked statu-esque standing over the headstones. Like a granite guardian angel protecting what was left of my family.

"Patricia," Helen said, "weren't you wearing those clothes yesterday?"

Without missing a beat, Patricia answered, "I love this dress, I always wear it two days in a row."

Hoping to change the subject, I interjected, "You're here early. Are there any pre-meeting conversations to catch up on?"

"Minus, you're as see-through as a glass door at a shopping mall. What have you two been up to? Don't answer that. I don't want to know."

"Sounds like you've been talking to my father."

"Yes, his style is contagious," Helen affirmed.

Patricia's rosy blush glowed in the mid-day sun. "Helen, I assure you that your imagination dwarfs reality," she said, ending that conversation.

We sat on the grass around the Filbert clan and Helen filled us in on her morning chat with Pops.

"Your father is quite upset, Minus. He thinks Brian's abduction was orchestrated by a distant relative. Paul has been in touch with Patricia's father—who by the way likes your car—and he feels there is a lot of history at play here."

"Really, he likes my car?"

"Don't get distracted, Minus," Patricia warned. "He used to have a '67."

"I finally have some family history," I said to Patricia.

"Savor it," she put an end to her family lore.

Helen regained the helm. "Apparently, something happened during the westward migration that is affecting us today."

"Any chance Wyoming has come up in conversation?" I inquired.

"Yes, Jackson Hole to be precise."

"They have ski resorts there," Patricia added.

Helen and I both looked at her.

"Well, they do," she said, standing up for herself.

"Any other tidbits?" I asked Helen.

"Just," Helen turned to Patricia, "your parents say hi."

Patricia got up and walked away. Away from the Filberts. Away from the Kellys. Just away.

"There's something not good in her past," Helen told me. "I don't know what it is, but I can feel it from both sides of the grave. I think your father knows, but he isn't telling."

"Should we follow her?" I asked.

"She'll come back when she's ready."

I took Helen's hand. "Thank you," I said. "Have you ever been to Wyoming?"

12

WYOMING

Wyoming?

Maybe a few stragglers from a wagon train had given up trying to reach the West Coast and decided to homestead this future resort mecca. Still, they're quite a bit out of radio range to orchestrate a head heist.

Doing a little research, before running off to the Grand Teton slopes, seemed advantageous. Luckily, I'm working with two women who are a hell of a lot smarter than I am. Left to my sleuthing abilities alone, we would probably end up in New Jersey.

We divvied up the tasks. Patricia's job was to check the identities of the potential buyers of the tomb. My job was to locate the person who advised me to bid on the Oakland School District contract. Helen was tasked with tracing Patricia's family members back to the fur trading days. From all of that, I hoped to solve this case, Patricia hoped to get a ski vacation, and Helen…I'm not sure what Helen wanted.

Kathy didn't get back to me until Monday. So much for time and a half.

As it turned out, a Nevada bus dealer had sent me the details on the Oakland sale.

"Why would another dealer want to give me a contract?" I asked Kathy, not expecting an answer.

"People like you, Minus," Kathy surprised me with a response that clinched the time-and-a-half pay.

She gave me the name of a dealership just over the border in Tahoe. I gave him a call.

"Hello, my name is Minus Filbert," I said to the receptionist at Nevada Bus Services. "May I speak with Jimmy Walsh?"

"He's on the other line at the moment. Can you hold?"

"Of course, that's my favorite pastime."

"Thank you," she said, as if everybody made that comment. I made a mental note to come up with a new line.

While I was on hold, Nevada Bus Services used the opportunity to sell me buses. They claimed to be the best in quality, customer service, and price, working with school districts all over the western states. By the time Jimmy came on the line, I was ready to put in an order for a fleet of minibuses.

"Hello, this is Jimmy. How can I help you?" a gruff voice announced, sounding like it had seen the butt end of too many cigarettes.

"Hi, this is Minus Filbert. I represent Blue Bird Buses in San Francisco. I wanted to thank you for throwing me a bone."

"I've heard the best things about you," Jimmy said. "I just referred you to the Oakland School District."

"Exactly, that's what I was calling about. I'm a little unclear as to how my name had traveled to Nevada."

"That is a little confusing," Jimmy tried to prepare me for a verbal shell game. "You see, my cousin's brother-in-law, in Wyoming, clued him into the Oakland deal. Sean, my cousin who has a bus dealership in Utah, had heard great things about you from his sister's husband."

"Wow, that's quite a convoluted series of referrals. By chance, do you have the name of the brother-in-law? I would like to thank him too."

"Sorry I don't, but Sean can help you with that. Let me get you his number."

Jimmy passed on Sean's contact information, allowing me to continue searching for the Irishman who started all of this.

As it was closing in on noon, in my eastern neighboring states, I called Sean before lunch took over his priorities.

"Hello, this is Sean. How can I help you?" There was no receptionist directing calls.

"Hi, this is Minus Filbert."

"Minus, I've heard so much about you. What a surprise. My brother-in-law has told me all about your bus-selling prowess. I hope someday to build my own little empire."

"Umm, thank you. You've caught me a little off guard here. My colleagues in San Francisco aren't nearly as complimentary as you."

"We're a pretty small town here. We just say what we think."

"That could get you fired most places," I said and quickly continued, "You're a breath of fresh air."

"We got a lot of that here, too," Sean informed me.

"I'll have to try it sometime. What I'm calling about, is to thank you for referring me to the Oakland School District for the bus bid. That was a genuinely nice gesture I don't often see."

"My pleasure, Seamus couldn't say enough good things about you."

"I take it Seamus is your brother-in-law?"

"Yep, he lives in Jackson Hole with his dog. My sister passed several years back."

"I'm sorry to hear that," I said, being a little taken aback by the lightness of his tone.

"She's never far from him. You see, he runs the cemetery there. We like to call it, 'Souls in the Hole.'"

I had to hold my tongue. Everything that came to mind would derail the investigation.

"I like that," I finally formulated a response. "I'd like to give Seamus a call and thank him personally."

"Sure, let me get you his number. Can you hold a minute?"

"It's my favorite pastime," I chanced, enlisting a belly laugh from Sean.

After leaving Sean in stitches with a joke about two bus salesmen who walk into a bar, I had to take a break. This felt like a journey through an Irish version of *Brigadoon*.

While decompressing, Helen called to say she had located Patricia's great-great-grandparents at a cemetery in Jackson Hole.

"Well, we're right on target," I said. "I'm just about to call the director of *The Souls in the Hole*."

"Excuse me?" Helen understandably questioned.

"It's a long story. So, who are we dealing with in Wyoming?" I asked.

"Mr. and Mrs. Brendan S. Kelly. They stayed behind during the migration because Bridget, the Mrs., became ill and couldn't continue the trek."

"It looks like we're getting a lot of information leading us down a Jackson hole."

"Was that a joke?" Helen asked.

"Not if you have to ask," I conceded.

I made my final call to Seamus feeling ill at ease with the unworthy praise I had been receiving. It was lunchtime, and I was eager to meet Patricia at the food truck.

"Hello, Holy Souls Cemetery, how may I help you?" a soothing woman's voice answered the phone.

"Hello, may I speak to Seamus Finnigan?"

"Certainly, who may I say is calling?"

"This is Minus Filbert."

"Please hold," she said, putting me on hold and missing out on my wit.

I began this phone search listening to sales promotions in Tahoe. Now, I was being dazzled with the promise of eternal life with a mountain view. I like my lovely view in Brisbane. My *will* clearly states that I am to be buried under the cushions on my sofa.

"Hi, this is Seamus. I'm out of the office right now, please leave a message and I will get back to you before you die."

I left Seamus a message saying who I was and asking him to give me a call before my heirs disconnected my phone.

With my calls completed, I was ready for lunch. Patricia and I had planned to meet at our favorite outdoor eating establishment, where we would compare notes and share a dessert.

*   *   *

When I was young, a food truck did not offer the type of food my parents ate. That is why I frequented them. I remember dear old Pops telling me I'd go blind eating *that food*. Or did I get that confused with something else? No matter, the mobile establishment Patricia favored was excellent.

When I arrived at the curb, Patricia was already in line. "May I cut in?" I submitted my request.

"You can go to the end of the line!" she said, with a glare in her eye. Then a smile on her face. "I can be intimidating, can't I?"

"I wouldn't want to meet you in a dark conference room," I said, taking my place in front of six other customers.

After ordering, we stepped aside to await the miracle of the culinary arts. A visual reconnaissance was also carried out to secure a place to sit.

"How's your morning been?" I opened the conversation with a little small talk.

"Not so fruitful. All the interest in the tomb was from developers wanting to flip the property. No one I would even *consider* selling to."

"Well then, the good news is," I said, with my endless optimism, "we can now focus our attention on Wyoming."

Patricia asked, "What did you find out?"

"First and foremost, I learned what a great guy I am. My stellar reputation stems from the Grand Tetons to the Pacific Ocean. That's all everyone is talking about."

"Positive reinforcement is usually a good thing, but I'm not sure it helps us here." Patricia found the words to talk me down.

"I know, but a fellow can dream."

"Dream on, my good fellow. And when you awake, can we get back to reality?"

"Exactly what part of this last week feels like reality to you?" I asked.

"Right now does. The two of us talking. The smell of the food truck. The homeless guy digging through the garbage. Reality is all around us and within that reality is a world we don't understand, but that does not make it any less real."

"I like my reality to make sense," I orchestrated all that existed.

"It making sense is your perception of reality," Patricia said, further confusing my delicate grasp on life.

"I'm sorry, I went to public school. Reality was avoided there. I *can* tell you when Columbus sailed the ocean blue."

"Minus, you have a wonderful sense of survival."

"Until I figure that out, I will take it as a compliment."

Patricia was summoned to collect our lunch through the small window in the big truck. We then went about securing a dining spot. The second preferred location we had identified, became free. The side door to the Heritage Bank was out of the wind and in the sun. A good spot for an autumn perch.

The terrazzo steps were oh so warm on my derriere. "I'll have to remember this when I'm feeling cold at the graves," I said to Patricia. "I bet the headstone would make a great keister heater."

"You would sit on your parents?" Patricia asked, with disgust.

"Of course not," I was quick to clarify. "I *would* sit on Brian."

"You must be feeling better about finding him."

"Now that I know reality doesn't have to make sense. And that my warm butt and Brian's disappearance are part of the same perceptive mechanism. I know that as long as my backside is toasty, Brian is somewhere to be found."

"I am not even going to try to follow that avenue of reasoning, as long as you're happy with it," Patricia said, exercising her eyeballs in a clockwise rotation.

My phone rang just as I took a bite of the chicken sandwich. It was Seamus. I chewed as fast as I could, counting the rings before it would go into voicemail. My mouth was still processing the herbed chicken on sourdough when I hit accept.

"This is Minus," I said, sounding like I had just gotten out of the dentist.

"Hi Minus, this is Seamus in Jackson. I got your message and wanted to get right back to you. Sorry if I'm disturbing your lunch."

His introduction gave me just enough time to swallow and say, "No problem, I was just finishing up."

"I quite often eat at my desk," Seamus filled a little more time, allowing me to take a sip of my soda. "To what do I owe the pleasure of your call?" he asked, making me wonder if he knew who I was.

"I was calling to thank you for turning me on to the Oakland School District bus deal."

"My pleasure," he said, putting my insecurities at ease. "After all, it's right in your backyard."

"That it is. By the way, since you're in the *dearly departed* industry, how is it you know about the needs of the Oakland School District?" I approached the question with as little suspicion in my voice as I could muster.

Mr. Finnigan was ready for that question. "I have a friend who's on the school board here. He's studying the procedures of larger school districts. *Education is everything*, he's always saying. He heard about the deal through the grapevine."

"Nice to know that my name carries well in Jackson Hole. But I'm still trying to work out how I fit in?"

"You sell busses," Seamus reminded me.

"Some weeks I wonder about that. Let me rephrase the question. Why me?"

Seamus wasn't so quick to come up with an answer for that. I waited patiently on my end of the line, anticipating a clever response that would explain everything.

Ending the silence, he returned to the conversation sounding like a politician on trial. "I heard your name from someone, but I can't remember who."

"I do that all the time," I said to put him at ease. "If the name comes to you, please let me know. I would like to give him my thanks."

"I will certainly do that," Seamus replied, noticeably less nervous with the misperception that he had pulled the wool over my eyes.

To keep the momentum of my investigation from faltering, I followed up with a question about Wyoming. "I have a friend who is ski crazy," I said, starting Patricia's eyes rolling again. "She was wondering if you had any recommendations?"

"Tahoe. There's great skiing there," Seamus answered, obviously not a member of the Jackson Chamber of Commerce.

"If I'm not mistaken, that isn't in Wyoming," I pointed out.

"No, but it's where I go."

"Is this a case of the snow being whiter on the other side of the mountain?" I said, wondering why he was sending me away from Wyoming.

"I also have family there, so I can hit two snow bunnies with one snowball," he said, putting a new twist on an old cliché.

"Interesting, Tahoe has come up twice today," I added to get his reaction.

"I'm sorry, Minus, I just realized that I have a meeting to attend. If you have any other questions, don't hesitate to give me a call."

We made our hurried goodbyes, then Seamus was gone. I looked at Patricia, who smiled and said, "I like skiing in Tahoe too."

"It looks like you may get a grand tour of western ski chalets and cemeteries. Hopefully not one as the result of the other," I informed her.

"What is your aversion to skiing? You're not scared, are you?" Patricia poked fun at me.

"I take umbrage at you insinuating that I have an irrational fear of smashing into a tree, breaking every bone in my body, creating a lifetime of pain."

"You must show me your glass bubble sometime," she said, sounding a little too patronizing.

I smiled back at her. "Gladly, you might want to try it out."

We spent the rest of lunch enjoying our truck grub and watching the wheels of industry turn.

Once lunch had been consumed and the recyclables, compostables, and redemption-less materials had been disposed of in the proper receptacles, Patricia went back to enabling renters to become massively in debt homeowners. I went home to have a nap.

* * *

When Helen called, I was just surfacing from a dream about green snow separated by a white picket mountain range.

"I've got some interesting information," Helen excitedly began the call.

"Helen, can I call you back? Nature calls."

"Sure, did I wake you?"

"Your insight is commendable. Talk soon." I hung up.

I completed my rising rituals by putting on a pot of coffee. The aroma of French roast activated my nervous system enabling my brain to begin processing rational thought. I took this opportunity of induced clarity to return Helen's call.

"How are you?" I asked before getting down to business.

"I'm regretting getting into education instead of investigation. This detective work is more fun."

"It's never too late for a career change. You could become an SPI," I suggested.

"What's that?" Helen took the bait.

"Spirit private investigator. I don't know how much call there is for that, but I bet there's very little competition."

"If you ever get tired of selling busses," Helen offered, "I'm sure I could find you a job as a career counselor in a high school."

"I'll keep that in mind. What did you find out?" I asked, changing the subject from my father's identity.

"I found a trail of Kellys stretching from the Mississippi River to California. I only went as far back as St. Paul, Minnesota, where Patricia's relatives had settled after emigrating from Ireland. The interesting thing is, it wasn't the potato famine that had them leave Ireland."

Helen stopped. I believe for dramatic effect. So, I felt it was my duty to say, "Really? What was it then?"

"Her great-great-great-grandparents were hired by a French bootlegger to set up a whiskey distillery in the newly named city of St. Paul."

I interjected, "I knew she had to have come from good stock."

"Minus?" Helen said, then thought better of getting into it with me. "You are your father's son."

Even though, in this case, that was not meant as a compliment, it warmed my heart to be with someone who knew Pops.

Helen picked up her report where I had interjected. "Anyway, Declan Kelly and his family eventually moved on, heading west."

"May I put forth a possible trail for Patricia's heritage?" I lobbied Helen.

"Be my guest. I have a feeling you've found out a thing or two, also."

"I have a simple theory, consisting of Jackson Hole and Tahoe. Any chance those places play into the story?" I said, keeping my interruption short.

"Among other cities, yes," Helen confirmed my hypothesis. "It seems we're closing in on something. I would like to discuss it with Patricia present. Are you okay waiting for a full answer?"

"Sure. What are you doing for dinner?"

Helen described the frozen meal she had planned to put in the microwave and eat on her lap.

"That sounds cozy. But how about I find a place to eat between you and Patricia, and we meet there?"

"Perfect. Detective work makes me ravenous," Helen admitted.

"Great, Italian okay with you?"

I Googled East Bay Italian restaurants and found a ☆☆☆☆, $$, Osteria that favored Helen's location. I offered to pick Patricia up at home and chauffeur her to dinner.

"That's extremely sweet of you, Minus," Patricia said, "but I don't mind driving."

"Okay, let me rephrase the offer. I would like to pick you up and take you to dinner."

"Thank you, Minus." Patricia then proclaimed, "Life is not about the destination. It's about the journey."

13

THE JOURNEY

I woke up with the sun in my eyes.

This was not a welcome start to the day, so I pulled the covers over my head to ease the discomfort. There was a softness to the sheets, a fresh, clean scent I hadn't smelt since my mother had stopped doing my laundry.

The dream I had just woken up from was fading, but I still felt its presence. Keeping my eyes closed and the sheets pulled up, I could feel sleep pulling me back, enticing me to leave the sun to its daily journey. While I postponed mine.

Sometime later—sometime much later—I surfaced again, like a whale breaching the waves only to submerge and breach again. I hadn't slept this peacefully since, well, my mother stopped doing my laundry.

Still, I had no memory of dreams. No feeling of impending doom, just the scent of summer vacation. Reluctantly, I peeked out from under my cotton fortress to see a room that was not mine.

I was alone. I like being alone. But I felt I shouldn't be alone, not here. Not in a place that wasn't mine. A place that was Patricia's.

"Hellooo?" I softly called out, unsure if I wanted to hear a reply.

No reply, but there was movement. Quiet footsteps approaching the bedroom. I waited for Patricia to come through the door, but no Patricia.

"Hello," I said again, apparently giving Patricia's cat permission to jump on the bed, scaring the hell out of me and it.

"Sorry, kitty, come back," I called, to the sound of feline feet running down the hall.

Oh, great, I've alienated the cat. The one creature that could have been my ally. It was time to find the catnip and make amends.

A robe had been strategically placed on the foot of the bed and slippers perfectly aligned below it. I slipped into both and made my way down the hall in search of coffee and the cat. One must keep one's priorities straight.

By the time I sat down with my cup of coffee, the cat had forgiven me and perched upon my lap as I looked out the kitchen window.

I could have driven home last night, but when Patricia offered to put me up, I accepted her kind gesture. However, the combination of Chianti and grappa caused me to fall asleep within seconds of collapsing on the sofa. How I got to the bed will be a topic of conversation with my hostess.

Patricia's kitchen faced the forested Oakland Hills. There's a peacefulness about trees. A calm descends when sitting at a window, with a cat on your knee, coffee in your cup, and a blue sky framing the view.

From Brisbane, these hills create a textured horizon. My current vantage point, though, had details I found curious. Patricia's view was in direct sight of the row of eucalyptus trees that protect the Kellys' plots from public scrutiny. That can't be a mere coincidence. For all of Patricia's laissez-faire attitude about her family, she still keeps an eye on them. It could not have been easy to find such a kitchen window.

One of the benefits of being a salesman is the ability to *not* work at home. Patricia and Helen have been enslaved by their corporate lords, whereas I am free to run myself into financial ruin. I decided to sit a little longer and contemplate my next move.

The cat and I sat undisturbed until Fluffy noticed a delicious-looking bird foraging in the yard. Forsaking my lap for breakfast, it shot out the cat door. I feared not for the little birdie. That is one fat cat.

No longer bound to the chair by feline shackles, I showered, refilled my coffee, and called Patricia.

"How'd you sleep?" she asked, as part of our morning greetings.

"Like a 185-pound log," I answered, giving away too much information.

"Is that how much you weigh?" She allowed me the opportunity to lie.

"Fully dressed," I fibbed, then changed the subject. "When did you leave?"

"Sometime between you mumbling incoherently in your sleep and the sun coming up. When did you come to life?"

"Sometime between the sun coming up and now."

"If we're going to find Brian," Patricia refocused our focus, "we will need to be a bit more accurate than *sometime between.* Will you be ready to leave for Wyoming tonight? I've already booked the tickets."

It all came back to me. Helen had ordered the fettuccine with clams, Patricia the gnocchi, and I the lasagna. Then, throwing caution to the wind, we decided to head out the next day to Jackson Hole. The search for Brian was in full swing.

"I hope Helen's research is accurate," I said, remembering the Chianti-laced conversation regarding the patriarch of the Kelly clan. "What time is our flight?"

Patricia filled me in on the details before running off to another meeting.

I made the bed, cleaned up the coffee grounds, and washed my cup. Looking out the kitchen window, I witnessed the birdie teasing the cat. That was a good reminder for me to lose a few pounds.

Two hours before the flight, Helen, Patricia, and I convened at my place to take one car to the airport. The consensus was to drive Helen's Toyota, since it was the only one of our vehicles that had not been designed to cripple the rider in the back seat.

Helen had packed a small carry-on to get her through the three days we had given ourselves to find Brian. Patricia had a suitcase the size of a steamer trunk, and I managed to fit all that I needed in my computer bag. Individuality is a beautiful thing.

The trip to the airport was thankfully quick. Because, after transferring five pounds of the contents from Patricia's bag to Helen's, and mine, we had just enough time to get to the gate. Security was the usual nightmare, worsened by having my pockets filled with women's underwear.

Once seated at the gate, I finally had time to look at the flight information. The plane was to board at 7:40 p.m. and arrives in Jackson at 12:07 p.m. tomorrow. That's fifteen hours. I thought Wyoming was on the same planet as California.

"Patricia, may I ask you a question?" I softly approached my travel agent. "Did the airline not have a stop in Dubai?"

"It sure took you long enough to catch on, Minus. I was going to route you through Cape Town but thought the South Africans have been through enough hardship."

"That's most thoughtful of you," I said, then shut up.

The flight's seating arrangement put Helen and me next to each other, with Patricia directly in front of Helen. After taking off, Helen leaned forward to ask Patricia a question through the gap in the seats. Next to Patricia was a very polite and generous airline patron who offered to switch seats with Helen to facilitate their conversation, putting me next to Buck, who loved to talk about hunting.

* * *

During the two-and-a-half-hour layover in Seattle, I asked my travel partners how they enjoyed the first leg of the trip.

"The time just flew by," Patricia was first to answer.

Followed by an equally exuberant Helen, "I don't know where the time went. How about you?"

"I learned how to kill a moose," I said, putting a pall over the table. "May I buy you guys a drink?"

With the refreshments ordered, Helen filled me in on her flight conversation with Patricia.

"I had been wondering what happened to the nightmare man who was pressuring Patricia," Helen said. "He hasn't made an appearance since he smashed your car, Minus."

"Good question, Helen. I completely put him out of my head." Turning to Patricia, I asked, "Do you feel like going through it again with me?"

"Sure, there's not much to tell. During my visit with Brian, I felt Maurice's presence. But since then, nothing."

"Could you tell if he was with Brian or with you?"

"I hadn't thought about that, but Helen wondered the same thing. Was he blocking Brian or stealing him? I don't know."

"Do you have any clues as to who this guy is? Any reference he may have made that would give us a lead? The aftershave he uses? Anything?"

"Minus, you almost went a full thought without making a joke," Helen pointed out.

"Yeah, traveling throws me off," I admitted. "I don't get it, we started off dealing with a cemetery plot for sale and now we're sitting in the Seattle airport chasing ghosts."

"You're right," Patricia continued my thoughts. "The family plots are no longer the focus. Brian's skull being whisked off has taken us away from our original purpose and onto a plane headed for Wyoming. If I were a suspicious person, I would say we were being manipulated."

"Exactly," Helen kept the conversation on track, "maybe Brian got in the way of the sale, and now unknown forces are working on damage control."

"For clarity," I chimed in, "it's actually three planes, so we still have eleven more hours to talk in circles before we get to Jackson. Does anyone want another drink?" I called for the next round.

The second leg of the flight was with a different airline, putting us through security again. I had given Patricia her underwear back, making the process less embarrassing. Helen, Patricia, and I had been plugged into whatever seats were available on this fully booked flight. My seating companion was a young Asian man wearing a very red robe. He seemed content within his meditations, so I focused my attention on the view. It seems no matter where I sit on a plane, the wing is always outside my window. The laws of aeronautic physics seem to change with my seat assignments.

Lift, drag, weight, and thrust had a successful union. We were once again airborne, headed in the general direction of Jackson Hole.

The moonless night was illuminated by a flashing red light on the wingtip. When above the brash concerns of the land, the stars become a backdrop for imagination. A stage for dreams to play out on. A pillow for my head. Sitting in a plane full of people, I dozed off with solitude as my companion.

My hibernation instinct kicks in when I stop moving for more than five minutes. Internal physical functions slow while mental stimulation becomes enhanced. Then the dreams come to life. Sleeping in public can be uncomfortable for those around me. I tend to talk, mumble, and grunt in my sleep for reasons I have not figured out, occasionally punctuated with a kick or some other form of flailing. The seat belts on a plane are little protection for my fellow passengers.

I dreamt I was sitting in the window seat that I was sitting in, looking out the window I had been looking out, but the stars were gone. The wing light still flashed red. With every illumination, I caught a glimpse of a shadow.

This silhouette had a familiar contour. It was motionless, standing erect like Jesus on the mount. Its cloak flowed in the breeze (I believe for dramatic effect because the plane was traveling at 500 mph). The wing light suddenly stopped flashing. Many long seconds passed before a solid white light took its place.

The faceless demon was back.

Excellent, we must be on the right trail. Maurice looked at me with a blank stare. Which, of course, one would expect from a faceless demon. I didn't feel scared, even when he started pulling the flaps off the wing. He was just another player in this mystery.

I didn't yell at him. No need to wake up the other passengers.

The Tibetan monk was slumped in his seat deep in meditation. No one else on the plane seemed to be put out by this apparition's deconstruction of the plane's engine, so I just enjoyed the show.

When he received no affirmation from me, Maurice went about ripping holes in the fuselage. Not wanting to witness my fellow passengers sucked out into the chilly air at 30,000 feet, I stopped his effect on my mind. Just like that, the plane was whole again. Grumpy was gone.

Since I seemed to be getting rather good at controlling my subconscious, I decided to stay asleep and enjoy a candle-lit dinner in Paris with Patricia. Helen opted to remain on the plane.

Just as we finished the shared order of *moules*, the flight attendant announced our imminent arrival into Denver, which woke me up. Damn!

Denver was kind to us. Even though we had to deplane, the gate of our last leg to Jackson was the same as our entry into Denver. All we had to do was sit in the terminal for five hours.

The airport bar was packed when we squeezed into the remaining open table. I recognized most of the patrons from our series of flights. It would appear that the convoluted nature of this trek drove most travelers to drink.

"Did you see the show on our last flight?" I addressed my companions.

"Yes!" Helen said with excitement. "I'd been wanting to see *An Original DUCKumentary* for a long time."

Patricia and I had no response for that, so we just looked at her.

"It was really good. I enjoy a good love story," she continued, hoping that would explain her excitement.

It didn't.

Patricia subtly redirected the conversation by agreeing that though she loves ducks, I might be referring to the visit from our spooky friend.

"I saw him," Patricia said. "He was very entertaining until he started pulling the fuselage apart. I bailed at that point."

"Me too," I said, then asking Helen, "Did you see him?"

"Sorry, the ducks were really cute."

We ordered drinks, hoping to compress time to something survivable.

As unique as the Denver airport building is, after two hours, I was wanting our faceless friend to return and entertain us with a grand dismantling of the gate. In the time frame of this journey, we could have peaked Everest.

On the other side of the terminal, I saw my Buddhist travel mate. He was sitting cross-legged on the floor facing a wall. I translated his meditation into modern Western life by ordering another drink.

We muddled our way through the remaining three hours by playing *I Spy*, which Helen was *really* good at.

Once back in the air, the sojourn to our final destination was uneventful. I napped while Helen and Patricia went into overtime with *I Spy*. The restful sleep was welcome.

14

WELCOME

At long last. Jackson.
Nestled in the Jackson Hole Valley.

We made our way to the hotel. Assuming it hadn't gone out of business in the last fifteen hours.

"Welcome!" Loris said.

I knew the woman behind the desk was Loris because her baseball cap said so. Embroidered above the brim was:

Hi, I'm Loris

Welcome to Jackson

I felt very welcome.

"Thank you, Loris," Patricia said, taking on the check-in duties. "We have two rooms reserved under Kelly."

I looked over at her. "That doesn't seem very nice to put Helen all alone in a room."

"In your dreams, Minus," Patricia referenced one of my favorite places.

I smiled and stowed the memory of Dumbo's ears.

"Do you get very many visitors from the San Francisco area?" I asked Loris to stop Patricia's last comment from hanging in the air.

"Sure do!" she said. "We get folks from all over coming here."

"I hear you have a nice cemetery near town," Helen joined the conversation.

"We have two. I'm partial to Holy Souls. You don't have to be a mountain goat to visit your relatives. Seamus keeps a tidy spread just outside of town. Gets lots of visitors too. Whereas Aspen Hill is convenient if you ski into a tree."

"Is there a tax benefit for buying your aunt a hole here?" I asked, hoping I wasn't being too cheeky.

"I don't know, but Seamus seems to do a good business."

Patricia completed her transaction with Loris. With that, the San Francisco gumshoe detectives went up to our rooms for a nap. Silently, we had agreed to put off the investigation for a few more hours.

Not wanting to sleep into the night, I set my alarm for three p.m. At four o'clock, I finally dragged myself off the bed, barely missing the floor. Once I had located my equilibrium, the door between our rooms became my destination. As unremarkable as this portal was, it denied access to my friends.

Tap, tap, tap. I delicately knocked on the barrier.

Patricia called out, "Huh!"

Obviously, not wanting to be woken up, I attempted to draw her out with a friendly question. "Where are we?"

"Minus, go lie down," she answered, not ready for my humor.

"Patricia? You haven't eaten Helen, have you?"

"I'm sorry, Minus, I just woke up from a bad dream," Patricia reassured me that Helen had not been fricasseed.

"Okay, why don't you guys get yourselves together? I'll be here trying to figure out the coffee maker."

By the time the women crossed the threshold separating our quarters, I had successfully made a cup of coffee with what looked to me like a button-making machine. Feeling a certain pride of accomplishment, I offered to brew up a couple more for the team.

"No thank you," they both declined, with an edge of disdain.

"Are you guys okay? That was coffee I offered, not prune juice."

They looked at each other, seemingly communicating with female Bluetooth. Patricia was chosen to deliver the message. "Those little plastic cups are too wasteful," she proclaimed.

"That's a reason to turn down a ritual? They're really small containers," I rationalized my desire.

"So is sand," Helen said, putting things in perspective. "Get enough of it and you've got a beach."

Conveniently, I heard a stomach growl and was able to change the subject. "Any chance you guys are hungry?"

"An early dinner would be great," Patricia suggested.

"I'm starving," Helen offered an insight to her current physical condition.

Using my advanced detective skills, I scoured the town of Jackson online. A Thai restaurant, within walking distance, served as enticement to lure us from our protective oasis. Snow was not yet decorating the trees, but it was cold. Far beyond cold. Cold would have been a welcome relief from the lunar surface outside. None of us had packed clothes for this weather. I doubt any of us owned clothes warm enough to prevent cryopathy.

We walked fast, taking turns acting as a wind block. Reaching the restaurant, Helen commented on three landscaping trucks parked along the curb.

"Does anyone know the culinary level of gardeners?" she asked.

"Looks like there might be a lawn and garden conference going on inside. There could be fresh herbs to be had," Patricia speculated.

Helen and I looked at her.

"Maybe?" she kind of stood up for her theory.

We entered the dining room to the sinus clearing fragrance of garlic and cumin. Even if the food was bad, we wouldn't know it until two in the morning.

My partners preferred a booth. This put us seated at a window behind a group of three landscapers.

"I can't imagine hiring that bunch to sweep out my French drain," I whispered to the gals as we slid into the booth.

"Minus, you can be so judgmental," Patricia said.

"Really? Would you like me to talk to them about trimming your trees?"

"Maybe later," Helen postponed judgment.

With our orders taken, it was time to devise a strategy that would break this case wide open. Since I was the most judgmental, I took the lead with possible sleuthing scenarios.

"I think these Cro-Magnon horticulturists are stealing skulls and bringing them to Jackson Hole," I began the brainstorming.

Whether or not my partners agreed with my hypothesis was hard to tell, but they were quite fetching sitting with their mouths open.

"Did you think about that before you said it?" Helen asked.

"It's just a primer," I replied. "Now it's your turn to make a fool of yourself."

"Thank you. I think I'll pass. Patricia?" Helen passed the baton.

"Thank you, Minus, for setting the bar so low. However, before we start accusing the local florists of body theft, we should have a word with Seamus," Patricia playfully put me in my place.

"Okay, but don't be surprised when I say *I told you so.*"

"You wouldn't do that," Helen said.

"Don't count on it," Patricia countered.

"She knows me well," I warned.

Patricia proceeded to raise the bar. "There was something about Loris referring to Holy Souls cemetery as Seamus's spread that was curious. With that name, I assumed it was a Catholic franchise. So, I looked it up and found out that Holy Souls is not affiliated with any church. Instead, it's a private company under the corporate umbrella of Titan Moon Distributors," Patricia said, hoisting the bar up a notch.

She let the news sink in with her dinner mates. One of whom loves a conspiracy.

Helen, who isn't big on conspiracy, asked, "You aren't thinking this is a conspiracy, are you?"

"I have no idea. It's just that Seamus's spread is owned by a corporation that distributes things."

"When did you find all this out?" I asked.

"Just before my nap," Patricia answered, reinforcing my next question.

"What was your bad dream about?"

"I was hoping you wouldn't ask. Can we pretend you didn't ask?"

"No!"

Patricia looked at Helen for help, but their personal Wi-Fi was down. "Okay," she relented.

Patricia looked out the window for a moment before going into her story.

"Brian is here," she began. Then she stopped.

"You spoke to him?" Helen asked.

"No." Patricia paused again.

"Are there any full sentences in your story?" I asked.

"Maybe."

"Minus, let her think. You know how hard it is to make sense of a dream," Helen stood up for her roommate. "Why don't you play with your utensils while Patricia gathers her thoughts?"

I have an uncanny ability to bring out the smart-ass in people. Helen was certainly finding her voice with me.

"There are two cemeteries in town," Patricia suddenly announced, still gazing out the window. "One has been here a long time and the other for less than thirty years. Brian is heading towards the latter. My family is in the old one." Patricia fell silent again. Her eyes followed each car as they drove by our window.

The moon was beginning its rise from behind the water tower at the edge of town.

"I have a terrible feeling about the place," she said, leaving the bar dangling.

Silence engulfed the booth as her statement hung over our heads.

After pretending to bend my spoon twice, I was unable to hold my tongue. I sheepishly reminded Patricia, "You said it was a bad dream. What was the bad part?"

"That's not part of the investigation. The important thing here is that I met with my great-grandmother."

"I'm glad to hear we have a mole in the cemetery. Does she know where Brian is?" I pushed the point.

"Minus, if you didn't have such a diverting smile, I would smack you," Helen verbally smacked me.

"Okay, let me rephrase that. What information does Great-Granny have?" I asked Patricia while looking at Helen.

"Are you talking to Helen or me?" Patricia asked.

"I think I'm talking to myself, but if you have an answer, it would be welcomed."

Patricia did have an answer. "Nana said there have been a lot of souls coming and going recently in Jackson."

"Nana?" I said. "You call her Nana?"

"That's what she wanted me to call her. I think it's kind of sweet."

"Just asking," I said, then let it drop.

"Nana feels that it's far too dangerous for us to be doing this on our own," Patricia continued. "Bad people are doing bad things at Holy Souls."

"Bad people are doing bad things everywhere," I said. "Last time I saw the news from the Capitol, I couldn't sleep for a week."

"DC will make this look like a walk in the park," Helen said.

"Great, I was hoping it would be easy," I feigned delight.

"With you here, Minus, everything is easy," Patricia flattered me, along with Helen's nod of agreement.

"I sense a manipulation," I alleged. "How do you propose we do this skull grabbing?"

"We'll work that out later. For now, I think we should pay a visit to Holy Souls," Patricia suggested, ending the conversation.

* * *

Back in the room, we did a web search for a place to buy heavy woolen coats. I suggested a balaclava for Brian, but my partners thought that was in bad taste. Girls!

The remainder of the evening was spent watching *America's Got Talent* highlights. At one thirty, I got up and slinked off to my room. We were going to have a big day of visiting the dead.

15

VISITING THE DEAD

The morning came early.

Well before the antler arch in the town square cast its jagged shadow on the empty street, I stood under the iconic sculpture and studied the calm of Jackson. Rest was complicated. The dreams were confusing. Wyoming is *damn* cold in late autumn, but the frigid morning air was a relief from my tortured sleep.

During the day, this town is buzzing with activity. In the pre-dawn hours, there is a peacefulness created by the surrounding landscape. As I stood beneath the antlers of a thousand creatures, I thought about the skull of my brother. An odd concept to grasp. Before this all started, Brian had been mostly a memory. Then a voice in my head. Now, I'm in search of his head. I couldn't understand why a person's soul would be tied to a hunk of calcium. If the human consciousness is to continue after death, it made no sense to me to be constrained by a physical attribute. I wondered what would happen to those cremated or ground up in a chipper?

These thoughts came to me at six a.m., for which I had no answers.

I found my way back to the hotel café while the sun was still considering whether it would make a showing. With my hot coffee in hand, I settled next to the fireplace in the lounge and waited for my companions to search me out.

Find me they did. Looking like a pair of downtown city folks, Helen and Patricia stepped off the elevator dressed for a luncheon at the Four Seasons.

"Howdy, ladies," I said. "May I buy you a drink?"

"You haven't been causing trouble, I hope?" Patricia replied with a question, leaving my question open.

"Only if buying a cup of coffee is a criminal offense," I brought the topic back to my original question.

"I'd love a drink," Helen said, leaving Patricia to say the same.

"Wonderful. Have a seat while I fetch 'em."

I shot into the restaurant while they made themselves comfortable in front of the fire. When I returned, with three steaming mugs, we sat quietly watching the flames consume its fuel.

"How'd you both sleep?" I broke the silence.

They looked at each other transferring information via Fe-Fi (female Wi-Fi). Patricia answered, "Uneventfully."

"I've been thinking," I stated my new concerns. "What are we doing? Are our lives so boring that we must chase after ghosts? Or, are we all nuts having a communal dream at an asylum in Napa? My middle-class upbringing didn't prepare me for spirit hunting. I think this is crazy. How are your coffees?" I politely ended my rant.

Patricia was the first to respond to my moderately controlled outburst. "Did something happen, Minus?"

"Yes. I've finally come to my senses. None of this madness is real. The mountains are real. The autumn trees are real. Even the tourists are real. Dead people are dead."

That killed the conversation rather quickly, leaving us looking at the hearth, which confined a blaze that danced along the ceramic log. The fire was hypnotic. As we watched the flames, they changed shapes creating forms that sparked our imaginations.

Then, as if thrust into a Harry Potter book, the flame dimmed for a moment before returning in the image of Brian. "Trust your thoughts," he said before returning to a formless conflagration.

Aware of each other through the corners of our eyes, we stared at the fire.

"Did you see that?" Patricia asked.

"I think so," Helen fessed up.

"Damn," I said. "There goes that theory."

* * *

Breakfast was a western treat. The Teton omelet was as filling as the view itself. With a full belly and a new look on life, we drove to Holy Souls Cemetery in our Mustang. As I was in charge of transportation, I had specified a pony with the rental company. Though, I had not anticipated being relegated to the back seat. Since neither of my companions were willing to squeeze into the torture chamber, which Ford had created for the second-string passenger, I became the political prisoner strapped to the water board.

Antlers are a commodity in these-here-parts. Not only are they made into giant civic arches, chandeliers, and cribbage boards, but they make a wonderful gateway to the afterworld. Holy Souls was designed to impress. I was impressed. The OMGs from the front seats gave evidence to the impressions of those sitting erect.

We drove through the impressive display in search of the office, where we hoped to find Seamus.

The grounds were beautiful. Trees covered with red and gold leaves were artfully planted throughout the cemetery. It was so beautifully landscaped, I almost wanted to die just to stay. Or, maybe it was the loss of feeling in my cramped legs that made me think that way.

The office wasn't far from the entrance, so I was soon relieved of my death wish. Seamus was standing outside waiting, as if he had been given a heads-up to our arrival.

"Welcome," he greeted. "Welcome to Holy Souls, Jackson's holiest place."

I hoped he hadn't paid a marketing firm for that phrase.

Patricia and Helen easily got out of the car to greet Seamus, while I extracted myself using primarily upper body strength. Once out and having regained partial use of my legs, I joined my partners and the director.

"I see you've met the advance crew," I said, bringing up the rear. "I'm Minus."

"Yes. Thank you. I didn't realize you were coming out this way," Seamus said with a hint of annoyance in his voice.

"I was speaking with my good friend Patricia here about skiing in Wyoming. She got so excited about the idea of risking her precious nervous system with a little downhill exhilaration that Helen and I couldn't resist joining her."

Seamus looked at Patricia and said, "We have some of the best skiers in the world interred here."

"That's convenient," I said to deaf ears.

"To what do I owe this visit, aside from skiing?" Seamus asked, trying not to sound nervous.

"A personal thank you for referring me to the largest deal of my career," I answered.

"I was told the Oakland School District had put the order on hold," Seamus said with his finger on the pulse.

"News travels fast around here," I quickly responded, hoping to fluster him.

"It is the cyber age after all," he said, without flustering.

"So true. Sometimes it seems faster than human thought," Patricia added.

Not giving away her connection with the Oakland School District, Helen commented, "Hopefully, it's a temporary delay."

We were invited into the office for a hot drink and doughnut holes. The warmth of the room was like a brick wall greeting us at the threshold.

"Is this the crematorium?" I asked, bringing a smile to Seamus's face while inciting audible sighs from my companions.

"No, we have very effective insulation," Seamus said as he opened a window. "Would anyone care for tea?" he quickly changed the subject.

Helen got right down to business. "No thank you. We were hoping you could help us find Brian Filbert's skull."

I could not believe what I had just heard. Patricia's jaw on the floor let me know that I had heard what I heard.

"Have you lost contact with a relative?" Seamus asked without missing a beat.

"Brian is Minus's brother. We heard he had come to Wyoming."

"Well, you've come to the right place. I'm rather good at tracking down lost souls. Tell me what you know."

We brought Seamus up to speed since Helen had already shown our cards.

"It sounds like you were hoping to find Brian under my office floor," Seamus said, causing me to feel a little like an idiot since that is precisely what I was thinking.

"That would be silly," I said. "But I *would* like to have a look in your closet."

Seamus gave me a sideways glare.

"That was a joke," I assured him.

"You haven't seen my closet," he joked back. I think.

"All joking aside," Patricia said to Seamus. "Are you familiar with this kind of spirit theft?"

"We specialize in the relocation of souls. Our goal is to keep those who have passed in touch with the living. Theft is not our business," Seamus stressed.

"I'm sorry, I didn't mean to insinuate anything. I was just hoping you could help us find Brian," Patricia clarified.

"If I sounded short, it's because others have accused us of theft, and I assure you it's not true."

Helen stepped in using her experience dealing with irate parents. "Mr. Finnigan…"

"Please, call me Seamus."

"Thank you. Seamus, your integrity is not in question. If I had doubts about your motives, I would not have been so forthcoming. Please try to understand our position of vulnerability. We're grasping at straws."

"My apologies, Ms. Wheeler."

"That's not necessary, Seamus. And please call me Helen."

"You can call me Minus," I chimed in. "Patricia, are you okay with being called Patricia?"

Patricia nodded.

"How long have you lived in Jackson?" Helen asked Seamus, attempting to put the investigation back on the rails.

"It will be five years next February," he confided. "The company I work for transferred me here to set up a distribution hub for the western states. It's a huge operation just outside of Sheridan. We house everything from marshmallows to hot tubs."

"You said the company you work for. Are you still employed in the same outfit?" Helen picked up on the tense.

"Yep, once I had gotten the Titan Moon complex up and running, they asked me to oversee the resurrection of Holy Souls."

Patricia observed, "Holy Souls seems like quite a departure from big-screen TVs. You must be a man of many talents."

"Nicely put. I could use you in my marketing department," Seamus said to Patricia with just a little too much charm for my taste.

"I don't mean to interrupt this friendly exchange, but can we get back to the subject at hand?" I said, sounding more jealous than I had intended to. Patricia looked over at me with a coy smile while Seamus searched for something in his desk drawer.

"Here it is," he said. "I knew he couldn't have gotten buried too deep. Have a look at this," Seamus announced, holding up a small piece of bone that looked like the remains of his lunch. "I would like you to meet my uncle Bob."

"I would shake his hand," I offered, "but I don't to see one."

Seamus studied the fragment of Uncle Bob. I don't know if he was expecting it to grow limbs or if my comment had him formulating a way to eighty-six me from his office.

"I can appreciate a family member who takes up very little space," I continued, hoping to distract him from asking me to leave. "Does he mind rooming with paper clips and Post-Its?" I added, to further confuse the moment.

"Uncle Bob gets around more than I do," Seamus said, surfacing from his ruminations. "This may be a small piece of Bob's skull, but it's enough to enable him to visit me. I have a large family, all of whom have a piece of him. These shards allow Bob to travel throughout Wyoming and part of Utah. He's having the time of his afterlife."

Helen asked, "Did you take this job because of your uncle, or did he come with the position?"

"Uncle Bob died when I was a kid. His skull was divvied out to everyone in the family. I've been able to talk to him my entire life. Bob is the reason I jumped at the opportunity to get this job."

"Seamus," I had to ask, "what does all of this have to do with school busses? You didn't know me from Adam, yet you referred me to the Oakland School District."

"That was a directive from the VP of Titan Moon. He told me you were the son of a close friend and wanted to do you a good turn, anonymously."

"I don't do well with convoluted plot lines," I confessed. "Are you telling me that I have to go up another level to find out what the hell is going on?"

Seamus was rather adamant that going up another level was as doable as being buried at Arlington National Cemetery. "My boss is as accessible as the president of Argentina. He's far away and well protected."

"I do speak Spanish," I said.

"Well, that won't help you here," Seamus replied, seemingly not getting the joke. "The head of Titan Moon is a Neanderthal when it comes to tolerating dissention."

"Are you telling me, he'd crush my head without a second thought or that he has a prominent brow?"

"You've got that right on both counts," Seamus assured me.

Patricia was deep in thought when I turned to ask for her take on the situation. She was staring at a photograph hanging above Seamus's desk. The picture was not at all decorative. It showed the progress of heavy earth-moving equipment on a hilltop above a cemetery.

"Is that here?" she asked.

Seamus replied without looking at the photograph, "No, that's one of our sister cemeteries. Titan owns quite a few facilities around the country. That particular one is in the Pacific Northwest."

"Looks like a big project," Helen added. "I've seen a new college campus go in with fewer machines."

"There's a lot of money in the dead," Seamus unabashedly said. " Nationally, over seventy-five hundred people die a day. That's one every twelve seconds. They take up a lot of real estate. Even when they're cremated, ashes are often entombed."

Since pulling out Uncle Bob's bone, Seamus had been casually sitting on the front edge of his beautiful, European walnut desk. He now went back around to the vintage brown leather chair, which one rarely sees outside of Goodwill, and leaned on its back.

"Exactly what would you like from me?" Seamus asked.

"Just your help," I said.

Seamus looked up at the stained-glass window above the entry door that depicted a sunset over a mountain range and said nothing.

Patricia, Helen, and I looked at each other hoping someone had the next move if he said no.

He then looked down at the three of us, who were still looking at each other. This went on much longer than anyone was comfortable with, so I characteristically said, "Does anyone feel like lunch?"

A sense of relief fell over the room as if a difficult decision had been postponed. Go figure.

With that, we all headed off to Seamus's favorite eating joint, Burger Heaven.

* * *

"The bacon and egg burger is a great choice," Seamus complimented Patricia on her order. "I always get it for Sunday brunch. It tastes like a day off."

"Is Sunday your only day off?" Patricia asked him.

Seamus was noticeably solemn hearing the question. "People die every day of the week. Sunday is the day for me to live."

With burgers in hand, we found seats near the fireplace.

The western decor of Burger Heaven was at once clever, evocative, and tacky. The use of antiques and Hollywood headshots to create an ambiance of the Old West had me feeling like I was vacationing on the backlot of MGM Studios, circa 1950.

I came right out with the standing question, "So Seamus, any thoughts on my request?"

"It's amazing how a burger can clear one's thoughts," Seamus began. "I've been working for this company much longer than my ethics should have allowed. I believe something underhanded has been going on, but I haven't wanted to face it. Maybe with your help, we can work it out. Or get ourselves killed trying."

My plan coming to Jackson was:

We would visit Seamus.

He would confess to soul-stealing.

Then give me back my brother.

This detective stuff sure has a lot of moving parts.

"Excellent," I replied to Seamus. "But can we spend a little more time discussing the part about getting killed?"

"Did I mention that my boss is a Neanderthal?"

"Yes, you did bring that up in passing," I confirmed his reiteration.

"If y'all are up for the task, I'm ready to do-si-do with the big boys," Seamus revealed his Southern roots.

We raised our eggnogs and made a toast to unity.

"May Burger Heaven seal our bond. And may hell's servants fall at our feet," I decreed.

"Sounds good, but doubtful," Patricia commented, with Helen and Seamus agreeing.

"Denial has done me well thus far in life," I stood my ground, "and I'm not about to forsake it now."

Although a little early in the season for eggnog, we enjoyed its warmth and the promise of Christmas to come.

*　*　*

Having consumed a heavenly feast, we found ourselves back in the office of Holy Souls. Stifled yawns dominated the conversation, but this was not the time for a nap.

"Before we get too far into our discussion," I said, opening the skull deliberations, "I would like to put forward a concern. Since these spirit folks can hang around unnoticed, what tactic can we use to avoid them eavesdropping? Short of getting inside of a giant microwave."

"That's a great idea," Seamus congratulated my inadvertent genius. "I know just the place."

We donned our winter woolies and ventured into the resting grounds of those who would spy on us. I hadn't given much thought to the occupants of the many stone markers, statues, and crypts that made up this post-mortal village. Now, I wondered if they were watching our every move. More likely, they were off dealing with their own afterlives.

Seamus led the way to the largest building on the grounds. The structure looked like a bomb shelter in a James Bond movie, without the armed guards. We were ushered into a cavernous room where the walls were lined with thousands of names.

"Welcome to the most densely populated space at Holy Souls," Seamus began his tutorial. "This public crypt currently holds more than twenty-five hundred souls. The building was designed to house a total of forty-seven hundred comfortably. Within these walls, our words are lost in the shear mass of thought."

"Doesn't that drive the occupants crazy?" Helen asked.

"They're able to tune out the noise but unable to focus on any one voice," Seamus clarified.

"How do you know this stuff?" I asked.

"Uncle Bob tells me everything."

"Everything?" Patricia asked.

"I trust Bob! I'd trust him with my life."

"From the sound of Titan Moon, we all may be trusting him with our lives," I brought home our risk.

Patricia asked Seamus, "What do you think is going on here?"

"It's hard to tell. Bob has not gathered any hard information, even though his senses tell him things aren't right. I feel the same way. It's like when you wake up from a dream. You're left with a memory you can't remember."

"I thought that was just getting old?" I commented.

Seamus gave me the look I get so often from people and said, "Don't you take anything seriously?"

"I'll be holding a forum on that at the end of the investigation. For now, try not to let it bother you."

Helen saved the moment by suggesting that we all meet with Uncle Bob.

"I think he would like that," Seamus said. "He doesn't often get to speak to the living, outside the family."

"Good idea," I said as if I was heading the panel discussion.

"Let's meet at my house," Seamus offered. "Bob can monitor if any other spirits are listening. As long as we're here, can you fill me in on what you know?"

We took turns relaying our stories, of crypts and coercion, food and phantoms, busses and brothers. Seamus seemed to especially like the parts with dogs.

Time was moving on. As it does. So, I suggested heading out into the brisk autumn air and reconvening at Shea Seamus.

"I have to stay here until five today," he reminded us, being the only person in the room who was working. "Shall we meet at my place at six thirty? I can make dinner."

A home-cooked meal was unanimously considered to be a unique experience in our lives.

"Two questions first," Seamus continued. "Is anyone a vegetarian, and Helen, how are you able to talk to Minus's father?"

"We all eat meat," Helen answered, looking back on our shared meals, "though Minus has an irrational disdain for liver."

I thought irrational was a bit harsh. I preferred to think of it as a healthy avoidance.

"As for my communication with Paul, he was an important person in my life."

"It still seems odd to me," Seamus said. "From my experience, I've only heard of family members being able to have direct contact with the departed."

Helen pointed out, "Both Patricia and Minus have had waking contact with Maurice. I would hope neither one of them has that bad fruit hanging from their family tree."

"Yes, another question for Uncle Bob," Seamus said, leading us back to the main door.

But there was no door.

Along the portion of the wall where the door had been, there was now more wall.

We stood looking at a wall like pilgrims in Jerusalem.

"I think you should fire your contractor," I said to Seamus.

"Will that comment be addressed at your forum?" Seamus asked.

"Future events are beginning to look doubtful. I'll get back to you on that."

"There's no need to worry or to sack O'Leary Construction. This vision has been planted in our heads. The door is still there. We are just being tricked not to see it," Seamus attempted to make me feel better.

It didn't work.

"I gather you're going to tell us to imagine the door where it was, and it will appear," I said, falling back on personal experience.

"You've done this before?" Seamus asked, nodding in agreement.

We stood in silence, focusing on our entry point, unable to conjure up even an exit sign.

Finally, Helen asked, "Do you guys see the door?"

Patricia was the first to admit she was still looking at a stone wall.

"Seamus?" I put the responsibility back on him.

"I'm working on it," he promised. "This usually works."

"Usually works?" I said with a bit of urgency in my voice. "Does this happen often?"

"Only when I start looking where I'm not supposed to."

"Do you have a mantra you use in these situations?" I requested.

"I can't say I do," Seamus said as he analyzed the barrier between us and where we wanted to be.

"Is anyone feeling hot?" Patricia asked.

I was suddenly struck with a chill that went deep into my bones. "I'm freezing," I told her. Then, being a gentleman, I offered, "Would you like to exchange subliminal suggestions?"

"If you would like to get warm," Helen interjected, "you could stand next to the fire over there," she said, pointing to the end of the room where a snowstorm was raging.

I turned to Seamus and asked, "What do you see?"

"You don't want to know," he said ambiguously.

"Is it really that bad?" I pressed.

"Not really. I just thought you wouldn't want to hear about the majestic waterfall ending in a crystal blue pond."

"You're right."

"They need me, but I think they see you as a threat," Seamus theorized.

The situation looked to be custom orchestrated. I'm in the arctic north, the women are fighting wildfires, and Seamus is ready to retire to the Bahamas.

"I've got an idea," I said. "It's as if they are using cookies to trace our likes and fears. Let's all talk about the strongest reason we would want to stay in this room. Except for you, Seamus. Maybe you could have a strong desire to book a flight to Hawaii."

Patricia said, "I can't think of one thing that would make me want to stay here."

"Okay, the floor is open for other ideas," I acquiesced.

With that proposal shot down, Helen suggested, "Why don't we use our other senses and see if we can feel the door?"

Seamus, Patricia, and I looked at her, stunned by the simplicity of the solution. Patricia was the first to recover. She walked up to the twenty-foot-high blockade and placed her hand on its surface. Within moments, Patricia took hold of an invisible handle. Slowly, she pulled open the stealthy hatch to reveal a winter scene straight out of *White Christmas.*

"Do you guys see a snowstorm out there?" I asked, receiving nods of affirmation from all. "Okay then, let's go."

Patricia held the door for Helen and Seamus to step out into the snow. As I walked past, I put a quarter in her hand and said, "You'd make a good doorman."

She looked at the coin and replied, "You'd do well in Europe."

* * *

We safely made our way back to the hotel under the expert driving skills of the snow bunny, Patricia. Generally, I need to see the road to navigate my way through town. The omission of a view out the windshield didn't seem to faze the skier behind the wheel. I think it was more a dismissive attitude towards survival than an innate sense of direction.

* * *

When my cell phone rang, I had been napping for three hours.

Abrupt awakenings send my synapsis into turmoil. It took a moment for my brain to process where I was and who might be calling me. Gaining partial use of my tongue and enough mobility in my right arm, I accepted the call.

"Hello, this is Minus," I said, trying not to sound like I had just woken up.

"Did I wake you?" Seamus said, proving my failure to sound coherent.

"No, I was choking on a chicken bone," I replied. "How are you?"

"If that's the benchmark, I'm great."

"How was your day?" I said, sounding like a loving wife.

"After our adventure in the mausoleum, there was nowhere to go but up."

"Or to Fiji," I reminded him of his preferential treatment.

"Yes, it's nice to know I have some allies in *The Wall*."

"The Wall?" I asked, wondering what made this noun proper.

"That's my nickname for the mausoleum. This is a big place. Giving simple names to the various areas of the cemetery helps me keep track of who is where."

"You have a computer, don't you? Aren't the ghosts in the machine?" I asked.

"My method feels more personal. Ultimately, the placement of the body is of little importance. Death is a great equalizer," Seamus further confused me.

"It sounds like a recipe for segregation to me," I said.

"You seem to have a deeper understanding of the internal workings of a cemetery than most," Seamus complimented my insight. "Did your brother fill you in on the soul alliance?"

"He did mention a few dos and don'ts. Mostly don'ts. I got the sense that there is quite a spirit hierarchy down low."

"I don't completely understand it," Seamus began his theory. "Which I believe is intentional on their part. Periodically, there's an abrupt switch in direction, which makes me think they have a political system like the living. No sooner have I set up a new system than I'm directed to do it upside down. It's like the Wyoming winters: inevitable, annoying, and comforting. Uncle Bob gets the pleasure of being the messenger. And I get the pleasure of Uncle Bob."

"Why do you think we have this special relationship with the dead when most people don't?" I asked.

Seamus was ready for that question. "I think everyone is in contact with someone. They just don't want to appear to be nuts. The ones who do talk about it look nuts. Proving the point."

"I'll try to remember that when being interviewed by Oprah," I made a verbal note-to-self.

"Do y'all still want to come over to my place for dinner and speak with Bob?"

"Are you originally from Texas?" I asked.

"Yes. The word y'all is like a verbal tattoo. It never goes away," Seamus explained.

"At least you don't say soda pop."

"Sorry, I lived in Milwaukee as a kid. I say that too."

"Well, that was a size twelve foot-in-mouth," I apologized. "What time would you like to see us?"

"Let's stick with 6:30. I think you'll enjoy Jackson's rush hour."

"I can't say that anyone has said that to me before."

"It's Texas hospitality," Seamus assured me.

* * *

I found myself the last one down to the lobby. This gave me pause. I really must review my primping rituals.

"What took you so long?" Patricia said with a smile, having seen me in the morning at home.

"Couldn't resist, could you?" I skirted the question.

"Minus, you are the only man I know who cleans the bathroom every visit. You know they have maids here?"

"I would think this would be considered an admirable trait. Are you suggesting that I should become a slob?"

"Not at all. You do look a little like a Nepalese shaman with your toilet brush scepter. I'm just saying let the hotel staff do their job."

"That statement could be considered insulting to a Himalayan, you know."

"I'm sure they have nothing against maid service," Patricia presumed.

With that conversation put to death, I said hello to Helen. "How did you sleep?"

"I didn't," she answered.

"I thought you were tired."

"I was. And still am. After leaving Holy Souls, I began having a noise in my head. When I tried to sleep, the sound turned into voices. So many voices, it almost sounded like a hum. Except for one. One persistent voice tried to cut through the din by saying my name over and over again. Barely audible, I finally realized he was saying *hell-on-wheels*. Your father would call me that, though it didn't sound like Paul. I assumed your brother was reaching out to me since no one else would know that nickname."

"I don't get it. Seamus said souls can only speak directly to family members. Yet both you and Patricia have had contact with Brian."

"Hopefully, Uncle Bob will have some answers," Patricia naively offered.

"The dead have been extremely circumspect when it comes to sharing information. I'll be quite surprised if Bob even shows up," I allowed myself to verbalize a subconscious feeling.

"What's up, Minus?" Patricia asked with a squint in her eye.

"I haven't heard boo from Brian. I'm feeling a little left out."

Patricia put her hands on my shoulders. Looked me square in the eye. Smiled. And didn't speak.

I don't know why, but that made me feel so much better.

"Thank you," I said.

Patricia turned to Helen and asked, "While we were waiting for Minus, you told me Brian was trying to tell you something. Have you figured out what that was?"

"I did."

"Excellent, Minus's porcelain scrubbing will not be for naught." Patricia kept the bathroom digs going. "What did he say?"

"He recited the words, *Said farewell to my last hotel.*"

"What the hell does that mean?" I asked.

"That's the first line of Paul McCartney's song, *Helen Wheels*," Patricia quickly pointed out.

"How did you know that?" I questioned her knowledge of a truly obscure reference.

"Everyone knows that," Helen answered. Indicating it was only obscure to me.

"I concede, I'm more of a melody person. So, what does it mean?"

"He's telling us he'll be here soon," Helen deciphered our first clue.

"How do you know he's directing us forward and not backward?" I suggested.

"There's no way to know for sure which way to go. We just have to follow our communal nose."

"Shall we see what Bob has to add?" Patricia said, directing us to the door.

16

THE DOOR

*We found ourselves
standing outside the front door of
Seamus Finnigan.*

Seamus lived on the outskirts of Jackson, putting his house somewhere between nowhere and a bison paddock. His grand log mansion rose in the foreground of the Teton Mountains with the splendor of a pagoda at the foot of Mount Fuji.

The door before us stood eight feet tall with a rustic patina from years of exposure to the harsh Wyoming elements.

In the form of a bull, with the bulk of a battering ram, a large brass knocker hung in the center. I took the bull by the horns to announce our arrival. Two pounds of metal hitting the receiving knob produced a barely audible sound.

Such is life, to be emasculated by the effigy of a steer.

Seamus was quick to answer my tapping. I assumed a camera was involved in his promptness unless Uncle Bob was keeping track of visitors.

"Welcome," he greeted. "Please, come in."

Once through the doorway, Seamus quickly closed and locked the castle gate.

"Are you expecting an onslaught from the hordes?" I asked before my polite side could stop my mouth.

"No, I love the feel of locking this door. It's like living in a mausoleum without being dead."

"Is that a good thing?" Patricia asked.

"Living grand while living, is living," Seamus said, not answering Patricia's question. Although it sounded poetic.

He directed us into the great room, which was also living grand. The ceiling was high enough to fit the Times Square Christmas tree with space on top for *The Winged Victory of Samothrace*.

I kept my mouth shut.

"Can I get y'all something to drink? I was just making a hot toddy."

"You read my mind," I said.

"That's not allowed," I heard Seamus mutter under his breath. After receiving affirmative nods from Helen and Patricia, he headed into the kitchen, leaving his nosy guests to look around the room.

"I wonder if Titan Moon supplied the house," Helen said, as she walked around with her mouth more open than closed.

The building was constructed of large wooden columns and beams repurposed from an ancient Japanese temple. Immense lidded Greek urns stood alongside pillars of stone supporting massive ceiling joists.

I was in such awe of my surroundings that I failed to register whether Helen was being rhetorical or just inquisitive. Until she followed up by saying, "This place is above the pay scale of anybody who works for somebody else."

I did have to agree with that. The last time I was in a house this grand, I was ushered out by presidential security for peeking in closets.

"Are you suggesting that Seamus owns Titan Moon? Or, that Seamus is house-sitting for Mr. Moon?" I asked.

"Either way, people with this much money are not easily sepa-rated from it. Those that threaten their status quo put themselves at risk," Helen attempted to get a message to me.

"You're being a bit cryptic here," I pressed for clarification.

"Okay, how about this? We need to watch our asses."

"Oh, got it."

During this deep philosophical discussion, Patricia stood quietly looking out the window into the back garden, which was magnificent even this late in the year. Whoever maintained the grounds was a genius at botanical planning. The colors of spring would be hard-pressed to compete with this winter palette.

"Are you okay?" I asked Patricia.

She nodded, almost imperceptibly, continuing to stare through the rimy glass.

"Are you fixated on squirrels?" I attempted to break through her silence.

Helen responded for Patricia, "What are you talking about, Minus?"

"I had a dog that would stare out the back window at squirrels," I justified my comment.

"There's a door in the yard," Patricia said softly.

Helen and I walked over to the window to see what she was talking about. Sure enough, there was a door in the yard. No walls or roof. Just a door, standing erect in what looked like a lily pond.

We remained focused on the door until our host entered the room. "Are you watching squirrels?" Seamus asked.

When we didn't answer, he realized what had caught our atten-tion. "Oh, the door. I forget it's out there."

Helen shifted her view from the garden to Seamus, asking, "Does it lead anywhere?"

"I don't know. It's locked."

Patricia broke her gaze from the mystery tambour and asked, "How can it be locked? It doesn't have a jamb."

Before Seamus could answer, I said, "A door is locked if it doesn't reveal its passageway."

"Excellent insight, Minus," Seamus congratulated me to the stunned looks of my detective team.

"How did you come up with that?" Patricia asked.

"It just came to me. I'm still trying to figure out what it means."

"Doors are intended to close one space off from another," Seamus stepped into my conceptual dilemma. "I believe there is something behind that door. I just don't know how to unlock it."

Before I had decided to write a book on the sale of a mausoleum, I thought this weird metaphysical stuff was only in the movies. I lived in a world where the Jackson/Timberlake halftime show for Super Bowl XXXVIII was my most surreal experience. Still, I needed to delve deeper into why and how the door stood just at the surface of the water feature.

"Is it floating?" I asked.

"No," Seamus answered. "It's suspended above the water with no means of support. Now come get your hot drinks before I need to put them in the microwave."

Seamus directed us to a large, round, glass-topped table in the center of the room. We seated ourselves at the four corners of the round table.

"With this much distance between us, we may need to break out our cell phones," I observed.

"That will only help if you have a sim card for the afterlife," Seamus kindly pointed out the purpose of our meeting.

With that, Seamus passed out the hot toddies before settling into a connection with Uncle Bob.

Our host's conversation with his uncle did not make for good theater. There were no aberrations or ghostly howls. Seamus sat mostly still with only the slightest nod of his head to indicate the exchange taking place with Bob.

"Uncle Bob says welcome," Seamus finally broke the silence. "He's thrilled to have some outside interaction."

Helen asked, "Is he able to hear us, or do you have to talk to him?"

"He's not the computer in *Galaxy Quest*. He can hear and see what is in this room, but he does need to speak through me."

"I love that movie," I admitted.

"Hello, all. I'm Bob O'Connor," Seamus announced.

"Hello, Bob," Patricia said.

Helen followed, "We're honored to have an audience with you."

"How's it going?" I said, trying to lighten the proceedings.

Bob greeted Helen and Patricia by name, but when he got to me, he said, "When I was a kid, I had a friend we nicknamed Comma. Is that what happened to you?"

"Minus is my given name. It was easy to live up to. Comma sounds too stressful for me."

"You've piqued my interest. Why would the name Comma cause anxiety?" Bob asked with a hesitation in Seamus's voice.

"I can't imagine going through life not knowing when to be used properly," I answered.

"Oddly, that never crossed my mind. We called him that because he had a big head and skinny legs," Bob said, revealing the cruelty of the nickname.

"Bob," Patricia broke into Bob's and my bonding, "Minus has a bit of a problem that we are hoping you can help with."

"I'm happy to do what I can. Seamus speaks very highly of y'all."

"Thank you," Patricia continued. "Minus's brother, Brian, was dismembered and his skull was transported across state lines. We believe he was brought to Jackson Hole. Do you think you can help us find him?"

"Thank you for the recap, but since I was in Seamus's office today, I'm already on the case. While y'all were in the big house experiencing global warming, I was following a lead."

Bob stopped speaking, leaving Seamus to nod and shake his head in private conversation.

"Bob has a question that I'm not able to adequately answer," Seamus said, finishing his head exercises.

"What would you like to know, Bob," I asked.

"How does Paul McCartney fit into all of this?" Bob regained the helm through Seamus.

Helen was quick to ask, "How do you know about Paul McCartney?" Leaving Patricia and myself still forming the letter "H" with our lips.

Uncle Bob was enjoying our response to his name dropping. "I thought that might get a rise out of you. I do enjoy a little dramatic effect. Truthfully, I much prefer Perry Como's *Catch a Falling Star*. Now that is a song with a positive message."

Why Perry Como had come up in the conversation was an absolute mystery. Dean Martin or Frank Sinatra I would understand. But Perry Como?

"We believe Brian is being censored," I explained. "He's using the song to get through to us."

Helen leaned forward on the table with her hands clasped. She had the look of someone with a question. I waited for her to speak but no question emerged.

"Did you want to say something, Helen," I asked.

"No. My back is getting a little sore. Continue," she nudged.

"Did you find out anything else?" I asked Bob.

"You bet I did," Bob said with excitement. "I learned that the Berkeley Bubbleheads are coming to town to play our local team, the Jackson Holes."

"Bob…?" I said.

"Yes…," Bob answered slowly.

"Do you know what the deal is with the door floating over the pond in the backyard?" I asked to preempt any blow-by-blow spirit sports dialogue.

"I don't have a clue."

"Any thoughts, suspicions, or fantasies about it?" I followed up.

"I think it's dangerous. My suspicion is; it's dangerous. Why the hell would I have any fantasies about it?"

"Fantasies are a way of coping with danger," I answered.

"That type of thinking is a good way to get yourself killed."

"Is that a general disagreement with my philosophy or specific to our current situation?"

"Do you talk like that when you sell busses?"

"Truthfully, I haven't sold that many busses."

"Go figure," Bob gave his opinion of my sales technique.

"Were you this codgity when you were alive?" I asked.

"I've mellowed in my retirement. If we had met when I was alive, you would now be carrying your head under your arm."

"I see why Seamus has such warm feelings for you."

"I like you, kid. Let's see what we can work out with this investigation." Bob warmed up to me. "Tell me, why are you so obsessed with this door?"

"I have a feeling that my team and I are going to chase all over Wyoming looking for clues. Then end up back at the threshold of this portico trying to find a way in. I would rather cut to the chase and break the code now."

Walking over to the window, Seamus identified himself as the speaker by saying, "Since the day I moved into this house, that door has been a hanging question. What makes you think it's a postern to another realm?"

"Let's say, there's something about its anti-gravitational abilities that raises it above the average garden gate," I suggested.

Uncle Bob regained his voice through Seamus to give his two cents on the door. "I've been curious about this aberration along with Seamus. My conclusion is; a door without a frame is merely an obstruction. It's not keeping you out, but it is blocking your view."

Helen asked, "Is there something behind it that we should see?"

Seamus or Bob said, "Yes, absolutely. There's an Indian paintbrush in full bloom."

"You folks do things funny here in the Wild West," I said. "Isn't it a little early for wildflowers?"

"There's a wonderful greenhouse out back," I assumed Seamus said, sensing Bob was not a gardener.

"May we see it?" Patricia sang out. "I would love to visit summer."

I could see Patricia gushing over a bouquet of peonies or roses, but an interest in greenhouse botany certainly caught me off guard.

Seamus stood at the window nodding his head, apparently conversing with Bob. When they finished their silent discussion, Seamus turned back into the room. "If we make a quick dash through the yard," he said, "we shouldn't need to put our coats on. Don't dawdle, though. There's a northerly, which comes down from the mountains and cuts right through my yard that can freeze the balls off a brass monkey."

With that image firmly set in our minds, we dashed through the yard, past the mystery door, and into the greenhouse before our un-coated bodies shut down from hypothermia.

Inside, the temperature was at least forty degrees warmer. I could feel every cell in my body reaching out to allow the local virus strains free entry as punishment for the excessive temperature fluctuation.

Looking around the glass enclosure, I decided whatever my body threw at me was worth it. We were in a room full of flowers that shouldn't be open for another four months. The Indian paintbrush larger and more vibrant than in Death Valley. Every form of spring beauty was also blooming as if winter had been shut down.

"How did you do this?" Helen asked.

"Fertilize," Seamus began. "Give a plant enough food, water, light, and heat, and it will follow you to the gates of hell."

"You make it sound like Faust's garden," I said.

"Plants don't have souls," Seamus said. "Sometimes, when I'm here alone, I am concerned for mine."

"That's a good way to make your guests look over their shoulders. What are you getting at, my friend?" I asked.

"There's a peacefulness among the plants. I feel a calmness in my life. It's a balance in nature that makes me want to take up residence here."

"Be careful what you wish for. I think I saw a euphorbia wink at you," I warned Seamus.

We split up to take in the cavernous conservatory of flowers. There were plants, trees, moss, and lichen from all over the world. Add a boat ride, and you'd have the wonder of *Pirates of The Caribbean*.

Magnificent as the garden was, I couldn't help thinking that nothing about this place seemed profitable. Why would a giant distribution company be growing exotic plants?

"Seamus," I said, as I approached him down a long corridor lined with some kind of tree that looked like it would eat your young, "is this a project supported by your employer? I can't imagine you would have the time to prune all these shrubs."

"Titan Moon has their fingers in many ventures. They pay for this giant terrarium and I get to enjoy it," Seamus said while stroking a plant with a leaf the size of Michigan.

"I don't understand how a garden fits into corporate domination of the dead." I made an accusation of Seamus's employer.

"This facility was already here when I moved in," Seamus said. "I assumed it was a pet project/tax deduction for one of the top brass. Do you think it plays into the company's afterlife endeavors?"

"This place feels like it has a purpose beyond a mere hobby. My senses tell me not to get too comfortable."

I continued my walkabout, unable to focus on any one sight for very long before some other floral wonder would grab my attention. Somehow, I made it through the hothouse jungle without taking root myself.

Both women had circumnavigated the complex, in opposite directions, to find themselves back at the entrance looking at me.

"Nice place," I said.

"Incredible," Patricia upped the praise.

"Absolutely awesome," Helen capped the hyperbole.

"Does everyone still have all their body parts?" I cautioned. "That was the biggest Venus flytrap I have ever seen."

Seamus joined us, asking if we were in the mood for a mai tai. "I'm always craving a summer drink when I leave this paradise," he justified the seasonal cocktail.

With a communal nod, we all agreed a cool drink under a swaying palm tree sounded nice and stepped back into the frigid north.

Helen entered the yard first. After a couple of steps, she stopped. In turn, Patricia and I did the same.

Point of view, perspective, position. Three Ps, for three people standing in one place, looking at a floating door perfectly framed by the window we had previously been looking out of into the yard.

"Interesting," I said. "Shall we discuss it over a cocktail before our joints seize up from the cold?"

There was no dissent to my suggestion of postponing the discussion.

17

THE DISCUSSION

*The mai tai was outvoted
by a consensus for Irish coffee.*

By the time we made our way into the house, even Uncle Bob had opted for a hot drink.

Team Brian looked out the window while Seamus and Bob went about brewing a pot of joe. From inside, the door looked like a decorative feature. From the other side, it felt like an entrance to the house.

Patricia opened the door deliberations, "I imagine we're all thinking the same thing. If we enter this room via that door, we might end up in a different place."

"That's exactly what I was thinking. Except for the *we* part," I answered. "We can't all keep putting ourselves at risk. If there is a way through, I should take it."

"That's an excellent idea," Patricia agreed. "Best to keep a backup team on the outside just in case."

"That's right, just in case," I agreed. "Exactly what do you think *just in case* entails?"

"The usual. Being ripped apart by demons summoned from the dark regions of the afterworld."

"Have I ever mentioned how much fun you are to be around?"

"You asked."

Helen continued to look out the window giving no indication of her opinion about my being torn apart by demons.

Patricia stood behind her. For a moment, the silence was comforting. As long as no one spoke, no decisions would be made.

Patricia then put her hand on Helen's shoulder and broke the silence. "Are you okay?" she asked.

"I need to be the one to go through the door," Helen answered. "There's a reason Brian is singing *Helen Wheels*."

"Coffee is served," Seamus said as he entered the room with a large tray of goodies.

I had a feeling that Helen was just about to reveal a secret. A big secret. A secret that was now going to have to wait, because she was first to belly-up to the bar, leaving Patricia and myself staring at each other.

Once our whiskey-fortified coffees were in hand and a heaping plate of cookies filled the other, we sat down to address the hanging question.

"You were saying?" I said, looking Helen straight in the eyes.

"I would like to be the one to go through the door."

"No, you said you *need* to go through the door," I reminded her.

"I did?"

"Yes, just before you hinted at a secret."

"I did?"

"Would you like me to change the subject?"

"Would you?"

"No!"

Patricia intervened, seeing that Helen and I were working at odds. "Minus, don't push her. Helen, when you're ready, you can tell us why you want to keep Minus from being torn up by tiny demons."

"What is this fixation with me being disemboweled by Satan's minions? You seem to be getting some perverse joy from the thought."

"Save the arguments until you're married," Helen broke back into the conversation. "I think I would be better suited to negotiate my way through the afterlife. After all, I do have experience dealing with the state legislature."

"May I ask a question?" Seamus or Bob asked. "Have you guys figured out how to open the door?"

That brought the conversation to a screeching halt. In a mad rush to have our limbs extricated from our torsos, we had forgotten we were still locked out. I felt like I had just flunked out of, *Detective Techniques for Idiots.*

"Bob has studied the door for years," Seamus continued, clarifying the identity of the speaker, "and still has no idea how to go through it or if it's even important."

Patricia pointed out, "Maybe it's for the living, not the dead."

"I've worked with Uncle Bob to come up with the magic phrase that would unlock the door. My heartbeat hasn't seemed to make much of a difference. The most we've been able to do is incite the water lilies open and close. Mind you, that is kind of fun. We've concluded that to get through the door, one needs more than curiosity."

"Could it be, all we need to do is ask permission to enter?" I suggested. "Did anybody notice a mail slot?"

Patricia ignored my contribution and posed to Bob, "You said earlier that the door was a visual obstruction rather than a passageway. That it blocks the view. Yet, when you go around it, the view is still there. If it's blocking sight of something and you must go through it to see that, then the door *is* a portal."

"I love human logic," Bob replied, making Seamus laugh. "You expect everything to make sense. The laws of nature don't apply here. Hence, a door that floats vertically above water. When you see the living room window perfectly framed by the door, your sense of logic creates a story that has you off and running with visions of demonic fairies. Now, *that* is a door blocking your view.

"Maybe the door is a clue. Or, maybe it means nothing and you're being distracted from your original mission," Bob hypothesized.

"Answers don't come easy around here," I said.

"Answers don't come easy," Bob expanded the scope.

I thought about Bob's theory. I studied his logic, the conceit of the door, and life in general. Having weighed all the information in less than fifteen seconds, I knew what to do.

"I would like to take a closer look at the door," I said. "I don't want to leave without at least ringing the doorbell."

"Bundle up," Bob suggested. "It's going to be a long wait."

"I'd like to go with you," Helen volunteered.

"You're just dying to get sucked into the abyss, aren't you? I would welcome your company though."

I looked over at Patricia, prompting her to volunteer to stay inside and have another Irish coffee. "I'm sure you two can handle it," she said. "The three of us would look like Jehovah's Witnesses handing out pamphlets."

"How do you come up with this stuff?" I asked.

"Life experiences," Patricia explained. "I never answer my door for that reason."

I love Patricia's perspective on life; self-preservation through avoidance.

Helen and I gathered our coats and thermal sundries then ventured back into the yard. Patricia curled up in an overstuffed chair with her fresh Irish coffee and waved as we set off on our adventure.

"Why do you think Patricia didn't want to come with us?" I asked Helen as we stood in front of the door.

"I was wondering about that too. Very unlike her wanting to be left out."

No mail slot. No doorbell. Not even a welcome mat. This was the most dismissive entrance I had encountered since the principal's office in high school.

Not wanting to be dismissed, I said, "I'm looking for my brother Brian Filbert. His skull has been stolen and I want to take him home."

"That's a direct approach," Helen said.

"Well, *open sesame* seemed a bit hackneyed."

I waited to see if anybody had heard my call. The door just hung there like a leaf on a spider web. I looked at the door. I looked at Helen. I looked at the lilies opening and closing. Then everything was gone. I hate when everything is gone. It just isn't natural.

* * *

There was no light, and there was no darkness. No up or down, in or out, or now or then. There were no senses, just existence. I knew I was, but I didn't know where I was.

"Hello," I said to no reply. "I gather someone heard my message. Will you show yourself?"

There was only silence. Not the silence of early morning or the quiet of the Sonoran Desert. This was a silence of the mind. The perception of hearing was not present. The construct of the physical world was gone. I had never felt more at peace. There was nothing to worry about. Nothing was important. Nothing was insignificant.

I knew I wasn't dead, but I knew I was with the dead. This reality did not feel like the place Brian, Bob, and my father had inhabited.

What I had asked for were answers. What I had gotten was truth. No one was there to skew my thoughts. I was put in a void to find the truth, but without guidelines, I was not lost, just stationary.

"Hello," I said again, hoping to obtain a little assistance with my freedom.

Still, the silence of eternity.

I felt no fear. I always feel fear, but not here. I had to remind myself why I had come to the door. I knew this was not my place. I needed to find my brother. And I knew I needed to go back to Helen and Patricia because they were now my family.

"Excuse me, may I speak to the spook in charge?" I said, falling back on my sense of humor, which usually would keep me out of trouble.

"You are an odd one," I heard a voice say.

"It got me out of the draft," I said, speaking the truth.

"Unlike your brother."

"You sound like the person I came to see."

"I am who you came to see, but I am no longer a person."

"That sounds sad," I said.

"Individuality is necessary in the living world, but here, we are stronger when we become one."

"Strength is something that is used to defeat. What are you trying to conquer?"

"Fear. There is no need for it here. Fear is a basic instinct that carries over far beyond its usefulness."

"I had a fear," I confessed. "That my brother would not be found. Do you know where he is?"

"Yes."

"I'm all ears," I responded to the word I wanted to hear.

"Yes, is a simple answer to a complicated situation. I can tell you where he is, but not where *the where* is."

"I'm sorry, did you just start speaking Latin?"

"I can if you like."

"No thank you, that was a joke. My father went to Loyola University. I've heard enough Latin."

"Do you take anything seriously?" the voice said.

"I take seriously that I'm having an out-of-body conversation with someone whose name I don't know."

"I represent many souls. My identity isn't important."

"It's important to me. I would like to know who you are and why you are helping me."

"You speak like you are in the position of power here."

"I am."

"I beg to differ. This is my realm and I have the information you need."

I was starting to enjoy this dialogue. Dead people think they know everything.

"There's a reason you brought me here," I began my argument. "I don't think my problem is of real concern to you. I believe you need me. And that puts me in a position of power."

"You're quite insightful for a jokester."

"Humor is a tool," I answered, turning his backhanded compliment into a compliment. "What motivates you?"

"Serving my community," he began. "I have a charge to help my constituents."

"Sounds like an elected position."

"No, I'm appointed."

"So, what is it you do?"

"I didn't bring you here to discuss my credentials."

"That's okay. I don't mind veering from the set agenda."

"Okay," my faceless, nameless, and selfless host conceded. "I'm the spokes-soul for the *Consortium of Souls*, which orchestrates the relocation of skulls. The afterworld cannot physically affect the material world. The Consortium is tasked with bridging that gap. My job is to work with the living to enable the dead to communicate with their families."

"I get it. You oversee the movement of cranial cargo."

"I hadn't thought of it in those terms, but yes. We helped set up a physical company that relocates sections of our clients' skulls all over the world."

"Clients?" I asked. "That denotes the exchange of currency."

"We don't use money here."

"No, but you must have dental work because I feel like I'm pulling teeth."

"A client is a soul in need. In this realm, every soul is equal. All have a right to be with their families. As technology has made it easier for the living to relocate, my job has gotten considerably more difficult. That is why the Consortium created a physical company to do the relocation of those who wish to stay close to their loved ones."

"I gather this company is called Titan Moon Distributors?"

"I see you've done your homework," the Consortium spokes-soul gave me credit for Patricia's dream works. "That company has gone rogue with the new leadership finding mortal clients who are more lucrative. I'm afraid your brother got in the way of one of their projects."

"That's just like Brian. He was always standing in front of the tanks."

"Well, he's gone up against a Goliath here. Titan Moon has brokered a deal to take over the hilltop above your friend's family plots. Their piece of land is essential to the proposed expansion. Until you and your brother got involved, they were going to have a free path to the top of the hill.

"I don't understand why an established plot would stand in the way of the expansion."

"Patricia's family are not only located right in the gateway of the new section, but they also have one of the best views."

"It's sounding to me like some folks in your realm are more equal than others."

"That is a direct result of the corruption within Titan Moon and is where you come in."

"I can't say I like the sound of that."

"It's the only way to find Brian. I don't mean that as a threat. We have to weaken Titan Moon if we're to find all the stolen souls."

"More people are missing?"

"Thousands. The company has been busy creating chaos, Minus," the Consortium spokes-soul said, before taking a dramatic pause.

"We would appreciate your help," he released, or increased, the tension. Depending which side of the statement you're on.

"Why me?"

"You're a good man," the spokes-soul answered, creating questions in my mind rather than making me feel all warm and fuzzy inside.

"May I ask what the deal is with the botanical super dome?"

"If you're referring to the conservatory, it was a *way station* of sorts. Before Titan Moon went bad, souls who had been lost would be brought there to convalesce. Those who had long been away from the living would find comfort with the plants as they met with a transition counselor. This helped them adapt to a new afterlife.

"The corporation still maintains the grounds, but we have no idea what their plan is for the facility.

"Minus?" the voice of the Consortium abruptly said.

"Yes," I tentatively answered.

"Will you help us?"

Since all I had to lose was my job and maybe my life, I was all in. "How can I turn down a spook with a problem?" I said. "What's the plan?"

18

THE PLAN

When I returned to my body,
Patricia was standing in front of me
staring intently into my eyes.

"Hello," I said, which sent her falling backward almost into the pond. "Sorry, I didn't mean to scare you."

"Where the hell have you been?" she shot back. "We've been trying to get through to you for ten minutes."

Helen, the second half of the *we*, didn't seem at all stressed. She gave me a smile and calmly asked, "Where'd you go?"

"Hard to say. Seems they hadn't paid the electricity bill, so there were no lights."

"Minus!" Patricia growled. "Be serious. It's not funny."

"I don't know about that. I saw the smile on Helen's face," I said, digging my grave a little deeper. "I am truly touched by your outrage. I will try to be more thoughtful," I conceded.

"I had an informative conversation with the man behind the door. I would be happy to share it with you, inside, with a hot drink. My consciousness may have been out of the cold, but my body was growing icicles."

We scurried into the house to be greeted by Seamus holding a tray of steaming cups of Mexican hot chocolate. As if someone had sent him our drink order in advance.

"Your intuition is uncanny," I said.

Seamus smiled.

* * *

We settled into the great room with our drinks to discuss the next steps. I asked, "Bob, are you with us?"

"Still here," Seamus said for Bob. "I heard about your conversation."

"Word travels fast in the afterlife. I was under the impression that what's said behind the door stays behind the door."

"I didn't hear any specifics," Bob quickly acknowledged. "My cousin is part of the Consortium of Souls. It appears we will be working together on this project."

"Welcome to the team," I said. "It's good to know that there's a back door to the door."

"I assume you're okay with joining the team?" I asked Seamus.

Seamus smiled.

Patricia and Helen had become quiet since returning to the house. I wasn't sure if it was something I didn't say or an intense love of Mexican hot chocolate. Either way, I felt I had an emotional knife at my throat wanting everything in my pockets.

"I apologize for not being disemboweled during my journey," I addressed my partners. "I get the sense you two would like to correct that oversight. What's the problem?"

Stone-faced, yet still able to communicate in their unknown language, Patricia was elected to air the grievances.

"You scared the hell out of us, Minus. Disappearing from your body has brought home how dangerous this situation is. We have to work together to keep each other safe. I don't know what you found out behind the door, but while you were gone, Brian came to Helen."

I turned to face Helen. She was looking into her hot chocolate like it was a portal to another world.

"Only for a moment," Helen said, holding her focus on the comforting beverage. "He wants us to stop trying to find him."

"Why would he want that?" I asked. "We're paid up through tomorrow night at the hotel."

"What?" they both said.

"Just an aside. Brian was always frugal."

"Never mind that," Patricia continued. "Brian said that they will do anything to get us out of the way."

"Who are 'they?'" I asked.

"We have to assume it's Titan Moon," Helen said. "That's all Brian said before he was gone, again."

"Well, that ties into my out-of-body tête-à-tête. It appears we three are a pain in the ass to somebody who likes to sit."

"Minus, is there any chance we can get through this without you joking around?" Patricia inquired.

"Very little," I assured her.

My hot chocolate was now temperate, as were the moods of my colleagues. "But I will try," I said, attempting to warm things up.

"So, what did you find out?" Helen reopened the investigation.

I had to put myself back into the void I had shared with the voice. The experience was starting to resemble a dream. It was like reading a novel with no words, only thoughts.

"Titan Moon was created to help souls be near their families," I began relating my novel experience. "I met with the spirit partner of the physical corporation. They call themselves the Consortium of Souls. I assure you, as silly as that sounds, I'm not making it up.

"In the past several years the terrestrial sector of Titan Moon has gone bad, selling burial land to the highest bidder. The man responsible for the change is the company president, Ronald Stump. He is a terrible man who has brought in some of the worst humans corporate society has to offer in an attempt to dominate the dead.

"With the help of our friends in the cloud, our job is to bring down the bad guys. To do that, we must stop looking for Brian," I said. "Sound familiar?"

"Is the plan to go to the *Washington Post* with dirt, then wait for Brian to come home?" Patricia asked.

"It sounded better when the Consortium said it, but that's just an option, not the plan.

"The Consortium doesn't want to bring down the whole company, just Stump. The service Titan Moon offers is still needed."

Helen pointed out, "How do we know that the Consortium of Souls isn't also the bad guys?"

"My senses tell me to trust them," I said, surely comforting no one.

* * *

The morning came early once again. The dreams that had become part of my night, were gone. I felt I had lost both a friend and a foe. My sleeping companion had forsaken me.

I woke up alone.

The fireplace in the hotel lobby was warm and aberration-free as I waited for my fellow tourists. We needed a break. Today was a day to take in the sights of Jackson Hole.

* * *

"What would you guys like to do today?" I asked, once we had given our breakfast order to the waitress.

Helen and Patricia looked at each other.

"Hold on. No secret conversations. I would like to be part of the moment."

"You're right, Minus," Patricia said. "We shouldn't exclude you just because you're a man and have limited communication capabilities."

"Thank you for recognizing my genetic shortcomings. I feel more included now."

"Will you two stop it?" Helen stepped in. "Today is a day of fun and relaxation. I for one, would like to go shopping."

"Now that's a good indoor activity," I said. "I thought you might suggest a sleigh ride."

"Do they have those?" Patricia showed interest.

"Actually, I think it's a little too early in the season," I conveniently assumed, having had enough of freezing my ass off.

* * *

While wandering the streets of Jackson, I wasn't sure if we were being watched. If the bad guys were trying to work out what we were up to, they would have to wait until we figured that out ourselves.

Patricia and Helen walked in front of me, acting as a windbreak. The occasional gust of warmth from a store's open door had me longing to purchase something I didn't need. The sleigh ride was starting to sound good.

Truth be told, I do like cold weather. I like it when I'm inside and it's outside. So, why were we window shopping? Which, by definition, is the cold side of shopping in the winter. At the risk of being accused of female profiling, I suggested that we go inside and buy a dress. Surprisingly, this sexist plea for warmth went over well.

My timing was impeccable. I had found the most expensive store in town. Stepping through the door, Helen asked, "Are you buying?"

I was so relieved by the sultry air that engulfed my face and hands, I inadvertently said, "Sure." I could always sell my stock in Amazon.

Inside, the environment was not just a relief from the Wyoming winter, but reminiscent of the sensation behind "the door." Overpriced women's clothing rarely sparks a sense of well-being within my already over-leveraged mind. I felt something odd was about to happen.

When I caught up to Patricia and Helen, they were standing perfectly still, looking deep into the store. I followed their gaze to the Giorgio Armani section.

"Hold on, guys. My Amazon holdings won't cover that."

Neither of them moved.

"Guys…? Gals…? Helen…? Patricia?"

No response.

I stepped in front of them. No change in their gaze.

"Hello?" I tried once more to make contact.

I opened my mind to see if I could follow where they had gone.

That didn't work. I looked around to see if people were starting to notice two women staring at Armani.

As luck would have it, the staff had just put out a fifty-percent-off rack, and all attention was now focused on last season's leftovers.

"Guys, can we find someplace a little more private to have this out-of-body experience?" I implored my colleagues to regain conscious thought.

I tried once again to contact whatever was arresting my friends' attention. I put my mind back in Seamus's frigid garden, standing before the door.

"Minus, I'm busy right now. Can we talk later?" the voice of the Consortium said, then was gone.

I looked around to see if anyone had been aware of the voice. The sale rack was still going strong and we were drawing the same interest as a full-priced blouse.

I feared the focus on the sale rack would begin to wane. Unless the establishment upped the sale to seventy percent, someone was going to notice two women in a vertical coma.

Suddenly, an idea came to me. I could pretend to be a mannequin salesman with Helen and Patricia as my floor models. I raised Patricia's arm to look like she was waving to a friend.

"What are you doing?" Patricia said, causing me to jump back, finally attracting a little attention from the sale rack.

"I'm making you look like a jet-setter to avoid the embarrassment of being unconscious in public."

"Are you two at it again?" Helen said, joining the party.

"I think we should go somewhere to discuss what just happened," I said, heading out the door into the brisk fresh air.

19

FRESH AIR

"A mannequin?" Patricia said for the fourth time since entering the café.

"Okay, it wasn't a great idea, but I had to think on my feet. What would you have done?"

"I would have pretended to be holding a meaningful conversation with you like I always do," Patricia said, with a great big smile.

"Now that we have the *unconscious in public* protocols down, can we move on to what happened in your absence?"

"We can't tell you," Helen said.

"I'm sorry, did I just get demoted from *brother of the missing?*"

"It's important that you not know the plan," Helen continued. "Patricia and I will be going home, and you will stay here."

I didn't know what to say to that non-plan of a plan. Firstly, I'd gotten used to them being around, and secondly, without a plan, I'm just a guy wandering the streets of Jackson. That may be an okay thing to do in San Francisco, but here they don't take kindly to hobos.

"Will you at least leave me a pair of gloves?" I pleaded for mercy.

"Don't worry, Minus, you're in good hands," Patricia tried to calm my panic. "You have an army to back you up."

I looked around the room. The table next to us was occupied by an elderly woman doing a crossword. Next to her was an elderly man doing a crossword. Aside from that, I couldn't see the army. "Are they conscripted or volunteers?" I asked, trying to get a handle on being commander-in-chief.

Both women shook their heads, as they sometimes do when I speak.

All I could get out of my partners was; they would be leaving in the morning and I would be contacted. It seemed rather cavalier of them to leave me alone with only an unseen army at my side.

As we walked back to the hotel, I suggested having one last dinner before I was sent off to war.

"Minus, will you stop that?" Patricia said, holding her head in her hands. "You are not being inducted into the Foreign Legion. If we thought you were in any danger, Helen and I wouldn't leave. Isn't that right, Helen?"

"That's right, Patricia. We would never use Minus as a decoy to safely skip town," Helen answered, with not enough levity in her voice for my comfort.

"I am forever thankful for your unfailing dedication to my well-being," I said, before getting back to making dinner arrangements. "I saw a French bistro a couple of blocks back that looked fun. The one with the guillotine in the front window. Shall we eat there?"

That got a smile out of them both.

After freshening up in our rooms, we once again met in the hotel lobby. With a quick glance at the fireplace, we were off to the gallows.

"Are you feeling any better about staying here on your own?" Helen asked as we stepped into the cold night air.

"Me, worried? I know you both have my back; I feel well taken care of."

"That's why I called ahead to the restaurant to assure the blade is sharp," Patricia said, knowing my low pain threshold.

The meal of fine French food was fantastic, including delicacies that most peoples of the world would not think of eating. The last to leave the restaurant, we slipped back to the hotel to prepare for the day of separation.

* * *

After sending my support group through security, I sat in the Jackson airport, thinking about the last thing Patricia said to me.

"Don't worry, Minus. Someday we'll be telling our children about this experience."

Before I could ask if these were our children or respective of our separate lives, she was swept into the metal scanner.

Helen gave me a wink, then stepped through the portal, leaving me with a single directive; not to worry.

The bench I was sitting on reminded me of The Yard as I looked around the departure lobby. I was alone. The people were like ghosts floating through the terminal. Ticketing kiosks were lined up like headstones in a cemetery. This brought me back to the job at hand. And gave me an idea. It was time to go back to All Souls.

* * *

"Good to see you, Minus. Where's the rest of your team?" Seamus greeted me into his office.

"My partners had to get back to San Francisco. Something about keeping their jobs. I was elected to stay behind to fight the good fight."

To what do I owe this visit?" Seamus quizzed my motives. "Bob has nothing new to report. It's been darn quiet around here."

"I realized I didn't have much of a chance to check out your facility last time. Do you mind if I take a stroll through the grounds?"

"Not at all. Would you like company?"

"Thank you, but I would like to spend time with my thoughts. I'll come back through to see you before I leave."

I started where the land was flat and the graves simple. The headstones were modest, each telling the story of the occupant in a single line; "Good father," "Good son," "Hell of an accountant." Every form of individual was interred here, giving tribute to the American way. They were all just people. People who had lived their lives as millions had done before them and as yours truly was doing now. The thought of a greedy corporate goliath disturbing the peace they should be enjoying came raging into my body. My brother's skull had been stolen. Thousands had been gathered up, for reasons I still didn't understand, and taken from their families. So many souls unable to get help. I started to sweat and shiver in the winter air. I took a deep breath, trying to clear my mind. The air was cold and clean. Hitting my lungs, it created a sensation of clarity, purity, and pain. My head began to spin with thousands of faces engulfing me.

* * *

The space around me was black. The cold was gone. Replaced with nothing. I was not behind the door. I felt eyes on me but could see none. I could feel hands touching me, but no one was there. Voices echoed in the distance, but there was no vista. Still, I was not scared. Since there was nothing there, I felt no fear.

I waited for the voice of the Consortium's spokes-soul, but all I felt were memories. Wordless thoughts that encompassed my life, leaving me with a sense of home. I could easily stay here and be at peace.

"You adapt well, Minus," a voice rose from the silence. I didn't recognize the spook who spoke.

"Most people don't do well when they can't see their surroundings," the voice continued. "We assume you have some experience with this out-of-body work."

"It's becoming a way of life," I said. "Are you part of the Consortium of Souls?"

"No, we are the Council of Skulls."

"You're kidding?"

"Did we say something funny?"

"Yes, but I have a feeling that is my issue," I confessed. "Between skull collectors and corporate titans, you must keep busy."

"There are many people who deal in skulls. Some work for us, some for Titan Moon, and some have a strange hobby."

The Council voice was silent for a moment before they got down to business. "We were told that your brother is missing, sending you on a journey to find him."

"I wouldn't call it a journey. It's more of a mission."

"Any endeavor where one learns and grows is a journey. A mission is just blind faith."

"Knowledge hasn't played much of a part in this search," I replied to a statement I didn't really understand.

"You found us. So, you've learned something."

"I don't see the connection between being drawn out of my conscious mind and obtaining a bachelor's degree in skull hunting."

"Who taught you to talk like that?"

"It comes naturally."

I felt myself slipping away from the voice. Seamus's face was starting to appear before me. It was too soon to go back to the cemetery, so I asked the Council, "How can I help you?"

"Thank you, Minus. You're learning."

I was back in the comfort of the darkness with the knowledge that one does not joke around with the Council.

"We've been monitoring the movement of skulls all over the world for eons," the Council voice continued, "except for Papua New Guinea. They had it right early on, by burying their ancestors' bones under their huts. If the Western world had been so wise, we wouldn't have to deal with this mess, but getting back to *your* question, can you swim?"

"I was the dog paddle champ in sixth grade. Why do you ask?"

"You may need to tread water. We've traced a large number of skulls to a privately owned body of water near Jackson Lake."

I felt I should remind the Council, "You know it's winter in Wyoming. You're not suggesting I go ice fishing for skulls, are you?"

"Of course not. That would be too dangerous. We were thinking more of a scuba diving expedition."

"May I approach this from a different angle?" I asked. "Why would Titan Moon dump the skulls in a lake?"

"Water is different from land. You've heard the phrase, lost at sea?"

"Of course."

"When skulls are in water, they are lost to the people on land. It's kind of a loophole in the afterlife."

"Can this wait until summer?"

"We thought you wanted to find your brother."

"Why were my friends sent away?"

"What? Weren't we just talking about your brother?"

"No, we were talking about me going into frozen water with no one to watch out for me."

"You don't trust us."

"Put yourselves in my place. A voice in the dark asked you to dive into a frozen margarita after dispensing with your support group. What would you do?"

"We can always try ice fishing for skulls if you like."

"That's not the point. Why did you send Patricia and Helen home?"

"We didn't. That was the Consortium's idea. We thought they should stay."

"I like your idea better. So why did the Consortium have them leave?"

"That was not discussed with us. The Consortium is a separate entity. They are not subject to our input."

"I'm going to have to think about this," I finally realized. "Can I get back to you with an answer?"

"That's a reasonable request. When you're ready, we will contact you."

"How will you know when I'm ready?"

"You'll tell us."

"And how do I do that?"

"By saying you're ready."

"Oh, thank you. Can you tell me the location of the lake?"

The Council told me the lake's location before sending me back to my body. I was now in Seamus's office after being found in the flatlands of the cemetery staring into a frozen bouquet of lilies.

I enjoyed a Dutch eggnog with Seamus, then went back to the hotel bar to consider my options.

Option 1: Stay in the bar until I become homeless and destitute.

Option 2: Stay in the bar until it's time for bed and think about it tomorrow.

Option 3: Go to Jackson Lake.

It was not a hard decision. Number two was a winner, though it turned out to be more difficult than anticipated. Staying in the bar until bedtime was easy. Not thinking about my situation was impossible. I lay in bed for hours staring at the textured ceiling, finding faces in the design. My mind kept running through the scenario of becoming trapped under the ice as my oxygen tank ran out.

I've never been a hero. I don't want to be a hero. I just want my brother back. If I have to risk becoming a hero to help Brian, than so be it, I will. But don't make me kiss babies.

* * *

By morning, the snow on my windowsill had accumulated to create a topographical map of the Tetons. It was a new day. A perfect day for a dip in a frozen lake. The headache from the fortified eggnog and two Manhattans was barely incapacitating.

Having decided to go ahead with the skull hunting, I consulted with the Council then checked out of Jackson's Wort Hotel, with fond memories of my traveling companions.

The cars in the hotel parking lot were wrapped in ice. The night had been cold, and the day wasn't looking to be any warmer. Standing next to my rented pony, I took a deep breath. I wanted to feel the reality that surrounded me before settling into my automotive cocoon. The cold, the clean, the memories of Jackson.

Once encased, I set the navigation for Jackson Lake, forty miles north of Jackson. I missed my friends but enjoyed finally being behind the wheel of a Mustang. Wyoming's snow-covered mountains were breathtaking when viewed from a heated driver's seat.

* * *

I pulled up to the Jackson Lake Lodge, where a room had been booked. The Council apparently had a connection with the management or plenty of American Express points.

The car was warm, and the view filled me with a sense of well-being. I felt close to Brian. Looking out at the mountains, I pondered the many souls lost in the wilderness, unable to find their way back, before and after death. Did the Council of Skulls deal with this type of search and relocation? Could a school bus salesman from San Francisco help the lost find home? Assuming the school bus salesman survived the frigid waters of the lake.

I'd been told to check in and wait in my room for instructions, which was a little too cloak and dagger for me. Instead, I went down to the bar.

"What can I get you?" the barman asked.

"Is it too early for an Irish coffee?" I questioned him.

He looked up at the clock and studied it for a moment. I hadn't intended it to be a difficult question. It was more rhetorical than anything else.

"Probably," he finally answered. "Would you like a single or double-shot?"

"On second thought, I think I'll have a warm cider."

I took my apple juice over to a window table that looked out on the Grand Tetons and awaited my orders.

After two ciders and an Irish coffee, double shot, the room went dark.

"You were supposed to stay in your room, Minus," the Council voice scolded me.

"You booked a room without a view," I shot back.

"Oh, we'll have to talk to Charles about that. His grandson is the manager there."

"He might also want to check on the credentials of the bartender. How are you?" I added, to see if I could get a non-plural response.

"We are fine."

It was worth a shot.

"There's a person in town who works for Titan Moon," the Council got right to business. "His name is Samuel Herbert. He owns a canoe rental store in Colter Bay Village."

The Council stopped speaking, leaving me with a *who* and a *where*, but no *why*.

"Minus," the Council returned, "the waitress is asking if you would like another drink. Go back and talk to her."

Suddenly, a woman was standing in front of me saying, "You okay, hun?"

"Yes, I'm sorry. I was mesmerized by the view."

"The sunset will knock your socks off, sweetie. Can I get you another drink?"

"I'm okay for now, thanks, but don't forget about me," I said, keeping my options open.

As she walked off, the room went dark again.

"That's why we wanted you to stay in your room," the Council voice chastised me.

"Well, you should have gotten me a room with a view," I stood up for my contrary behavior.

"Let's not go through that again. We need you to contact Mr. Herbert to find where the skulls are being submerged."

"I appreciate having something to do," I said, "but why don't you just follow him around until he goes to the dumping grounds?"

"We tried that, but some spirit always lets him know we're there. That's something we have to work out."

"You might want to start with Charles's grandson," I suggested.

I don't know if it was the conversation with the Council or the Irish coffee, but I was ready for a nap once I had received my orders. On the way back to my room, I was stopped by the woman at the front desk. "Excuse me, Mr. Filbert, we found you a room with a view."

It's good to have connections.

20

CONNECTIONS

I like lakes.
I like ice.
Lakes are pretty.
Ice is nice in my drinks.

Lakes with ice are dangerous. When my new buddy, Samuel, invited me out for a boat ride on Jackson Lake I was a little hesitant.

"There's a peace and beauty on the lake that can't be felt from the shore," he said, as I checked my life insurance policy for exemptions.

I had contacted Mr. Herbert the morning after the Council issued my directive. His office was in a small building alongside the water's edge, with the lake tour schedule posted just outside the shop door. As I stood reading the times for the insanity of touring the lake this time of year, Samuel came out to greet me.

"You're an adventurous one. Feeling up for a dip in the lake?" he said.

"I can't say you fill me with a great sense of survival," I replied.

"Don't worry, my last client is expected to thaw out by May."

"Do you have any hot chocolate inside? I'm starting to feel a little chill coming on," I said.

He ushered me into a small shop filled with all the trappings one would need for a summer day on the lake.

"You don't rotate your stock, I see."

"Why? Who's crazy enough to go on the lake this time of year?"

"Is the schedule on the door part of the summer stock?"

"No, you never know when a sucker will come your way."

"You're not doing a very good job selling me on a boat tour," I told him.

"Sure I am. We're still talking, aren't we?"

"That doesn't mean I will hire your services."

Samuel smiled.

"Okay, you win. How much for a winter tour?"

"It's on the house. I doubt I would ever get the money from your estate anyway," he confided in me.

Samuel and I hit it off swimmingly. He told me of his life in the merchant marine before settling on Jackson Lake. There was a calm about him. Unhurried, relaxed, and strangely nice for a skull thief.

I stretched out my hot chocolate until ice crystals began to form around the edge of the cup.

"Shall we go?" Samuel asked.

"Is it too late to ask for my money back?" I almost begged.

"That's the problem with free," Samuel reminded me, "there are no refunds."

With that, we headed out to the dock. Moored, adjacent to a sign recommending the use of condoms, was a small motorboat named *Titanic II*.

"Are you averse to having a successful business?" I joked.

"Lightning never strikes the same spot twice. Also, I have other income," he admitted. "I do this for the love of it."

* * *

The Council exists in a dark, safe environment, while life explodes from a bright, frigid world. The lake, the mountains, the land, sky, air, light, world are amazing when viewed from a frozen planet. As uncomfortable as my skin was, my soul was afire with the exhilaration of the ice age. I would have paid Samuel a thousand times what he was charging for this experience. Zero is a number that holds its value. I'm a big spender when it comes to free.

"Do you do many tours this time of year?" I asked Samuel.

"You're my first."

"What about the guy thawing out in May?"

"He isn't actually expected to survive."

"I'll try to fare better. How do you keep yourself going in the winter months?"

"I lease out a portion of a small lake I own just east of here."

"Do you have tours of your lake?"

"It's too small. I only bought it to fish. A company rents a portion, I assume, to take clients on fishing excursions. Lots of trout in that lake."

Now we were talking business. The business I came to talk about.

"Do you know where the corporation goes when they're on the lake?" I ventured to ask, hoping I wasn't giving myself away.

"I leased them the area with my favorite fishing hole. I miss going there, but they pay good money."

"Is there good fishing this time of year?" I continued weaseling myself into his life. "I haven't fished for trout in years."

"Do you like to ice fish?" Samuel brought up a touchy topic.

"Oh, yeah! I have quite a collection of ice fishing decoys. Do you think we could sneak onto your favorite site?"

"Sure, why not? This time of year, the company men don't come very often. Anyway, they were here just a week ago."

I knew if I kept opening my big mouth, I would put a trout in it. Changing the subject, I asked, "Do you have any more of that hot chocolate?"

"I might even be able to conjure up some brandy to reactivate the nerve endings in our fingers," Samuel said, giving me hope of living to see another day.

On our way back to the little shop on the lake, I asked, "Is your family from around here?"

"Not really. I grew up in Oregon."

"Why do you say, not really?"

"My grandfather told me that his grandfather died in Jackson Hole when they were migrating west."

Bingo! I felt like a real detective.

* * *

The warmth of the hotel bar was welcoming. I sat at my favorite table that looked out on Wyoming's majestic mountains and thought about San Francisco. I was missing my companions. Helen and Patricia had said not to contact them for reasons of secrecy. More cloak and dagger, but I was determined to show that I could follow *some* rules.

The dead and the living are not so different. Both become only memories when absent, allowing me to make up stories that keeps them with me.

In my mind's eye, I imagined the women of *The Oakland Ladies Detective Agency* scurrying around in trench coats. Patricia's was a pink Coach, double-breasted with big black buttons. I could see them hiding behind gravestones listening for clues that would break this case wide open. Other than that, I had no idea what they might be up to.

Once that little bit of fiction had been exhausted, I turned my attention to the problem at hand. I had arranged with Samuel to set out onto a frozen lake. Where we would cut a hole in the ice and somehow extricate an unknown number of skulls without looking suspicious. All the while pretending to ice fish, which I have never done before.

That was the plan in broad strokes. The actual essence of the scheme consisted of my hoping for a miracle.

I'm always hoping for a miracle. This time, I felt I had the clout of those spirits in charge of such things or who could put in a good word for me.

Watching the clouds gathering above the distant peaks did nothing to alleviate my feeling of dread. Adding a snowstorm to the scenario was sure to weaken my resolve.

I looked at my phone.

Then, at the clouds.

And back at my phone.

"No, I can do this on my own," I said to myself.

I pushed the phone to the edge of the table and ordered another drink.

The bartender and I had achieved a friendly rapport. I ordered drinks and he didn't editorialize. It was going to be a long night for us both.

My phone rang as the first Manhattan glass was being exchanged for the second.

"Hello, this is Minus."

"Hi, Minus, Samuel here."

"Hi Samuel, how did you know where to find me?"

"This is your cell phone, right?"

"Oh, yes…sorry. I lost track of time."

"Are you okay?"

"I hope so. What's up?"

"I just got word that the corporation is visiting the lake tomorrow. I think we should postpone our fishing excursion."

"That was sudden."

"It's very strange. They usually give me a few days' notice. This time, it sounds like they're in a big hurry to do something."

"Do you like a good Manhattan?" I asked.

"Sure, why do you ask?"

"Can you meet me at the hotel bar? I'd like to buy you a drink."

* * *

Samuel sat down just moments before his drink arrived.

"How'd you do that?" he asked as the barmaid walked off.

"Do what?" I responded, knowing perfectly well what he was asking.

"Never mind."

I offered him what was left of my fried calamari before getting down to business.

"Samuel, I need your help."

"I love calamari," he said.

"Thank you, but that's not what I'm meaning. I need your help with…" At this point, I realized I hadn't quite figured out what I was going to say. "…with a logistical issue, I've come up against."

"Do you think you could be a little more vague?" Samuel asked.

"Right!" I said, jumping to the point of my visit. "I need help finding my brother's skull."

Samuel said nothing. He just looked at me like I had asked him for the time.

"Okay," he said.

"Okay? Just like that? No, *what the hell are you talking about?*"

"I've known why you were here since you arrived."

"Oh!"

"Did they give you any tartar sauce for the calamari?" Samuel inquired.

"Sorry, I sent it back."

"That's okay," he forgave me my condiment transgression. "So, what are you thinking?"

"I'd like to watch these guys tomorrow."

"Sounds like fun."

Samuel surprised me once again with his willingness to assist.

"Why are you helping me?" I asked, suspecting he was truly a nice guy.

He stopped to look out the window. It was dark now. The mountains only existed in our memories.

"My great-great-grandfather was led to believe that the skulls being displaced were of those who abused their power. By visiting the living in an adverse manner. We refer to the behavior as *haunting*. Gramps and I felt the bottom of a lake was a good place for them.

"Once you arrived, he started doing more research and found out something quite different. These souls happened to be in the way of a corporate giant that wanted them removed."

"I don't get it. Just because I showed up, your great-great-grand-father decided to Google 'why are skulls being stolen?'"

"He likes you."

"So did my mother, but she just nodded her head when I spoke."

"What?"

"Never mind. Just emotional baggage. So, do you have a plan?"

"Of course. Is there more calamari?"

* * *

There was a fly in my room. This is not the time of year for any kind of airborne insect, so why was there a fly in my room? I could hear its wings as it followed a flight plan past my head every ten seconds.

Why is there a fly in my room?

After its fourth approach to the runway, I turned on the light. The clock showed 5:15 a.m. A time I had only read about in books. The brightened room must have thrown off my little friend because he stood just above the minute hand as if he were the cuckoo ready to chime.

Why is there a fly in my room?

I had no answer. I stopped caring because I needed to get to the lake to meet Samuel.

* * *

What is it about a frozen lake at 6:30 in the morning that makes you want to go back to bed? Maybe it was the appearance of soft white sheets with fluffy pillows in the snow.

Samuel and I settled in among a stand of aspens, not far from the fishing hole of suspected skull dumping fame. There was no way of knowing when the culprits would enter the scene.

It was cold. It was dark. The coffee was hot and dark. As long as the joe lasted, we could survive.

"Any chance you have an almond croissant in your satchel?" I asked Samuel, feeling left out in the cold.

"How can you be hungry after last night's calamari feast?"

"Excuse me, I was sustaining myself with the cherries from my Manhattans while you enjoyed the second plate of squid."

"Your choice."

"Thank you, what about a Danish?"

"Okay, I do have a cinnamon twist, but you have to share."

"That won't be hard since you have control over it."

Being the humanitarian that he is, Samuel gave me more than my fair share of the feast. I will never forget him for that.

At 10:00, as the sun began to act like a heat source, the persons of interest arrived on the lake with a bundle in hand. A small bundle. Not much bigger than a skull.

"Minus!" I heard Brian's voice say.

I looked around to see if he was going to show himself as the first time.

Samuel, obviously startled, asked what was wrong.

"My brother is here...somewhere."

"Minus, I'm in the bag."

I looked out at the lake. The men had stopped. They seemed to be waiting.

"What's going on, Brian?" I asked.

"Did you know you have a Cousin Mickey?" Brian asked back.

"What the hell does that mean?" I kept the conversation of questions going.

"You really need to mellow out, Minus. The man with the bag is your cousin."

The man with the bag looked like he had been on the wrong end of too many fists. If his nose were bent anymore to the left, he could sneeze in his own ear.

"Brian, I am mellow. WHAT THE HELL IS GOING ON?"

"You don't sound mellow."

"BRIAN!"

"Okay, I'll explain."

The men stood perfectly still on the ice while Brian went into a long-winded explanation of this long-lost relative who worked for Titan Moon. Brian had contacted Mickey, bringing him over to the "Force."

"You're kidding, right?" I said.

"Minus, I can't talk to you. Where's your sister?"

"I don't have a sister."

"Sure you do. Where's Helen?"

My mind went back to the fly in my room this morning. It made no sense. Nothing was making sense.

"Helen is not my sister. Is that bag a little too tight around your head?"

"Oh, Minus, you are so naive."

"Can we get back to Helen?" I tried to focus on one thing.

"This isn't the time or place for that conversation."

The men on the ice continued to stand still. I couldn't move. Samuel looked really worried.

"Minus, are you still with me?" Brian asked.

It took a moment for that question to sink in. "Is there anything else you would like to tell me?" I said without fully thinking about the repercussions of the question.

"That can wait. I don't want to overwhelm you."

"Thanks," I said, ready to move on.

"Why don't you come out of the trees and meet your cousin?" Brian prodded me.

I explained to Samuel that these people *probably* wouldn't kill us, and we needed to talk to them.

As we stepped onto the ice, Mickey reached into his coat. I grabbed Samuel and we both fell back behind a scrub oak, which was little defense against a gun but did obscure the lens of Mickey's cell phone.

"What are you doing, Minus?" Brian asked.

"I'm trying to keep from getting shot."

"Congratulations, you've avoided being posted on Instagram. Now, will you stand up and say hi to your cousin?"

I looked out from behind the bush to see Mickey and his partner having a good laugh.

* * *

Back at the bar, Mickey filled us in on his partner, Mikey. A cousin on his father's side. They both had joined the ranks of Titan Moon shortly after high school and had worked their way up to Chief Head Knockers—AKA security for TMD (Titan Moon Distributors). Brian had found them and managed to convince the two to help stop the skull thefts.

Samuel then made the virtual introduction of his great-great-grandfather to the table.

With all the who's who completed, we ordered lunch. Mickey and Mikey both wanted a burger, Samuel a Cobb salad, and I requested a pot of coffee. It was quite obvious who would be joining Brian and Great-Great-Gramps the soonest.

"So Mickey, have you and Brian come up with a plan to save the world?" I started the conversation.

"You are a cynical one," Mickey replied. "Your brother is quite a caring soul."

"Sorry, I have a tendency to take things less than seriously. I've been told it's an annoying habit."

"As long as you're aware of it," Mickey, the thug therapist, responded.

Samuel offered, "I would like to help. I feel responsible for perpetuating this crime."

"Thank you," I heard Brian say, instructing me to pass it on to Samuel.

"We have a team of six living and at least five dead," I gave a head and skull count, "I still can't see what we can do to stop the cranial expulsions."

"Don't be so morose," Brian said. "Remember, two of our team are women. They always have a plan."

I shared that insight with the table, which brightened the mood. With that, we enjoyed lunch and planned our trips back to San Francisco.

After spending the next twenty minutes discussing the best areas to stay, the best restaurants to try, and the best sights to see, Samuel asked, "Why are we going to San Francisco?"

We all exchanged curious glances before Brian stepped forward with the answer. "That's where the women are. Without them, it would be like ice fishing in Wyoming."

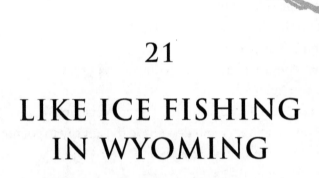

21

LIKE ICE FISHING IN WYOMING

By nature, I'm a loner.
Most of my life has been spent avoiding relationships.
The rest of my life has been spent getting out of relationships I couldn't avoid.

I now found myself in the company of six humans, two spirits, and a dog.

The great migration to San Francisco had begun. I flew home to change the sheets in Patricia's room before my guests arrived. Mickey and Mikey drove the company car, having convinced TMD that they needed to keep an eye on me. Samuel carpooled with Seamus, who had wanted to join the team with his dog Digger.

My flight was uneventful and relatively short. With the travel time clocking in at two hours and fifteen minutes, there was no comparison to the epic world tour getting to Jackson.

Helen was kind enough to break radio silence and offered to pick me up at the airport. Now that I understood our relationship, I was eager to have a little Q and A with sis.

"Did you know that we have the same father?" I asked Helen as I got in the car.

"It's nice to see you too," Helen replied. "I would have to be an idiot not to have known."

"I'm hoping that is not an assessment of my intelligence."

"Minus, your parents loved you."

"What does that have to do with you being my sister?"

"Are you hungry?"

"Excuse me. Did we finish the last conversation?"

"No, but I'm hungry and don't have the energy to go into it right now. I know a nice sandwich shop on Potrero Hill."

"I love that place," I said.

"Why is it, sometimes you know exactly what I'm talking about and other times you're completely clueless?" Helen asked.

"Food is a non-threatening subject," I gave insight as to how my brain worked.

We made our way to Eighteenth Street, on Potrero Hill, where a parking space was open right in front of Hazel's Kitchen. It seemed a squirrel had been sent to hold the spot for us. The little fellow had just stared down a Buick before running up a tree to let us park.

*   *   *

"Which one do you think is Hazel?" I asked as we ate our lunch in Helen's car.

"There is no Hazel, Minus. That's just the name of the shop."

"There has to be a Hazel, or they wouldn't call it Hazel's Kitchen."

"Do you think Mr. Macy is working a cash register at Macy's?" Helen attempted to put my assumption into perspective.

"Of course not, but he is the Santa Claus at Christmas," I said, killing that topic.

Helen owned a late-model Toyota SUV with a pristine interior. Hazel's secret sauce threatened the sanctity of the passenger's seat fabric. "May I have another napkin?" I asked as the seasoned mayonnaise ran down my chin.

"Your father is proud of you, Minus," Helen proclaimed, handing me a paper towel to clean a spot on my shirt.

"For what?"

"For bringing Brian back."

"Mickey and Mikey are bringing him back. I didn't think I could get him through security."

"You know what I mean, Minus. You found Brian."

"No, Brian found his way back. I just bought drinks for everyone afterward."

"I have a flailing stick in the trunk if you would like to use it," Helen offered.

"Thank you, but I have my own."

"Minus!"

"Yes!"

"Never mind. I'll take you home."

"Did I say something wrong?"

"No, you just wore me out," Helen finished the conversation and started her Toyota Nondescript.

"Before we go," I said, "where is Patricia?"

Helen turned off the Nondescript. "Why do you not accept what I've told you?"

"She's indisposed, is not an answer. It's a calculated misdirection designed to confuse me."

"Are you confused?"

"Yes."

"Then it worked. I'm going to take you home now."

* * *

The next day, shortly after Seamus, Digger, and Samuel had found their way to my house, Mickey called.

"Hey, Minus," his oddly comforting voice came out of the hands-free speaker in my car, "how's it going?"

"It's going well," I answered the polite, but unnecessary greeting. "We're just heading out for lunch. Where are you?"

"Brian wanted to visit the folks. We've stopped by his old haunting grounds."

"You're in Oakland?"

"Yes, but we have a problem."

"You wouldn't believe how much I didn't want to hear that," I said. "Go on."

"Your parents are gone."

I pulled the car off to the side of the road, since I'm not proficient at driving and panicking at the same time. "Gone, in what sense of the word?" I asked.

"How many senses of the word are there? Gone, as in not here," Mickey tried to clarify.

God, I longed for the day when I could just sell a school bus again.

"Do you still have Brian?" I asked.

"Of course, he's around here somewhere."

"What!"

"Sorry, just trying to lighten the mood."

"Don't move," I told him. "We'll be there in twenty minutes."

We parked in my regular space. Seamus lagged behind to take Digger for a walk. Samuel and I hot-footed it to the family plots.

At the gravesite, Mickey and Mikey were standing perfectly still with the skull-bag in hand. They literally had not moved. I could see why Titan Moon had hired them.

"Hi, guys. You take direction well."

"That's why Titan Moon hired us," Mikey said.

"Minus," Brian's voice came into my head, "this is not good."

I looked at the gravesite. It looked untouched. "Are you sure that they aren't just deep in a game of bridge?"

One would think you needed a pair of lungs to give a deep sigh, but apparently, even a skull can feel exasperated. "Minus, I love you, but you can be such a dope. They are not here."

"I'm just trying to look at the big picture," I said, further proving Brian's point.

"Mickey thinks it wasn't Titan Moon."

I looked at Mickey for an expansion on this theory.

"Titan Moon still thinks everything is going as planned," he said. "They would have no reason to steal your folks. Someone else did this."

"I'm already dealing with six humans, two spirits, and a dog. Now you're telling me there's more?"

"No. I just think it's not the dog," Mickey said.

That sounded more like a punch line than an answer, but I got the gist.

"Do you have any ideas, suspicions, or solutions?" I asked Mickey, then opened the question up to everyone.

After a long silence, Seamus offered, "I agree. Digger had nothing to do with it."

We stood around the graves like friends at a funeral, trying to figure out what had happened. Uncle Bob was the first to put forward a theory.

Through Seamus, Bob suggested, "They're still there. And they're not."

"Bob," I said, counting to three in my head, "was that a helpful statement?"

"Minus," Seamus/Bob continued, "Why do you think I'm here with Seamus? I could be with my nephew Mel or my great-nephew Sid. All three have a part of me. I choose to be here because I want to be here, but I can only occupy one part of me at a time. This method allows me more freedom. Only a portion of your parents' skulls has been removed. Look at the small hole under the gravestones."

Just beneath the marble epitaphs was a small circle that seemed obvious now. My thoughts went back to Wyoming and the plan to drill a hole in the ice to extract skulls.

"Are you suggesting that someone drilled into the caskets and removed part of their skulls?"

"Exactly."

"You know there's a concrete layer over the final burial?"

"Masonry bits. You can get them at any hardware store," Bob answered, being an experienced dead person.

"I wish I could have brought Great-Great-Gramps," Samuel interjected, "but he has never told me where he's buried."

I had to think why Samuel would bring that up. It kind of fit in with the conversation and was out of left field at the same time.

"Why do you bring that up?" I finally asked.

"Gramps is afraid of losing his home. He knows of souls who have been taken from their resting place and never returned. These people loved where they were, but the living were being selfish."

That statement scared me. I had imagined death as the ultimate freedom. No longer being commanded by the frailties of life. Now, it was sinking in. Knowledge is the sword and compassion the sheath. We must take what we learn and use it wisely. *The living needs to respect the dead.*

I couldn't think. There was too much to think about. I excused myself and began walking up the hill. Brian stayed with me but was quiet. I felt his presence as a comfort. When I reached the tomb on the hill that had started this mission, I remembered the game of souls. Was that a dream, or did I experience hundreds of souls at once? I wasn't related to any of them, so how did that work?

Looking back at the city, I asked Brian, "What's going on?"

Brian was silent, but I knew he was listening. He began speaking to me without words, without thought, without consciousness. I felt emotions. An entire language composed of feelings. He was filling me with what it was to be dead. The infinity of everything with the calm of nothingness. I saw the city as a place of promise. Filled with the potential of my life and the lives of everyone who lived there. I felt the multitude of souls that surrounded me. I felt grateful to be alive but longed to be dead.

"Okay, that's enough of that," Brian said, pulling the plug.

Just like that, I was back in my anxiety-ridden brain.

I sat down on the bench that looked onto Patricia's family. The people she had disowned, even before being pressured into selling. After Brian's tutorial on death, I could see why this property was so coveted. I felt like taking up residence.

"The question still stands, brother," I tried again for an answer.

"Minus, don't rush to get here. You need to fulfill your life. This place is unimaginable and eternal. I wanted to give you a sense of what you're fighting to save. Titan Moon is destroying peace for thousands of souls."

"Why me, Brian? There are far more powerful people you could ask to help."

"You weren't chosen, Minus. Patricia was. I'm afraid we got caught in the crossfire."

"They certainly found a funny way of romancing her. Who was the spook making her sell the property? Her cousin Maurice?"

"No, he's her brother."

Half the people I know have dead brothers. It seems to be a fad. I was surprised, however, that Patricia had not mentioned him.

"I gather they didn't get along," I surmised.

"On the contrary, they were twins and inseparable. He's trying to help her *and* the cause."

"You know he jumped on my car," I reminded Brian.

"Not in real life, Minus. Cut him some slack. By the way, where *is* Patricia?"

"I was hoping you could tell me. I haven't seen her since I've been back."

"Where's Helen?"

"Today? I don't know. If you're referring to a broader timeline, she picked me up at the airport yesterday. After dropping me off at my house, I assume she went home, though she did mention a movie she wanted to see."

"Wow, that's amazing!" Brian exclaimed.

"What, that she picked me up?"

"No, that answer. Is that what's going on in your head?"

"I edited that. You don't want to know what's going on in my head."

Brian was silent for a moment before taking a rain check. "We can talk about that later. For now, can we finish with Helen?"

"Gladly. What would you like to know?"

"Does she know where Patricia is?"

"Yes."

"Go on."

"Okay. Yes, she does?"

"Minus?"

"Yes."

"Are you mad at me?"

"Yes!"

"Why?"

"You just gave me a taste of nirvana and then threw me back into my hell hole."

Once again, Brian paused. I was starting to think they gave drama classes in the afterlife. Then, out of nowhere, he asked, "Do you like sautéed scallops?"

"Of course!" I answered, knowing I was about to be taught a lesson.

"When you order them at a restaurant, do you savor them?"

"Religiously."

"When the waiter takes your plate, do you tell him to fire the chef?"

"Of course not!"

"Then why are you firing me?"

It did seem rather unfair to treat Brian with less patience than some head cook I didn't know, who probably yells at his sous chef.

"Point taken," I said, "but you owe me a revisit to nirvana."

"Gladly. Now can we get back to Helen?"

"Sure. What would you like to know?"

"The same thing I wanted to know a minute ago."

"She's on her way now."

"Why didn't you tell me that in the first place?"

"I just thought you wanted to know if I knew something that you already knew."

"What?!" Brian almost yelled.

"You know. Kind of like a double spy thing."

"Minus! We're on the same side."

"Right. Sorry, Brian. I don't function well under surreal conditions."

Then, as if a character in a novel, Helen crested the hill. "Hi Minus, where's Brian?"

"He's around here somewhere."

"Hi, Helen," Brian said, "we were just talking about you."

"Minus didn't tell you I was coming, did he?"

"I think we've already beaten that horse to death," Brian said. "Shall we get down to business?"

Helen sat down and gave me a bump with her shoulder, then smiled and winked.

"Well, you're quite the cheery superintendent of schools," I said.

"I've got good news," she reported.

"Has Congress eliminated the electoral college?" Brian asked.

Helen and I both looked up and said, "What?!"

"Well, you know it's been wreaking havoc with democracy for a long time," Brian explained.

Helen turned to me and said, "He's starting to sound like you."

I winked.

"No," Helen said, "I just found out that Patricia isn't dead."

"WHAT?!" Brian and I sang out in a perfect third.

"Didn't I tell you? She went to visit her brother."

"As I recall, you were rather elusive as to her whereabouts," I reminded her.

"I didn't want to scare you."

"Thank you, I'm much calmer now," I said with as much sarcasm as I could muster.

"I'm sorry, Minus, but she asked me not to tell you."

"Does she know her brother was the spook trying to get her to sell the tomb?" I asked.

"Yes, when we got back, he visited her again. You would not have wanted to be him because this time he slipped by using her nickname and she ripped him a new face."

"What's her nickname?" I indelicately asked.

"She hates it. I've been sworn to secrecy."

"How about a clue?"

"Minus!"

"Okay, okay, I'll weasel it out of her later. So, what happened then?"

"He vanished again," Helen answered, turning to face the ocean.

The season had changed noticeably in the past week. The trees were stripped of their leaves, allowing the city to invade the hill. I watched Helen search the horizon for an answer. The urban skyline gave no indication of her response.

When Helen continued, she spoke softly with a hint of worry in her voice. "Patricia was terribly upset. She wanted to find him."

"How did she intend to do that?" Brian asked.

"It's incredibly sad," Helen began with the backstory. "Patricia's brother died young. I believe Zero was in his early twenties. He had been sailing with friends just outside the Golden Gate when the fog came in fast and thick, engulfing the boat as they approached the bridge. Zero was at the helm at the time and lost control, causing the vessel to hit one of the bridge's piers. Almost everyone drowned, including Zero. His body was never found.

"Patricia thought he had been lost at sea. Now she knows Zero had to have made it to land or he wouldn't be able to contact her.

"Yesterday, she rented a boat and went out under the bridge to look for him."

"If he didn't die there, why was she looking for him on the bay?" I asked.

"Because it was dangerous. She wanted to force his hand," Helen explained.

Brian asked, "Why didn't you go with her?"

"She wanted to be alone. I think there is a lot of baggage there."

"I know her brother; that would not be an easy family reunion," Brian surmised. "Where is she now?"

"In the shower," Helen answered.

"Thank you. She's at home, would have sufficed," Brian said, with a touch of embarrassment in his voice.

"She's not at home. She went to Minus's house."

"How'd she get in?" I asked in amazement.

"Minus, everyone hides the house key under the big rock outside the door," Helen informed me of my human frailty.

"I did toy with putting it under the ceramic duck, but thought that was too obvious," I attempted to justify my decision.

"Did she find her brother?" Brian got back to the crux of the matter.

"Yes, she did, and it went surprisingly well."

"I gather he didn't try to smash her boat," I said, recalling my own experience with Patricia's lovely brother.

"You're not going to let that one go, are you?" Brian said.

"Not as long as I can justifiably complain about it."

Helen used my last statement to further her report. "You are going to change your opinion of him very soon. Both of you."

"I didn't say anything," Brian defended himself.

"You eluded to it. Now may I continue?"

There was silence.

"Thank you," Helen continued. "Patricia believes he's trying to help."

"He sure has a novel approach."

"MINUS!" Helen scolded.

"Sorry! But it's true. With friends like him, as they say."

Helen closed her eyes. I could almost hear her count to ten.

"Boys, please just listen. If you feel like commenting, DON'T," Helen chastised. "Patricia didn't go into her family's history, but she made it clear that we need to trust Zero."

"My dog?" I asked.

"No, not your dog, Minus. That's Patricia's brother's name," Helen clarified.

"You're kidding?"

Helen put her face in her hands, I believe to suffocate herself, before taking a big breath and saying, "May I continue?"

"Sorry," I said.

"We need to trust each other, and we need to work together," Helen prompted. "Can I get you two to do what I say?"

"I will if Brian will," I said.

Helen's hands moved closer to her neck where they might be more effective at ending her agony.

"Helen, we will follow you to the gates of hell," Brian said.

"Nice reference," I agreed.

For some reason, this conversation had Helen looking like a Samurai searching for a sword to throw himself upon.

I capitulated to behave.

"Okay, I'm going to hold you to that, Minus," Helen said, sounding like a third-grade school teacher.

We made our way from the Kelly tomb, to the Filbert tomb, to find our "muscle" playing cribbage on the family plot.

"Who's winning?" I asked.

"Mickey," Mikey said, "he cheats."

Mickey smiled.

I noticed a lessening in our ranks. "We seem to be missing a human and a canine. Where's Seamus?"

"He took the dog for a walk," Mikey answered.

"I hope Digger doesn't pee on Crocker," I said. "We have enough trouble."

22

TROUBLE

Reclining on the sofa,
hair still wet from the shower.

Patricia was looking exceptionally clean with an internal glow. Her meeting with Zero, not the dog, seemed to have filled her with a sense of accomplishment and cathartic relief.

"Where have you been?" she asked as I took a seat in the white leather chair that had become my haven from the world.

"Just visiting the folks."

"Oh, how are they?"

"I don't know. They seem to have gone on vacation. I assume to the Bahamas."

"No, they're still around," Patricia confirmed my suspicion.

"I knew you had something to do with it. Digger isn't smart enough for this caper."

"Who's Digger?"

"Ah, something you don't know."

"Sarcasm?"

"More like…playful banter," I recovered from my snide comment.

"Excellent!" she said with a smile. "Are you pouring the wine?"

"It's only four o'clock."

"Not in Wyoming."

I unscrewed the cap off the New Zealand Sauvignon Blanc as Patricia regaled me with mariner's tales of monsters at sea.

"I imagine Helen told you where I was?" Patricia began.

"Yes, she said you went out hunting for dragons on the bay."

"I found my dragon."

"So I hear. What's with his name?"

Patricia was concise without revealing too much about her past. "My parents had an issue with a male child. I don't know why. By the time I realized something was wrong, I didn't want to know why.

"My brother and I are fraternal twins. Even though he was born first, they treated me like the number one child. That's why he took the nickname of Zero. He hated his real name."

"I can't say I would have been happy with the name Maurice."

"That's not his name. His real name was Frances."

"That's a nice name."

"It was spelled with an E instead of an I. He hated that. Instead, he wanted to be called Zero. It was a more direct affront to his masculinity."

That small insight into Patricia's childhood gave me a cynical view of the souls lying dormant in and around the tomb on the hill. I had read about such upbringings in the *New York Times* and filed them away as *something not to think about.* My parents may not have told me everything, but there was never an omission of love.

"There's more to it now, Minus. This has become bigger than all of us. We have to put a stop to it."

"If it's bigger than us, how can we put a stop to it?" I stated the obvious.

"Because we have to," Patricia said, with the confidence of a true fighter.

"In that case, count me in," I said, sitting a little straighter in my white chair.

This lovely sofa-reclining woman went on to hatch a plan that sounded totally ridiculous to me. Still, she looked so lovely reclining on the sofa. I would have followed her to the gates of hell.

* * *

The next day began at my house, with a gathering of the troops.

Patricia was firing up the coffee machine when Helen arrived. I was face down in my pillow listening to the sounds of morning.

It was Saturday. The street was quiet, though the air was filled with the chatter of birds. Trees surrounded my home. Within these trees was a world of creatures able to float in space. I envied them. I envied the dead for the same reason. I was face down in a pillow while the goddess, Gaia, had given the sky to the birds and the dead.

My envy was soon disturbed by the remainder of the team showing up with a din verging on a herd of bison. I shot out of bed to preserve my standing with the neighbors.

"Guys," I said, as I stumbled out of my room fumbling with the tie on my robe, "the mayor just called and asked if we were holding a political rally. Do you think you could keep it down to a loud roar?"

The gang blithely ignored my plea for quiet, except for Digger, who stopped barking and laid down under the dining room table. With that modicum of success, I retired to the shower.

When I came out of the bathroom, the house was silent. For a moment, I thought they had started the assignment without me. I stood perfectly still, listening to the starlings outside the bathroom window when I heard it. The sound started as a low rumble, barely discernible before it came charging into my head. "GARBAGE! I forgot to put out the garbage."

Just as the truck pulled up outside, I was able to drag the bins to the curb and dispose of life's unwanted.

When I went back into the house to see if Charlie's Angels were still assigning marching orders, I was met with silence. Occupying every seat in the living room was the team, eyes closed, heads down, unmoving. They looked like an audience at a vice-presidential fundraiser. I took the opportunity to get a cup of coffee.

"Minus," Brian's voice came into my head, "nice of you to join us," he said, as I sat down next to Patricia.

"Priorities, brother. It's been two weeks since I put the garbage out and the smell was starting to attract bears from Yosemite. What's going on here?"

Brian explained that the Consortium of Souls had put together the equivalent of a Zoom meeting in the spirit world. "Everyone is linked," he said. "Would you like to join?"

"Will I still be able to drink my coffee?" I asked, not wanting to be wasteful.

"I'll see what I can do about that. For now, I think it best to put the cup down."

"Hi, Minus."

Suddenly, I was being greeted by everyone.

"Hi guys, did I miss anything?"

"Not really," Seamus said. "Mickey was just telling us about the time he hid two hundred skulls in the giant urns lining my entry."

"How could Uncle Bob not notice them?" I asked, knowing a little bit about the subject.

Seamus had the answer at the ready. "Each skull was sealed in a Ziplock filled with water."

"Mickey," I directed my question to the skull stealer, "why didn't you put Brian's skull in water to keep us from following you?"

"I was told not to."

"By whom?"

"Zero."

Looks like the hen has come home to roost. It appears all roads lead to Zero.

"This is getting confusing," I said, wanting to verify my suspicions. "How can you talk to Zero?"

"Haven't you wondered how you, Patricia, and Helen are all able to see him?"

"It had crossed my mind," I said.

"I bet that was a short journey," Mickey mumbled.

"Excuse me?"

"Never mind… I'm sure you noticed that there's a Filbert buried on the Kelly land," Mickey said.

"Are you telling me we're related?"

"Goal, six points to the salesman! Would you like to guess the relationship for the extra point?" Mickey said, as a true football fan.

"I'm going to run the ball for two points," I played his game. "Patricia is my cousin three times removed."

"Was that a guess, or is that something you already know?"

"Goal!"

"If you boys have finished your pissing contest," Helen stepped in, "can we get to work?"

"That was fun, Mickey," I quickly added.

"Ditto, Minus," Mickey sneaked in a virtual high five before Consortium of Souls took the helm.

"I have called this meeting to bring you up to speed with the plan that Patricia and we have devised. Everyone will play a part, except for Digger. He's a bit of a wild card.

"As you know, our goal is to return Titan Moon to be a beneficial player for the afterworld. Starting by replacing Ronald Stump, as president, with Minus."

That caught me off guard. I hadn't been privy to this aspect of the scheme. "Patricia, you didn't tell me that," I complained.

"I didn't want to worry you without the group's support," she attempted to comfort me.

I had to think fast. "Can we back up and elect someone even less unqualified?"

"Minus, you can do it," the spokes-soul assured me. "Stump is a moron. He's mean and has inflicted a lot of damage."

"Thank you for the vote of confidence, but that doesn't make me feel confident."

"You don't have to take the job," Helen said, "just consider it."

Helen had become my anchor, my strength, my sister. "I'll think about it," I said.

"That's all we can ask," the spokes-soul said. "Now, let's get down to the plan."

With that, the timeline was set, the duties assigned, and the mission began.

* * *

When the spirit moves me, I am quite capable of entertaining guests. Before the gang headed off to their designated duties, I whipped up a little lunch for the troops. I make a killer mac and cheese.

Stump had sent Mickey and Mikey to spy on us. We, in turn, sent them back as spies for the good guys. I wasn't sure if they were double spies or just needed two incomes to meet their monthly bills. Either way, may the best side win their allegiance.

Jackson Hole felt like it held the missing piece that would free Titan Moon from the foul tendrils of Stump. The house of plants never truly left me. I had sensed a presence there. As if the grounds were occupied by something or someone, attempting to communicate with anything or anyone in the living world.

Seamus and Samuel returned to Wyoming in hopes of proving my newly found intuitions.

A sabbatical from the Oakland School District allowed Helen the opportunity to investigate why the Kellys, the Filberts, and the Wheelers had been put in charge of the fate of the dead.

Patricia relisted the tomb, hoping to draw in the bad guys.

I was instructed to pose as Patricia's driver. My life was starting to look like a Beatles song.

"Miss Patricia, may I ask you a question?" I made a request of my boss as I drove her to meet a potential buyer of the tomb.

"Sure, Minus, I'm an open book."

"Thank you, I'll try not to write in the margins. I understand everyone else's job in this scheme, but I don't get why I'm driving you. Titan Moon is fully aware of who I am. It's not a particularly effective charade."

"You're mostly here to protect me," she clarified.

"I'm your bodyguard?"

"Every land baroness needs one."

"I was counting on you to cover my ass. Can I be reassigned to kitchen duty?"

"Minus, when the bullets fly, you'll be spectacular."

"Yes, I'll go out in a blaze of glory."

"Not a bad way to go," Patricia agreed.

"Thanks. I'll try to remember that in my panic."

"Don't think about that, Minus. You probably won't have time to panic."

"You're a cheery little bird, Miss Patricia. Shall we move on to the business at hand?"

"Good idea. No need to dwell on the inevitable," Patricia finish our morose conversation before discussing the upcoming meeting. "These people we're seeing are shills from Titan Moon. M&M have been surveilling them."

"M&M?"

"It's easier to say," Patricia said, forever relegating Mickey and Mikey to *melt in your mouth, not in your hand*.

"Okay, but if the bullets start flying, I hope you have a plan because mine is to run like hell."

"You would take a bullet for me, Minus. I know you."

"Right through the heart," I said.

My usual space in the cemetery parking lot was occupied. The Finkleman family was back for another game of touch football. They had taken my parking spot. Not that I have a true claim to the second space from the right, but I am a creature of habit.

At the risk of being offside, I quickly visited the family plot while Patricia started up the hill. She was nearing the top when I caught up.

"Were the folks home?" she asked, knowing full well they weren't.

"Are you ever going to tell me where they are?" I complained.

"Yes," Patricia said cresting the hill with a smile.

On the far side of the property were two men in suits. One, tall and thin. The other, taller and thinner.

"Vegetarians," I said to Patricia.

She shook her head and proceeded to approach them.

"Hello, I'm Patricia Kelly. This is Minus Filbert," she said, extending her arm in my direction.

"Good morning, my name is Phillip," the tall one said. "This is Stretch," he introduced the taller one. "You have a beautiful spot here."

"Thank you. I find it a little stressful," Patricia added.

"I'm aware you're familiar with the company I work for," Phillip got right to the point.

"Yes, you are the folks who stole Minus's brother."

"An unfortunate decision. Why have you decided to put your property on the market again?" the taller one asked.

"I'm done with it. There's nothing here for me and you guys are a pain in the ass."

I wasn't totally clear on the plan, though I thought it involved deception. So far, almost everything Patricia had said was true.

"It's a business model that works for us," Phillip confessed. "We would like to buy the land, but your price has gotten quite a bit higher than market rate."

"Supply and demand," Patricia said. "I have the supply and I'm demanding the price."

I thanked my lucky stars that I was on Patricia's side. She would scare the hell out of me if I were Tall and Taller.

"I take that as, you're not willing to negotiate," Stretch said.

"Not at all," Patricia surprised us all, "but I want to talk to your boss."

"Slick?" Phillip asked.

"Who's Slick?" Patricia shot back.

"He's our boss."

"No, I want to deal with Stump!"

Skinny and Skinnier were noticeably surprised by Patricia's request. She allowed her clients to ponder the repercussions of saying no, before prodding them to respond. "I'm happy to go to him," she said, anticipating their response.

"We'll look into it," Phillip finally said. "Mr. Stump rarely sees anyone."

"Perfect, I rarely want to see him."

* * *

As we walked back down the hill, I asked Patricia how long she was planning on telling the truth.

"Until it stops working for our purpose," she said. "I've looked into Ronald Stump. This man has no relationship with the truth. Lies he understands. Truth, is our strength."

"That sounds risky," I ventured to admit.

"Embrace the truth, Minus. It's the only thing that's real."

The Finklemans' car was gone when we got back to the parking lot. That damn football though, was laying right in the middle of my usual parking space.

"Did I ever tell you my football story?" I asked Patricia.

"If you did, it went in one ear and got thrown away. I don't care for the game."

"That's okay, the moral of the story is: *Trust your thoughts.*"

Patricia stared at the ball for a moment before saying, "Someday, I would like to hear that story."

* * *

It was lunchtime when we rolled out of The Yard. Helen had suggested meeting at Nation's World-Famous Giant Burger. Naturally, I jumped at the opportunity to reward my salivary glands for years of yeoman's service with the best grilled cheese sandwich one can buy.

Helen was seated in my favorite window booth when we entered the restaurant.

"How did you know I like this booth?" I asked as we joined her.

"Brian told me," Helen admitted.

"Is he here?" I asked, looking under a napkin.

"No, he had to leave, but he did give me your order."

"I would find that presumptuous if I wasn't so hungry."

"I also ordered for you, Patricia. Zero passed it on through Brian. A cheeseburger with extra onions, fries, onion rings, and water."

"He remembered," Patricia said happily.

"The dead never forget," Helen said, sounding a little spooky.

"How'd it go?" Patricia asked Helen.

"Great, my research has been fruitful."

"Is this a private conversation, or can anyone join in?" I asked.

"Sorry, Minus," Helen said, fidgeting with the straw in her soda. "Brian gave me all the dirt he had on Stump. It's not pretty."

"I'm sure it could put a strain on your nervous system. What did he have to say?"

"I need a drink before I get into that," Helen said, picking up her Sprite.

"As long as it doesn't fog your brain," I warned her.

"I'll sip slowly," she promised.

Helen kept her promise. One slow sip after another slow sip until finally, I couldn't take it anymore. "Okay, go ahead and guzzle it, but don't blame me if you wake up with a hangover."

Once Helen sucked every last drop from the cup and had refilled it, she got down to storytelling. "Are you guys ready?" Helen asked.

226

Patricia and I looked at each other and agreed. Indeed, we were ready.

That's when our number was called. Helen quickly jumped up to get the order.

"Patricia, is she stalling, or am I impatient?"

"She is stalling, and you are impatient."

When Helen got back, laden with a feast from the gods, Patricia asked, "Are you stalling?"

"Yes," Helen answered to our surprise.

"Why, may I ask?" I asked.

"Because you both won't like what I found out."

"Can we have the good news first?" I requested, with Patricia's agreement.

"Sure, then I'll start at the beginning," Helen said, taking another long, slow sip of Sprite.

Helen continued, looking at me then turning to Patricia, "Our brother, Brian, is a hero."

"Why are you looking at me?" Patricia asked.

"Brian is your brother-in-law."

"Brian was never married," I quickly pointed out.

"Minus, there are a *few* things your parents decided not to tell you."

"Like?" I ventured to ask.

"Like Brian was gay," Helen kindly answered my question, then turned to Patricia.

"Zero?" Patricia screeched, causing the infant in the next booth to screech even louder.

"Yep, they were quite the couple," Helen acknowledged.

"I never knew," Patricia said in a hushed tone, not wanting to activate the baby again.

"Sure you did. You just didn't want to accept it. That's not all the good news. This whole episode has been devised to bring down Stump, and pull us together. We're halfway there."

"I guess that brings us to the bad news?" I said.

"That's a mixed bag," Helen explained. "Bringing Stump down is still good news. It's who Stump is, that's the bad news."

"Don't tell me he's the love child of Brian and Zero." I couldn't resist the imagery.

"No, he's—"

Just then, an extremely loud crash came from the kitchen, sending the whole room to their feet. A woman came out yelling, "It's okay. Nothing to worry about. Everything is under control." Then she slipped back through the swinging door like a bit player in a dream.

Everyone in the room sat down in unison while making comments about increased heart rates and spilled ketchup.

"Was that part of the story?" I asked.

"It is now," Helen answered, blurring the line between reality and fiction.

"You might want to get to the spoiler then, before the sky falls," Patricia sagely advised Helen.

"The sky is on our side," Helen assured us. "It's the terrestrials we have to watch out for. You're not going to like what I have to tell you. I didn't like it."

Patricia and I put down our sandwiches and sat back into the genuine Naugahyde seats, nodding for her to continue.

"Okay, it's your funeral," Helen began, before taking a bite of her burger.

She looked out the window, up at the sky, like a lost soul searching for an answer.

"Stump is my uncle," she muttered between chews.

"Helen, you really shouldn't speak with your mouth full," I said. "That sounded like you said, *bumps in my knuckle*. Although I feel bad for you, I can't imagine we've made this journey to discuss your arthritis."

Helen finished chewing and washed her burger down with a quick sip of soda.

"Patricia," Helen asked, "did you hear what I said?"

Patricia was silent. Her wide eyes gave evidence that she had heard something completely different from me.

"Yes," she finally admitted.

"Lovely, would you kindly translate for Minus?"

Patricia gave me a wry smile and said, "It looks like your family tree has a Stump."

In my mind, I attempted to hear Helen's words without the lettuce, onions, and pickles. *Stump is my uncle*, became crystal clear.

"No way," I blurted out. "You would have known that already."

Helen shook her head deep in thought. I could feel this was the hardest part of the story. A sadness fell over Helen's face, drawing the life from her eyes. Her posture softened as the steadfastness drained from her body.

"Before I was born, Stump had a relationship with my mother's sister. Until this morning, I thought my mother was an only child. Anyway, that travesty resulted in a pregnancy.

"The bastard promised to take care of her and the baby, but instead skipped town and disappeared."

Helen went silent. Patricia and I didn't know what to say.

"Her name was Helen. She died. Giving birth."

The entire room seemed to lose its atmosphere.

Pre-history. The time before each of us. The time that influences our lives before we can influence time.

Control. Is an illusion.

"The baby was put up for adoption and my mother never spoke of either," Helen said out of the silence.

"I'm so sorry," Patricia said to Helen.

"I'll kill the bastard," I said, hoping the security cameras didn't pick that up.

"Thank you both, but that won't be necessary, Minus."

"Somehow, I feel this isn't a coincidence," I said.

"No, it's not," Helen replied. "We have each been carefully chosen."

"I can't even think of a joke right now," I said, feeling defenseless.

"Good!" both Helen and Patricia said.

"What now?" I asked.

"For now, we need to continue with our plan," Helen said, before adding, "There's one more thing."

I waited for a crash from the kitchen. This time there was no dramatic prelude.

"He has to be brought down without destroying his reputation. The company has to be left squeaky clean."

"Any other restrictions that can make this an impossible job?" I asked, before pacifying myself with my root beer's straw.

"Minus, that question is music to my ears. There is one more thing. You have to meet with Stump," Helen said with a smile.

That indeed, did shut me up.

* * *

Everyone and everything had been put into place for the great afterworld redemption.

Brian's skull had been parceled out so that he could now act as our spirit cell phone. Bob had shared Seamus's coin pocket with Brian for the trip back to Wyoming, where they would poke around for information to free Titan Moon from the shackles of tyranny. The idea was that Brian would then report back to the team without incurring roaming charges.

Brian was always the adventurous one of the family. While I was home trying to figure out the lock on the bathroom door, he was out with his friends conquering childhood. Now, he was spearheading the investigation while I wanted to lock myself in the bathroom. Some things never change.

Not even in death.

23

DEATH

Everyone lay dead before me.
All the people in my life,
lined up like fallen soldiers in a morgue.

Why was I still living? They looked so at peace that I wanted to join them. But I couldn't. Someone was pulling on me. Forcing me to leave that room and pushing me into a place where the sun was shining, and a table had been set with the bounty of the rich. Lining the feast were the occupants of the morgue, laughing and singing in praise of those who had come before.

"MINUS!" Patricia yelled. "Wake up!"

I opened my eyes to find myself on the floor with sheepskin in my mouth.

Spitting out the bedroom rug, I looked up at Patricia.

"Did I wake you?" I said.

"Minus, is everything a joke to you?"

"When it scares the hell out of me, yes."

After helping me up from the floor and onto the bed, she sat at my side and fished a piece of lamb's wool out of my ear. With a comforting voice, Patricia asked, "What was the dream?"

"Is life better than death?" I responded to her question with an unknowable.

"It depends, do you like eating at nice restaurants?" she asked, bringing home a point of life's pleasures.

"I do, and I get what you're saying, but at some point, it all comes to an end."

"Until that point, we enjoy the menu," she attempted to persuade me to carry on.

I put my head in my hands, not wanting to impose upon the shoulder of my friend.

Patricia pulled me closer to her until my eyes rested aside her neck.

I was scared of losing the living. I was scared of losing the dead.

I was scared of losing.

I laid my head on Patricia's shoulder a little longer than common etiquette would suggest. It was hard and boney, with the scent of a rose. I could have stayed there all day. But instead, I pretended to pull myself together, allowing Patricia to further fill the air with the scent of coffee.

She was spending more time at my place than her own. I wasn't sure if this was because we needed to stay in close contact to fulfill our mission as the saviors of the afterworld, or because I had free laundry in my garage. Either way, I enjoyed her company.

Today, we were to begin our conquest against the forces of evil. Stump was in our crosshairs. The only thing missing was an explanation of my part in the whole scheme. I knew I was to be the leader, the savior, the kingpin. Now, I needed to be told how to do that. Unless Stump required a fleet of school busses, I felt ill-equipped.

Sleep should be a passive activity, not a marathon, and I needed to wash the night off my skin. While I lowered the local aquifers, Patricia took on the ritual of grinding the morning beans.

The water was soothing, covering my body like a protective suit, offering me a safe place to contemplate. I do my best pondering in the shower. This situation, however, had me stumped. No amount of water was going to bestow me with an answer.

As Patricia handed me my well-deserved cup of coffee, I asked, "How the hell am I going to deal with Stump?"

"You're pretty good at thinking on your feet. I trust it will come to you."

"Your misplaced faith in me isn't all that comforting."

"It should be. I never misplace anything."

I sat on my bed and thought about her statement, "It should be." Why should it? What is it about me that gives others the confidence that I can succeed? I certainly didn't feel that promise of victory. Was the world in denial of my limitations? Or, was I unaware of my abilities?

I looked at the clock. I looked at the sheepskin. I looked inside myself. I liked the rug the most. What I had to do was beyond me.

I again, lowered my head into my hands and the world faded. I plugged my ears and the world further receded into my head. All I could hear was the sound of blood pulsing through my veins. I closed my eyes and the world was gone. My body was gone. Only the din remained, like a million voices speaking at once. No one person standing out. Just a cacophony of souls depending on me to right a wrong.

"Patricia," I called out. "I need your help."

I continued to hold my ears, eyes clenched tight like an angry fist, when Patricia put her arms around me.

"I'm sorry, I can't help you," she said. "You need to work out your part in a way that's right for you."

"Brian told me that you were the chosen one. Why now am I in the hot seat?"

"Because I chose you."

I accepted that reason. It told me nothing while filling me with the warmth of trust.

I opened my eyes and released my ears from their confinement. "What now?" I asked.

"We wait for Stump to make his next mistake," Patricia said, getting me back on track. "That, I believe, will be soon."

"I like your confidence. Is there more coffee?"

* * *

To be human is natural. To be humane is a decision. Stump had chosen a humanity that was alien to me. How can we anticipate his next move when we don't think like him? Narcissistic, corrupt, and mean is a difficult psyche to comprehend.

Before I finished my second cup of coffee, the phone rang. I answered on speaker phone to keep Patricia in the loop.

"Mr. Filbert?" a calm and soothing voice said.

"Yes, but I'm not interested in a loan, thank you," I went into my standard phone response.

"I'm not a salesman, Mr. Filbert, this is Holy Hill Cemetery," the voice of eternal peace said. "My name is Michael."

"Oops, sorry, force of habit," I apologized. "How can I help you?"

"We've had an incident. I don't want to worry you, but your family's plot has been disturbed. It appears someone has stolen your parents' bodies."

"I should have guessed that," I said, suddenly realizing the plot.

"Excuse me? I don't understand," Michael said, losing his angelic demeanor.

"Please pardon my outburst, I'm doing the *New York Times* crossword," I attempted to recover from my happy response. "When did this happen?"

"The thieves managed to avoid being captured on any of the surveillance cameras. The best we can guess is sometime last night."

"Well, that's vague enough for me. Did you call the police?"

"We wanted to speak with you before doing that."

"Thank you. Would you mind if I look into this myself, before bringing in the authorities?"

"I can understand your hesitation. This is a sensitive situation," Michael said, once again sounding like his namesake.

"Thank you. I'll be there within the hour."

After I ended the call with the voice from on high, Patricia said, "He's in on it!"

"That's what I thought at first, but I think he's being a guardian angel for the cemetery. What say we head over there now? I'll buy you a breakfast burrito on the way," I said, knowing that skipping breakfast would *not* go over well with Patricia's daily vowels.

* * *

Patricia and I picked up a bacon breakfast burrito each, from Tiffany's. A small café in the Bayview district. As we walked back to the car, Patricia asked, "Which one was Tiffany?"

"Ask Helen. She seems to know about these things," I said, with an internal smile.

Michael met us at the scene of the crime, which looked like a crime scene. Dirt was piled everywhere, looking like a sounder of wild boar had come through in search of last night's dinner.

"I'm sorry you had to see your parents' graves this way," Michael tried to comfort us.

"It looks like someone was in a hurry," I said.

"This almost never happens."

Was the use of the word "almost" a slip of the tongue, or a request for a question? I decided to take the lead. "Has this happened before?" I played dumb.

"Not a lot. We've had an incident or two in the past, though no one ever reports it to the authorities."

All three headstones had been covered with mounds of dirt. It looked like the groundbreaking for a subway terminal.

"You said that the surveillance cameras recorded no unusual activity. Were they tampered with?"

"No, whoever it was, knew how to avoid them."

Michael then surprised me by asking, "Do you know who it was?"

I cocked my head at that question, which made me feel a little like a dog. "Yes," I said. "Don't you?"

"Yes," he said, looking sideways over his shoulder as if expecting a tree to fall on him.

"Will you help us?" I asked.

Michael looked down at the hole, shook his head, but said, "Yes."

"May I ask why? You know the other guys can get a bit testy," I pointed out.

"I heard you were working on bringing down Titan Moon, from my cousin over in section 5B. It's about time these guys were stopped."

"How did your cousin know about us?"

"There's quite an underground network here," Michael answered, not giving anything away while creating an anxiety in my chest that could crack a walnut. "But don't worry, they're all on your side."

I was starting to see my army.

*   *   *

Patricia looked quite happy as we drove back to the city.

"Contentment works well with your complexion," I said. "Do you wish to share anything?" I fished for the next step.

"Now that the tracer has been set, I guess I can let you in on the plan. Would you like to visit your folks?" Patricia offered.

"I knew it! The moment Michael reported the theft," I gloated.

"You're a clever one," Patricia said, giving me a wink.

I was directed to head home for the reunion. The meeting with my parents was to take place within the sanctity of my own house, in Brisbane.

The remainder of the ride was in silence. I hadn't spoken to my mother since her death. Through this entire affair, she had remained silent and I had made no attempts to contact her, even though she was who I missed the most. Our relationship was once my anchor to life. Her death was my hardest loss.

Once home, Patricia instructed that I sit on the sofa. She then slid over the small Tibetan box that sat on the coffee table and said, "Open it."

I didn't look at her or the box, only out the window. This story felt like it was all about me when the goal was to help others. First, I was going to write a book about the sale of a tomb. Then, I was to stop the sale of that tomb. Now, my deepest emotions were being summoned from the tomb in my heart. This isn't what I had signed on for.

The bay's waters were still.

Patricia was still.

I opened the box.

Inside were two black cloth bags with pull strings. I picked one up and pulled on the string. A shiny silver-bound votive fell into my hand.

"Hello, Minus," my mother said.

I began to cry.

Patricia sat down on the sofa and put her arm around me.

"Hi, Mom, are you okay?"

"Never better. You know how I loved to wear jewelry, well now I am jewelry," she said, referring to the pendant in my hand.

I looked at the skull chip, which had been carefully bordered with silver, terminating with a loop.

"You look beautiful," I complimented her. "I love what you've done with your hair."

"Your father opted for platinum, have a look."

I picked up the other bag, which was substantially heavier, and slid dear old Pops into my other hand.

"Hi, kid," he said.

"Hi, Pops. Where have you been?" I asked.

"We've been enjoying your view until you needed us."

The rest of the day and night was spent talking, crying, and laughing. We had plenty of time until the contraband bones of my folks would reach their destination.

Mom and Pops didn't need to sleep, unlike their son. Patricia had long since gone to bed by the time I pulled the plug. I was wishing Patricia could speak directly to my parents. They would get on well. I wondered if the folks could Bluetooth her through Zero, but I had no idea where to find him.

"Guys, I'm beat," I addressed my parents in a more familiar tone than I would have in my youth. "I have to go to bed. Please stay up as long as you like. Drinks are in the fridge."

* * *

The following day began with my father commanding, "Wake up, boy, the eagle has landed."

I didn't need to open my eyes. There was nothing to see. "Is this how you treat your wife?" I said. "I'm surprised she still talks to you."

"I'm nice to her. You, I don't have to be nice to until you're dead."

"Something to look forward to," I said.

I sat up, avoiding catching a glimpse of myself in the mirror. I have a striking resemblance to my father. Under the present circumstances, I didn't need the visuals to match the audio.

"What are you carrying on about?" I asked.

"The perps have arrived at their hideout."

"You didn't say that, did you?"

"Didn't say what?"

"You sound like a bad cop show. I think you need more sleep."

"Son… Get up!"

I hoisted myself to my feet and headed for the bathroom. Patricia was just coming out of her room. She asked, "Did you knock the lamp over next to my bed?"

"That was probably my mother. They seem to be in a hurry. You first," I said with a wave at the bathroom.

* * *

It was time. We were ready to uproot Stump. Within four hours of getting up, the three soul seekers were back on a plane with three souls in tow. Thanks to some parental herding, we made our flight to the Pacific Northwest.

A quick web search verified that Stump lived near the place my folks sensed their bones. Gig Harbor; a quaint and moneyed area of Washington State, outside of Seattle. Green and lush with crystal blue waters reflecting the snow-capped Mt. Rainier. The vistas were reminiscent of the verdigris of an ancient bronze. Every shade of green nature had to offer.

A lovely place to be spirited away to.

A great place to live.

I just wouldn't want to be dumped there.

Helen had met us at the airport still wiping the sleep from her eyes. Once we were on the plane, I said, "You look terrible."

"You couldn't find a nicer way to say that?" she yawned.

"I mean it in the most sensitive way."

"Coming from you, I'm touched. Do you mind if I take a nap?" she said, not waiting for an answer before closing her eyes and reclining the seat.

In turn, I took the opportunity for a little shut-eye, seeing Patricia across the aisle sound asleep.

* * *

"Minus!"

My eyes shot open. Brian stood in front of me. I was still on the plane, but all the other passengers were gone. Their bodies were seated, though the people were gone. I could feel no life around me, not like death, just empty.

"What's going on, Brian?"

"This is the other side of death, Minus. You've felt the peace and solitude of being with the dead. This is the loneliness of being with the living. It takes effort to focus on the lives of the living. Without concentrating, this is what the living world is like for me. You need to be careful. I don't want to see you here for a long time."

Experiencing death on the hill, I felt alive. This was a vacuum of warmth without the company of a chill.

"I get your point, brother. Why do you bring this up now?"

"Stump is a bad man. You have not come across this kind of evil before. Your life is important. All your lives have meaning; do not sacrifice them for us. Watch your back, Minus."

"Consider me duly scared," I managed to say without my voice breaking.

"I'm not trying to scare you. I don't want you to be scared. I want you to be careful," Brian tried to clarify his point to a card-carrying coward.

"I'll do my best," I said, wondering what that was.

* * *

When I next opened my eyes, Patricia was standing over me. I was in a hospital room. Helen was sitting in a chair at the end of the bed.

They both smiled. I closed my eyes, searching for an answer to the confusion in my head. That investigation was fruitless. I opened my eyes again in hopes that I would be back on the plane.

"Hi, Minus," Patricia said.

"I am in a hospital, aren't I?"

"Yes."

"Am I alive?"

"According to the cardiograph, you are."

I closed my eyes again. I wanted to still be on the plane, not a patient in a hospital. I can count the number of colds I've had on one hand. So, why am I here?

I opened my eyes once again and asked, "Why am I here?"

"Your heart stopped beating on the plane," Helen answered. "You died. For a moment. Luckily, the twelve-year-old boy in the seat in front of you had been taught first aid at school and he brought you back."

I tried to sit up, which sent Patricia and Helen into convalescent mode, holding me up while adjusting the pillows.

"How long have I been here?"

Helen looked at the clock and said, "A long time."

"Can you quantify that into hours, days, or years?"

"Twelve hours," Patricia said.

"I'm pleased that days and years didn't come up. When can I leave?"

"That's up to the doctor," Helen said. "For now, enjoy the rest."

Brian specifically told me not to die, so what did I do? Just like a petulant sibling, I was contrary. I died. I tried to remember death. There was no white light, no video of my life, not even a trailer for the upcoming show. Nothing, except then and now. I felt fine, a little tired, but I'm always a little tired. It's good to know that momentary death isn't overly taxing.

Once again, I tried to put myself back on the plane. There was no reason to die on the plane, except that my insurance paid out triple if I kicked off on public transportation. Still, with my lame insurance policy, it wasn't worth it.

I looked at Patricia and Helen, who were looking at me like I was a patient in a hospital, when the room went dark. Being in no mood to speak in the plural, I hoped I was in the audience of the Consortium.

"Minus, I would like to thank you for your diligence in helping us," a familiar voice spoke with an *I* statement. "Not too many people would court death to help the dead."

241

"Can't say I was intentionally asking death for a date night," I addressed the Consortium of Souls. "My intentions were quite the opposite and I don't see how it would help the cause anyway."

"Search your mind, Minus. The next world has welcomed you without cutting your ties to the living. You have experienced what no living person has before you. Search your feelings. Memory is fleeting. Emotions, control your mind."

That was a tall order. All I wanted to do was sleep. Sleep had become my friend, my refuge from the world. Still, I wanted to know what had happened, where I had gone, and why the hell I was in this hospital bed.

"Brian, can you help me here?" I reached out for assistance.

"Minus, trust your thoughts," Brian's voice echoed in my head.

"Guys, throw me a bone. I'm lying in a hospital bed after dying on an airplane. I've got two voices in my head telling me to trust what I think. That's not a recipe for rational thought."

"That's good," the Consortium of Souls offered, "rational thinking is what prevents you from remembering your experience in our world. Let go of what ties you to your life. Let go of your ego."

"You say that like it's as easy as dropping a ball. Ego has been with me for a long time, while all along being fed with a lifetime of accomplishments and failures. Reality and fantasy. But mostly, hopes and desires. I can't just stop being me."

"Yes, you can. You just don't want to. The idea scares you and it should," Brian said, rejoining the conversation. "Because you will die again. Don't worry, Minus. We will lead you back to your life."

"Why? Why do you want me to do this?"

"Knowledge," Brian said. "This is the strongest power we have. It fuels the truth. To believe in what you are fighting for, you must know why you are fighting."

"Can't you just send me a pamphlet on the subject? Anyway, aren't you the one who told me not to rush to death?"

"I'm in no hurry to see you every day in The Yard," Brian assured me. "I *will* make sure you have a very long life."

Always looking for the silver lining, I said, "Well, the upside of dying is; I won't have to come up with the co-pay for the hospital stay. What do I need to do?"

It took Brian a moment to process my last statement before handing me over to the Consortium of Souls. "Minus, clear your mind and listen."

I put myself back at the tomb on the hill, looking out to the ocean. This was the most peaceful place imaginable. I could feel myself sliding free. The fears of life melted away like snow from a tree, until I felt like a cherry blossom resting at the end of a branch.

"Very good, Minus," the Consortium said, "but you're a little too relaxed. We've got work to do."

"Sorry, I'm just trying to be a good guest."

"This existence you're about to enter is infinite and fragile. You can go anywhere but can't leave where you are."

"Isn't that a line in an Eagles song?" I said, showing that death had very little effect on my sense of humor.

"Brian," the Consortium said, "can you take over for a while? I need a break."

With that, the Consortium was gone.

"Congratulations, Minus, you are the first person to send the Consortium into sanctuary."

"I was just insuring a return ticket to my thousand-dollar-a-night room. What did you want to show me?"

"You need to follow my directions very carefully. If your heart stops again, with your body hooked up to a cardiogram, the nurse will come at you with a pair of jumper cables."

That's all I needed to hear to start behaving myself.

Brian's voice became soft and calming. "I want you to listen to your heartbeat. Follow its rhythm with your consciousness. It is the only thing that exists. It is all that matters. Imagine you are holding your heart in your hands."

I did what he said. My heart was warm and comforting, lying in the palm of my hand. Yet, it felt heavy with the weight of my life.

Like a quality wine glass. Strong and elegant, with a fragility that makes it precious.

"Now carefully put it in your pocket and come with me."

I followed Brian's instructions. Immediately, I was standing next to my brother in front of an endless wall littered with words.

"Hello, brother," I said, turning to look Brian in the eyes. "You look good for a dead person."

"Thank you, but all you're seeing is your memory of me. Minus, look at the wall and tell me what you see."

"It looks like a New York subway station in the 1970s," I said, not joking.

"Look closer."

I stepped up to the wall to focus on a small section containing innumerable handwritten inscriptions. They were voices of sadness. I could hear each word as I read. *"You said you wouldn't tell anyone." "That wasn't what I wanted." "Why did you betray me?"*

I stepped back from the wall, feeling my heart beating faster in my pocket.

"What is that, Brian?"

"That is the Wall of Broken Promises, Minus. This is where souls come to exorcise their sadness, pain, and frustration inflicted on them from the living."

I looked in both directions down the wall. There were millions of voices written along its borderless surface.

"These are all promises not kept?" I asked.

"These are just the ones for today. They will soon burn off and start afresh."

"I don't understand. Who made these promises?"

Brian looked at the wall as it was engulfed by flames. A firestorm ran from left to right, followed closely by a torrent of words re-covering the wall.

"The living," he said.

"Don't do this, Brian. I'm not a hero. I can't even think on that scale."

"We don't expect you to make the living keep their word to the dead, but they need to know the importance of doing so."

"That's still a tall order, brother."

"This is the end goal, Minus. Your job is to stop Stump. He has caused tremendous damage. You and I may be a small part of this fight, but we play a key role. Stump sees you as insignificant. That will be his downfall."

I could feel my sheltered heart. There was a tension in its beat, as if trying to escape the confines of this assignment.

"Calm down, Minus," Brian warned. "You're going to have the nurse hooking you up to the wall socket if you're not careful."

I took my heart out and softly stroked it until it fell into the rhythm of Ravel's *Bolero*. Slipping it back into my pocket, I asked, "How does this help me deal with Stump?"

"He has made promises that he hasn't kept. Those broken promises have created a weakness in his defense, making him vulnerable. Trust is a person's front line."

"We're not going to start with football analogies again, are we?" I asked.

"You understand what I mean, right?"

"I got it. I'll do an *end-around* and draw in his best players."

"That's the ticket, Minus."

I looked again at the wall of voices, the wall of memories, the wall of disappointment. Is one's word, only as good as the heartbeat of the person you give it to?

"Brian, did I keep my word to you?"

"Minus, you have never let me down."

Brian put his hand on the wall, then gestured at me to do the same. The moment I touched the infinite barrier, the pain was unthinkable, but I had to hold on to it. This was what I was fighting for.

Brian took my hand off of the wall and said, "It's a two-way street, Minus. These souls also have a responsibility to the living. They have the ability to protect those they have left behind."

"I don't understand. The dead can't touch the living."

"No, they can't, but they can influence thought. Think about the time you almost ran your pretty red car into a semi-truck."

"That scared the hell out of me. Good thing I looked back in time," I said, remembering the occasion when I was distracted while driving and almost became a hood ornament on a Mack truck.

"You looked back in time because I told you to. You sure had me sweating more than with most of your close calls."

"That was you? I thought it was just dumb luck."

"Luck is not dumb," Brian sagely offered. "It's the responsibility of the dead to protect those they swore to watch out for in pre-life."

"Do the dead keep their word?" I asked.

"Most do, even the ones writing on this wall."

"I'm ready to go back now," I said. "I have a job to do."

The next thing I saw was the nurse standing over me with a catheter.

"What's going on?" I shrieked.

"It's been far too long since you last urinated," she said. "We felt you may need a little assistance."

"No thank you, the sight of that device did the job. You might want to send in the janitor, though."

* * *

After a battery of tests, which surely put a strain on my health insurance, I was told to watch my salt intake. Then I was sent out onto the street to be hit by a bus or a runaway hotdog cart.

Patricia spearheaded my release from the hospital while Helen brought the rental car around. As unpleasant as the poking and prodding was during my stay, what came next was worse. I couldn't believe that a minor cardiac incident had allowed my partners to rent a Dodge Cavernous. Here we were in the Pacific Northwest. Surrounded by the beauty of majestic mountains and crystalline views. To now be schlepping around in a vehicle better suited as a shuttle bus for the elderly.

"Did Avis not have a Rambler station wagon available?" I asked.

"I'm sorry, Minus," Patricia said, "the agency just shot the last pony."

I let it go. No more distractions. It was time to bury Stump. I had my folks hanging on a leather strap around my neck, while Helen had a chunk of Brian's skull tucked away in her purse, along with a spare bit in my man-bag, just in case we needed to plant a tracer.

We checked in to our hotel, which was a stone's throw from Stump and the last place Mom and Pops reported themselves to be.

"Now that we're here," I began, as we waited for our drinks in the hotel bar, "can anyone tell me what I'm supposed to do?"

Brian was the first to speak with a suggestion to try the potstickers. "I hear they're the specialty here."

"Anything else?" I asked, hoping for either a plan or the full menu.

"You can go talk to Stump," Helen offered.

"Sure, point me in his direction," I joked.

"He's right over there," Helen said, pointing to the man at the end of the bar.

"That's convenient. Did you invite him for dinner?" I asked.

"Good insight, Minus, but he only had time for drinks," Patricia continued to reveal information previously withheld.

"Tell me you're joking," I implored.

I watched Patricia look over my shoulder and smile. "Hello, you must be Ronald Stump," she said.

I closed my eyes, putting myself back at the wall with the pain of countless souls raging through my arm and breaking my heart.

Giving my head the slightest shake, I stood and greeted my foe. "Ronald, we meet at last," I said, taking his hand. "I'm Minus Filbert. This is Patricia Kelly and Helen Wheeler. Would you like to join us?"

Helen pulled out a chair. Stump set down his drink before seating himself.

"I hear you had my parents' bones stolen and dumped somewhere nearby," I calmly stated, as I took my seat.

Stump picked up his drink and analyzed the viscosity of the liquid. "You're quite a detective for a school bus salesman and chauffeur," he said without taking his eyes off the whiskey.

"It doesn't take a PhD in sleuthing to be led by the nose. Why did you bring us here?"

"You do get right to the point."

"I'm paying for a rental car that I don't want to keep very long." I showed my impatience.

To regain control over the conversation, Stump directed a question at Patricia. "Ms. Kelly, why did you put the tomb back on the market?"

I could see the gears turning inside Patricia's head. She sat back. Then using some of the dramatic silence that the dead are so good at, she stripped Stump from controlling the conversation.

"That's personal information. What's your interest in the property?"

"I have clients who are wishing to relocate their family to the Bay Area. They like your view."

"The cemetery is expanding further up the hill," she informed him, "why not buy land there?"

"I have," he said. "The entire new section is mine. Your property is the gateway."

"Excuse me," I said, breaking into the conversation. "I would like to get my parents back."

"I know nothing about your mother and father, though I would be happy to help you find them," Stump said in code, assuming one of us was recording the conversation.

In fact, the three of us were recording this meeting, hoping Stump would tip his hand.

"That's nice of you. How do I accomplish that?" I asked.

"Funny you should ask; I was just speaking to Patricia about that very subject."

"I would like to offer you this," I told the CEO of TMD. "You help us find my parents' bones and we'll keep you out of jail. How does that sound?"

"A bit melodramatic. I don't see incarceration in my future."

"Indeed, and that's where we come in," I quickly added.

"I think we've hit a wall," Stump said, getting weary of the conversation and to the bottom of his glass. "How about you three come to my house tomorrow morning for brunch? I have a beautiful harbor view."

Helen, who had been silent throughout this entire exchange, accepted the offer. "That would be wonderful. What time would you like us to arrive?"

Personally, I found the invitation somewhat threatening, but I trusted Helen's perception and agreed to attend. Patricia smiled nervously.

* * *

The day of reckoning was upon us.

Samuel, Seamus, and Great-Great-Gramps had fulfilled their mission in Wyoming, helping us to prepare for the meeting with Stump.

Mom, Pops, and Brian were all present as we drove up to Stump's front door. Helen and I were tuned in to the afterworld. Patricia had been left to depend on the living. There was no sign of Zero.

The compound belonging to this corporate brute was compact but impressive. The iron gates entering the property looked more like Rodin's *Gates of Hell* than a welcoming portal. We drove through the grounds, which were green and lush with a hint of poison oak. I could feel my skin reacting to the toxins in the air.

I knew we were being watched but wasn't sure if it was a hidden camera or hired muscle from the local cemetery. It didn't matter. We had our own spooks watching our backs.

Stepping up to the front door, Helen rang the bell that echoed throughout the cavernous structure to the tune of Wagner's *Faust*.

"Interesting choice," I said. "Wagner is such an acquired taste."

We stood at the door waiting for what felt like an entire movement of the famed composer's *Ring Cycle*.

"Greetings," Stump's voice came from behind us, causing all to jump in fright. "I'm sorry, I didn't mean to startle you."

Doubtful, I thought, while saying, "Not at all, we were enjoying the concert. Is there a secret passage around here?"

"I like unexpected doorways," he said. "They expand my options."

"They also give you more places to be locked out of," I said.

"I have a lot of keys," Stump proclaimed, unlocking the front door and ushering the prey into his lair.

What is it about wealthy people and high ceilings? The ceiling of the vestibule we stepped down into rose twenty feet above our heads. The rooms of the house were terraced, but the roofline remained on a single plane. By the time we made our way down to the living room, at water level, the ceiling looked like it belonged to another building.

"Do you get much seepage here?" I asked, attempting to make conversation.

Stump chose to ignore the question that had Helen and Patricia looking at me sideways.

"Please have a seat. Brunch is almost ready. Would anyone care for coffee or tea?"

"Coffee would be nice," Helen replied, looking at Patricia, who agreed with the decision. I, in turn, declined, having been up since four o'clock drinking espressos in my room.

When Stump went out of the room, Patricia turned to me and said, "Seepage? Where did that come from?"

"It was just a thought. I wanted to get his reaction."

"And?"

"Inconclusive."

Through a doorway on the opposite side of the room from which he had exited, Stump rejoined us, saying, "Please, make yourselves at home."

He set down a tray of coffees with all the appropriate additives and chose the mug that had *The Boss* emblazoned on it. Stump took a seat after procuring enough milk and sugar to make it no longer coffee.

Helen and Patricia retrieved the two delicate porcelain cups and ignored the pollutants.

"Mr. Stump," I said, pausing to see if he would ask me to call him Ron, which he didn't. "I'm a little unclear as to why all this hospitality. The elephant in the room is obvious to us all."

Stump looked out the window at the bay and took a sip of his concoction. "We all know what we want, and we all think we will get it, but some of us have all the control," he proclaimed.

"You really shouldn't feel powerless. We are happy to work with you," I said.

"Thank you. I'm curious why you feel so cocky."

Patricia deflected the question, saying, "Minus is just naturally vivacious. Still, his point regarding working together could benefit us all. From where you sit, we may seem like three benign individuals, though I assure you, there's a growing force behind us."

"That sounds very much like a threat," Stump observed with an edge in his voice.

"Cancer is always a looming threat," I said.

Stump smiled.

Turning to Helen, he asked, "Ms. Wheeler, you've been rather quiet. I wonder if you have the same beliefs as your colleagues?"

"I'm sorry, I haven't been listening. My brother has been talking to me. He wishes to have a word with you. Do you mind talking to dead people?"

"Not at all. Some of my best friends are dead."

"Yes, I know. That's exactly what he wants to talk about with you."

For the first time, Stump appeared nervous, momentarily, before regrouping and beginning to speak with Brian.

"Good morning," Brian said through Helen. "This is a nice house you have. Do you get much seepage?"

"That seems to be a concern in your family."

"I see you're aware of my relationship with Helen and Minus?"

"I'm aware of everything," Stump gloated.

"I'd be happy to put that to the test," Brian retorted.

Stump remained stone-faced as he picked up his *Boss* mug and slowly sipped his bastardized coffee.

"Be my guest," he said, unable to hold the mug to his lips any longer.

"Are you familiar with the expression, *Keep your friends close and your enemies even closer?*"

"Of course. That's how I've gotten where I am."

"Once your enemies are dead, I'm afraid they are no longer close," Brian raised the ante, to create tension.

"I don't worry about the dead," Stump said, showing his weakness. "The dead have no control over the living."

"So true. We cannot make the living do anything they don't want to. Though, we can tell them things that otherwise would go unknown."

Stump appeared uncomfortable with this statement. I was uncomfortable with the statement. Hopefully, the dead have a protocol for the use of sensitive information.

"Do you ever wonder what happened to your old boss, Rock Bamana? Now he was a good man," Brian added to set the lance a little closer to Stump's heart.

"Brunch is served," came a familiar voice from the kitchen doorway.

Mickey stood at the kitchen, holding the swinging door open, looking like a short-order cook at Denny's.

"Excellent," Stump exclaimed. "Shall we eat?"

All rose as the lord and master headed for the deck on which a feast had been laid. Mikey was there to hold the chairs for the ladies. It was unclear whether I should know M&M, so I chose to play dumb.

"This is quite a spread," I said.

"It's all Mickey. He's my right-hand man and I would trust him with my life," Stump said.

"I had a dog like that," I said, glancing at Mickey through the corner of my eye. He gave me a private wink and went back into the kitchen.

"Don't get Minus wrong," Patricia went into damage control. "He loves his pets." Then, not to linger the point, she asked Stump to pass the bagels.

Brian's mention of Rock Bamana hung over the table like a glass skylight ready to shatter. Surprisingly, Stump was the first to raise the topic again. "Tell me, Brian, why bring up my old colleague?"

"I believe he was your boss, not your peer," Brian said through Helen.

"We were close," Stump continued to enhance his relationship with the man he had replaced.

Brian allowed that statement to decay in the air. The silence that followed felt like the waiting room at the IRS.

"I've had wonderful conversations with Rock," Brian continued.

"That's impossible," Stump showed his first card.

"Why would you say that?" my brother set the trap.

"Rock died at sea. He isn't able to communicate with anyone."

"You are so right. His yacht did disappear near the Farallones. Fortunately, he wasn't on it."

"It sounds to me like you're fishing for information," Stump said.

"The dead don't fish," Brian assured Stump. "I have all the answers. Indeed, I can answer questions for you."

Stump looked puzzled. "How do I know I'm talking to Brian Filbert and not Helen Wheeler?"

"Helen's prettier," I said.

Patricia, once again, stepped in to salvage the moment. "You can ask a question that Helen couldn't answer."

Our host put down his fork and sipped the mimosa Mikey had just served. I did the same. Helen sat back in her chair while Patricia took the opportunity to refill her plate with home fries.

"I keep a cash stash in my house," Stump said. "Where is it?"

Without hesitation, Brian answered, "The sock drawer in your dresser, next to a .38 caliber pistol with your father's initials engraved on it."

Maybe there was a rogue orange seed in his drink. Stump began to choke on his cocktail, hurriedly excusing himself to the restroom with Mikey patting him on the back.

Mickey stepped out of the kitchen with a tray of handmade samosas as Stump was whisked to the facilities. Not sounding at all alarmed, he asked, "Is everything alright?"

"There might have been a .38 caliber citrus seed in his champagne glass," I said.

"You're a real jokester," Mickey informed me.

"It has served me well thus far," I replied. "By the way, your fried tomatoes are divine."

Mickey shook his head and went back into the kitchen.

"Minus, are you determined to blow this whole thing out of the water?" Patricia asked.

"Patricia, humor is a tool. In the right hands, it can build a gallows."

I don't think Patricia agreed with my theory, but she let it drop.

The interlude, presented by our host choking, allowed us to enjoy Mickey's bounty. I ate as if it was my last meal.

When Stump regained his ability to breathe, he re-seated himself at the head of the table. "Sorry about that," he said. "I had something caught in my throat." After taking a sip of water, he added, "Where were we?"

"I think we were in your underwear drawer," I said.

Why that statement caught my colleagues off guard is beyond me. Patricia's head almost dropped into her hollandaise sauce.

"Thank you, Mr. Filbert," Stump said. "I must say your brother's insight was surprising. But, let's not play games here. Shall we cut to the chase?"

Helen put down her fork and finished chewing the last of her meal, then gave the helm back to Brian. "We want you to step down from Titan Moon and install Minus as president."

"Well, that went right past the chase and straight to the epilogue," Stump laughed.

"I'm not wanting to delay dessert," Brian said, channeling me.

"Mr. Filbert, you have not convinced me that all is lost."

"No, I haven't, Mr. Stump. I would be happy to do that."

"If you can, this is your opportunity."

Helen took a sip of water, chasing it with a slug of mimosa. "I've enjoyed many long conversations with your buddy, Mr. Bamana," Brian continued, once Helen had swallowed. "He's an interesting fellow."

Helen sat a little taller. "I imagine you're wondering how this is possible since you've submerged his skull. The urns in Seamus's entryway are more than decorative. They are also watertight."

"Was that a question or a statement?" Stump asked.

"Either one," Brian said. "It was designed to create anxiety. I'm carefully constructing a platform for you to hang yourself."

"I appreciate your attention to detail, but I bore easily."

"I'll try to keep it exciting," Brian said, going head-to-head with Stump's defenses. "Your late boss had an operation a few years before you had him killed. I'm sure you recall the aneurysm that nearly killed him. Rock had the foresight to convince the doctor to remove a small portion of his skull for safekeeping."

Stump looked unmoved.

"How's your anxiety level?" Brian asked.

"Less than my boredom level. Please continue."

"You're a trooper," Brian commended Stump. "Shall I bore you with the tedious details of Rock's death that you already know, or should Minus start having his business cards printed?"

"I'm pleased that my hospitality has you comfortable enough not to fear for the lives of your family members."

"I'm disappointed that you believe me unaware of their vulnerability. I assure you, I have not been remiss with their safety," Brian said, keeping his composure.

Stump sat looking thoughtful. Surrounded by the detritus of an elegant meal, he said, "Please continue. I'll try to stay awake."

"You're a gracious host," Brian responded.

Helen adjusted herself in her seat to look as confident as Brian sounded.

"Mr. Stump," Brian continued, "we are both aware of the unpleasant details of Mr. Bamana's murder and disposal. I see no reason to ruin a lovely brunch with that. I would rather focus on your weaknesses. You have surrounded yourself with employees by lying and misleading them. Not a recipe for loyalty."

Stump's cell phone sounded with a triumphant horn. "Hello, Seamus," he answered. "I'm in the middle of something. Can you make it quick?"

After listening for a moment, Stump said, "Yes, they're here now. I will keep that in mind. Goodbye."

Stump questioned Brian, "Are you referring to your perceived friendship with Mickey and Mikey?"

"Ah, yes, the truth of the matter. Power doesn't lie with the billions of souls that came before. Nor with the soulless billionaire here and now. This moment belongs to two men," my brother proclaimed.

Stump's phone once again announced a call.

"Yes," he said, not revealing the caller's identity.

Stump listened for a moment before hanging up without a goodbye.

Brian went silent. Helen had another sip of her mimosa. Patricia and I were scared shitless. This was the plan? To put us in the devil's den and hope that two thugs had truly turned over a new leaf? That might be okay for a dead person, but for someone with a heartbeat, it increased that heartbeat.

"May I ask a question?" I asked. "Any chance there are more corn fritters?"

Mickey, standing at the kitchen door for most of the conversation, disappeared. Mikey sat in the living room reading a magazine.

Suddenly, Mickey burst into the room, sending everyone to their feet, including Stump. He charged into the room, holding a tray of fritters.

"Sorry, I didn't realize how hot this was," he said, dropping the tray on the table. "Who would like more?"

It took a moment to regain our composure and appetite. Mickey took this opportunity to calmly serve his culinary genius.

After savoring the corn savory, I braved the question. "Mickey, it appears you and Mikey are the ones in power here. Mr. Stump feels you are completely loyal to him. We four are hoping that isn't true. Would you care to shed a little light on the subject?"

Mikey put down his magazine and stood at the opposite end of the table from Mickey.

Stump leaned back in his chair.

Everyone was silent. The tension was intolerable.

"You know guys," I said, "the dead have this drama thing down much better than you. Can we make a decision here?"

Mickey looked at Stump and said, "Sorry boss, blood is thicker than water."

Stump jumped up pulling out the .38 caliber pistol, engraved with his father's initials previously stored in his underwear drawer, and pointed it at Helen.

"Ron," I said, hoping to sound like his mother.

Stump hesitated. For a moment, he took his eyes off Helen to look me square in the eye.

"You may have the gun, but we have your future," I said, in hopes of freezing his trigger finger.

"My future is to be the last man standing," Stump proclaimed.

"Your future is to rot in hell," Mikey said, as he pulled out his gun and shot Stump in the head.

When Mikey's bullet entered Stump's skull, another bullet left the chamber of the .38 caliber pistol, engraved with Stump's father's initials, and headed in the direction of my lovely, intelligent, and kind sister.

Time slowed.

Nanoseconds became minutes.

I could see the bullet in my mind moving faster than my brain, but slow enough to watch. Drilling its way towards Helen, who stood between it and the wall I wished was in front of her. I wanted to move, but my body was still on Pacific Standard Time. Frozen in place like a corpse at a funeral.

No one was moving.

Only the spinning bullet had motion.

Helen was looking at me, unaware of its approach.

My race with time was approaching the finish line with time taking the lead. I was having to watch my sister die in slow motion. This was my chance to beat time. All I had to do was reach across the table and pull Helen out of the way, but my hands were bound by tiny neurons.

The bullet was so close to Helen's cheek that I wanted to close my eyes, unable to cope with what I was about to see. My lids were attached to my body, which was not keeping up with current events. Suddenly, Helen twitched as if she had been pinched, causing her to jerk slightly to the right.

I watched as the bullet spun past Helen's left side, knocking out her earring. Then, shattering a Roman-Greco urn, sending pottery shards bouncing off every hard surface in the room. One of them finding a receptive target in Stump's forehead.

My thoughts slowed. No one moved, except Stump as he hit the floor.

I looked at Helen to see her holding her left ear.

"Are you okay?" I asked.

"I seem to have lost an earring," she said, obviously in shock.

"I have it," Patricia announced, holding a gold hoop that was now shaped like a heart.

M&M immediately grabbed Stump's body and dragged it to the edge of the deck, where they tied a weight to his torso and a rope around his leg. About to toss him into the bay, I suggested removing the pottery from his head. Mikey took hold of the two-thousand-year-old piece of clay and tugged. His fingers slipped, leaving the shard firmly embedded in Stump's skull.

"Just like Stump," Mickey said. "Once he gets something in his head, he won't let it go."

M&M again attempted to remove King Arthur's sword to language not fit for my ears.

I got up from the table to stand over the petulant dead body of Stump. Taking hold of Excalibur, I gave Stump's head a kick and the shard released its hold.

"I always said Stump needed a good kick in the head," Mickey commented.

With that, the two employees of Titan Moon Distributors delivered Stump into the bay.

"You're good at that," I said.

"Plenty of practice," Mickey answered.

I held up the remains of a majestic vessel that had once decorated the home of an ancient and powerful man. If there's one thing this experience has taught me, it was not to be surprised by anything. Beautifully rendered on this ceramic chip was an image of a Centaur dispatching his enemy.

All I could think to ask was, "What now?"

EPILOGUE: WHAT NOW?

"I love this view,"
I said to Patricia as we sat on the hill,
looking out to the sea.

"You say that every morning," she said.

"And you say that every morning," I replied.

"I know," Patricia admitted.

"I could die where I sit, if I could sit where I die forever," I added.

"We can arrange that," Patricia assured me.

The tomb had been saved. Beyond the tomb was a new lawn with a killer view. My family had moved up with the Kellys. Mom, Pops, and Brian were each given a plot with a view of the sea.

No words could honestly describe the sensation evoked by the landscape. Beginning in the eyes and traveled through millions of nerves to rest in my memory with contentment.

"What about you? Does this place hold a lure for you?" I asked.

Patricia's folks had remained silent before, during, and after the fight for the dead. She tried to find Zero, but he had also shut down communication with both the living and the dead. There was a sadness in her that I couldn't break through.

"I like the view," she said.

"That's it? These people mean nothing to you?"

Patricia didn't answer immediately. Many imidiatelies went by creating a silence fit for the view.

"I like the view," she said again.

"I hope someday you'll share your past with me."

"It's not a life-enriching experience. I just want to move on. Speaking of which, you have a plane to catch."

"I was hoping you had forgotten that."

"You are the CEO of an international corporation now, Minus. Try to get your head around that."

"My head is just a figurehead. Brian really runs the place."

"You're right. Let me rephrase that… Let's go," she said, letting me know who the real boss was.

"Thank you. For a moment there, I was starting to believe my own press."

"I've got to keep you real."

I was now expected to lobby Congress for a bill to protect the sovereign rights of the dead. My message being, "Just because you're dead and in the ground doesn't mean the living can walk all over you. The dead are people too."

Helen and Patricia were a great help to me with this goal. Meeting with the members of Congress individually, we brought their loved ones back to speak to them.

History was made. This was the first bill ever to be passed by a unanimous vote of the 535 members of Congress and signed by the president, his cabinet, and the entire White House staff, including the maids.

* * *

Ultimately, no one cared what had happened to Stump. There were no inquiries into his disappearance. No news stories. Not even a mention in the *Star*.

It appears his true allies were less than zero.
But definitely, *not* Minus.

**It's never,
"THE END!"**

ACKNOWLEDGMENTS

Most of all, I would like to thank Stephen Houser. My friend, mentor, and luncheon buddy. Steve brought me into the world of writing and encouraged me to grow. With sandwiches and support, I grew.

Colleen P Oakes for helping me understand the phrase; *You can do better.*

Callie L Oakes for helping me to *do better.*

Margie Cleland for her support and excitement from the beginning.

Lin Chen Willis for telling me *I should write a book.*

CPSIA information can be obtained
at www.ICGtesting.com
Printed in the USA
BVHW092047050722
641403BV00007B/183/J